LET SLEEPING CATS LIE

LET SLEEPING CATS LIE

THE 9 LIVES COZY MYSTERY SERIES, BOOK FOUR

LOUISE CLARK

Book and cover design by eBook Prep
www.ebookprep.com

January, 2019
Paperback ISBN: 978-1-947833-57-9
Hardcover ISBN: 978-1-947833-58-6

ePublishing Works!
644 Shrewsbury Commons Ave
Ste 249
Shrewsbury PA 17361
United States of America

www.epublishingworks.com
Phone: 866-846-5123

CHAPTER 1

Roy Armstrong sat down on the porch steps in front of his Burnaby townhouse and settled his laptop on his knees. Then he opened it up and stared down at the screen, his fingers on the keyboard. To anyone looking his way, he was deep in concentration, pouring over some document or other. He was actually stewing about the arrival of Dr. Tamara Ahern, mystery woman.

Calling her a mystery woman wasn't exactly true, of course. He knew her name because she and his son Quinn had once been lovers. He wasn't sure how long-lasting their relationship might have been, but he knew Quinn had been devastated by how it ended.

He typed some gibberish into his latest work in progress, his mind far away. Quinn met Tamara in Africa, where she was working as a trauma doctor, providing medical services for civilians caught up in a vicious civil war. Quinn had been there, reporting on the atrocities that were inevitably occurring, when he met the dedicated, passionate, and determined Tamara. He'd used her in several of his stories, giving her a voice, making her the face of a cry for help from the outside world.

The reports had gone global. The images of suffering were horrendous, Tamara's despair at the limited services she and her team could provide, heartbreaking. Roy remembered the time and the clips vividly. His son was in the middle of a maelstrom, his beloved wife Vivien fighting a losing battle against cancer. Quinn had always been a risk-taker, and Roy had been proud of him, but at the time he'd wondered if he would ever see his son again, or if the two most important people in his life would be taken from him simultaneously. Quinn sent him e-mails and sometimes texts when he could, but those were always reassuring, telling his father he was safe and not to worry.

Not to worry. Of course he worried. He watched each and every one of those news reports. He hated them, but he did. It didn't take much imagination to realize that there was more between Tamara and Quinn than professional respect. Roy could see that his son had fallen hard for the beautiful and passionate Tamara. He wasn't so sure she was as smitten, but there was something there on her part too.

Then the unthinkable happened. The encampment where Tamara and her colleagues provided medical care was raided. The inhabitants, civilian wounded and noncombatant medical teams alike, were slaughtered. Quinn had been away at the time, filing one of his articles—thank God!—when the attack occurred. All he could do was stand by the broken and defaced bodies and report a crime against humanity. His anguish was clear for all to see.

And now Tamara was here, very much alive and upstairs in the living room of the house Roy shared with Quinn. He knew from recent news reports that she'd been kidnapped by rebels and had spent the past three years in captivity, so after Quinn introduced them he made his excuses and left the two of them to reconnect while he came out here to the front porch to pretend to work.

He typed some more gibberish while his mind grappled with questions. Why was she here? What did she want with Quinn? Was it love that brought her? Did she want to rekindle the passion had seemed to simmer between them in the heat of an African desert?

The giggle of an eight-year-old soon to turn nine interrupted his thoughts. He realized he had pounded out a whole page of nonsense and shut the laptop with an annoyed click.

Noelle Jamieson breezed past, her shadow and best friend, Mary Petrofsky, in her wake. "Hi, Roy! What are you doing?"

"Pretending to work," Roy said. He put his elbows on the closed laptop and rested his chin on his palms. "What are you two up to?"

"Mary and I are telling Mom that we're going inside."

"My mom wants to bake cookies," Mary added, in her usual serious tone.

Roy grinned. "Sounds like fun. What kind of cookies?"

"Chocolate chip," Mary said.

"The best!" Noelle bounced up and down a couple of times then headed for the house. "Come on, Mary. Let's run!"

They galloped away, charging up the Jamieson front walk and making quick work of the porch stairs. Roy shook his head, still smiling. Noelle was a delight. Three months ago, when Quinn and Noelle's mom, Christy, had been an item, he'd been looking forward to having her as a granddaughter he could spoil as his own. Now that too was in jeopardy. He decided Tamara Ahern wasn't high on his popularity list at the moment.

He heard the Jamiesons' door slam. A few minutes later he saw the long, lithe form of Stormy the Cat wending his way toward him. He straightened, ready for whatever was to come.

The cat stopped at the foot of the stairs and sat on his haunches, back straight, tabby striped tail wrapped around his paws. He stared at Roy, green eyes unblinking. *Who's the woman?*

The voice in Roy's mind came from Frank Jamieson, Christy's dead husband who had taken up residence in the cat after his murder. "Tamara Ahern. She once worked for Canadian Medical Services Abroad."

That's not what I meant.

Roy knew that. He also knew that Frank was jealous of Quinn and Christy's burgeoning relationship, and he had done all he could to crush it. He'd succeeded, too, back in March when he'd gone quiet for a time and made them all think he had moved on to whatever existed beyond death.

Roy shrugged. "She's an old friend of Quinn's."

Girlfriend.

Roy didn't answer.

Christy's upset. She saw Quinn hugging her.

"They hadn't seen each other in a long time."

Christy won't talk to me about Quinn, but I know she's sad.

Roy glared at the cat. "If she is, it's your fault."

Stormy lifted a paw and began to clean between the pads. Frank and Roy had had this conversation before. Frank didn't like to be reminded that he was now the alter ego of a cat, no longer the good-looking bad boy who didn't have to work at anything to get what he wanted.

Does this Tamara Ahern want to get back together with Quinn?

"None of your business." Roy tapped his index finger on the laptop. "If you want to help Christy, you'll leave this alone to play itself out."

The cat abandoned his paw cleaning to look at Roy once again. Roy swore he could see a devious gleam in the animal's eyes.

You think Christy still has a chance with Quinn?

"I think anything is possible if we don't interfere," he said. He tried to sound lofty. Instead, it came across more like a lecture from an old school marm.

The cat stood up, arched his back and stretched, then leapt up the stairs to rub against Roy's arm. *I'll try.*

Roy scratched behind the cat's ears. "Thanks."

I want what's best for her, you know.

Roy thought that was true, but he wasn't sure that Frank's version of what was best for Christy was the same as Christy's was for herself. The Jamiesons' front door opened, disgorging Noelle and Mary on their way back to the Petrofsky house to bake cookies. He was relieved when the cat went with them.

He opened his laptop again and this time he did get down to work.

CHRISTY JAMIESON LEANED against her refrigerator door and watched Ellen Jamieson, her late husband Frank's aunt, kneed a wad of dough with considerable enthusiasm and not a little satisfaction. Noelle had been and gone, with the promise that she would return for dinner. Now it was just Christy and Ellen chatting while Ellen worked her dough for home baked rolls that would accompany dinner.

"Mrs. Morton says the end of year concert is coming together well," Christy said. Mrs. Morton was Noelle's classroom teacher.

"When is it?" Ellen asked. Even though she was baking bread, her brown linen slacks were perfectly cut and the loose blouse she wore with them was silk.

"Just before the end of school. Oh, and there's a special assembly on the last day, a sort of year-end wrap-up. Parents are invited to attend."

"Good," Ellen said. Her attention was all on the dough. A month ago she had enrolled in a personalized cooking program provided by one of Vancouver's internationally recognized culinary institutes. Her class this morning must have been on making breads.

"I'll go upstairs and put the dates into my calendar," Christy said. "That way we won't miss them."

Ellen nodded. She was frowning at the dough as if it was a rival in a competition she intended to win.

Christy slipped out of the kitchen, leaving her to it. Adding dates to her calendar was a lame excuse, and if Ellen hadn't been so focused on her bread making, she would probably have called her on it. As it was, Christy needed some time to decompress.

She had been coming up the road with Noelle and Mary Petrofsky, on their way home from school, when a taxi slid to a stop in front of the Armstrongs' house and a woman got out. A young woman with pretty features and blonde hair tied in a knot at her nape. Her clothes were nothing special and they hung too loosely on her form, disguising her figure. Christy had stopped at her front walk, while Noelle and Mary bounded up the road to see what was happening at

Mary's house, and watched as the woman climbed the steps to Quinn's front door and rang the bell.

She shouldn't have stood there and gawked, waiting to see what happened next. She knew that. She was snooping into Quinn's life, something she had no right to do. But ...

Yeah, but. A few weeks ago, Roy had mentioned a woman Quinn had known in Africa had recently been released from captivity resulting from a brutal kidnapping. Her release was a good thing, Roy had said. If she was alive Quinn would no longer mourn her loss.

As she watched the woman standing quietly at the door, her hands clasped together in front of her, Christy wondered if this was the kidnap victim. And if she was, how Quinn would react when he saw her.

She didn't have to wait long. The door opened; Quinn stood in the opening. His hair was black, thick and springy to the touch. His eyes were dark gray, framed by long black lashes. They opened wide now, as shock registered on his handsome face. That was followed by dawning recognition, then open, joyous delight. Christy heard him say, "Tamara," then he stepped out the door onto the porch, opened his arms, and wrapped the woman in an embrace that spoke of familiarity and deep emotion.

In that instant, Christy knew some things were not meant to be. Like her and Quinn Armstrong, together as a couple. Sure, they'd split a couple of months ago. She'd taken the blame at the time, because she couldn't seem to get Frank out of her head, but now she wondered. Quinn's reaction to the arrival of the lost Tamara was too intense to just be pleasure at seeing an old friend return safely after a harrowing experience. He was still as tied up in her as Christy was in Frank. Maybe more so.

Reaching her room, she picked up her laptop, which was on top of her dresser, and settled in a reading chair positioned by the window. Opening her calendar, she put in all the important school dates, then scanned her emails. One was from Isabelle Pascoe at the Jamieson Trust about an upcoming event she thought a Jamieson should attend. Christy grimaced, moving on without replying. She'd toss that issue around with Ellen to see which one of them would take on the job. Ellen probably. She enjoyed the networking and socializing that went on at society events like this.

Another message was from Harry Endicott, the forensic accountant tasked with investigating the disappearance of the Jamieson Trust. He wanted a meeting next week. She frowned. Harry was working with the awful Samuel Macklin, former Jamieson trustee turned embezzler. Macklin had accepted a plea bargain in return for ratting on his fellow trustees. Part of his sentence was to make restitution to the Jamieson Trust by finding the funds he'd help embezzle, all done under Harry's watchful eye. Unfortunately, the money had gone through many twisted paths, not all of them ones Macklin had created. So far, the embezzled funds had proved elusive.

So why did Harry want a meeting? To tell her the money would never be found? Or that it had been?

A little quiver of excitement came to life in her stomach. What if Harry had good news? That he and Macklin had recovered the money? Even if it wasn't the whole, excessive, Jamieson pile, having extra funds would make life a little easier and provide a more comfortable future for Noelle.

She wrote Harry accepting the meeting, then she powered off the computer and headed downstairs to talk to Ellen about which of them should represent the Jamieson family at the gala.

CHAPTER 2

When the doorbell rang, Quinn was sitting at his desk in the basement of the Armstrong townhouse, deep in writing mode. He was focused on outlining a book on the murder of Vince Nunez, the rock band SledgeHammer's late manager. The idea had come not from his friend Sledge—also known as Rob McCullagh— the leader of the popular band, but from SledgeHammer's press agent. The murder had generated a great deal of media and fan interest, especially since Graham Gowdy—Hammer—the band's drummer, had been a leading suspect for much of the investigation. Hammer had never been charged, and the murder was actually done by someone outside of the band, but the press agent was afraid the suspicions would stick. She hoped a book written by someone inside the investigation would go a long way to clearing Hammer's name and reassuring SledgeHammer fans.

Mitch Crosier, the record mogul whose company produced SledgeHammer's music, was enthusiastic since the idea fit right in with his vision of cross-platform marketing for his bands. When Quinn agreed to write the story, he approached the publishing company that would soon be releasing his book on Frank Jamieson's disappearance and death. His editor loved the idea and contracts were drawn up. All he had to do now was write it.

And that wasn't going to get done if he was answering the doorbell every time it rang.

He waited somewhat irritably, listening for his father, Roy's, footsteps on the stairs, but heard nothing. The last time he'd seen Roy, he had been sitting at the kitchen table, laptop open, and was himself deep in writing mode. Evidently his concentration was one step better than Quinn's was.

The doorbell rang again. Quinn waited another few moments for sounds of action, then he muttered a curse, saved his work, and headed for the front door.

The townhouse was a multi-level structure, with the front door located on a landing between the main floor and the basement. Quinn ran lightly up the half dozen stairs from his level to the landing. He flung open the door, prepared to growl at whoever was calling, then simply stared, unbelieving.

"Tamara?" he said at last. "Tamara Ahern, is that you?"

She looked back at him. Her dark eyes, large and full of intelligence, were shadowed with uncertainty as she smiled rather tentatively. He hated the vulnerability he saw in that cautious smile. Tamara, his Tamara, had been fierce, demanding, bold. She dared people to give her a hard time and then fought them to a standstill if they did. This woman looked as if she needed protecting. She was too thin and those big dark eyes were full of shadows. A great wave of affection, mixed with concern, had him stepping onto the porch, then pulling her into a hug.

She stood stiffly in his embrace for a minute, resisting his attempt to connect, then she uttered a little sigh and laid her head on his shoulder. The rest of her body melted into his.

As she sank into him, Quinn registered a sound. He looked up and saw Christy Jamieson on the sidewalk, looking his way. Given the time, she must be just back from picking her daughter, Noelle, from school. She was wearing jeans and a loose blouse that nonetheless emphasized her curvy figure. The breeze had ruffled her short, red-brown hair and combined with the casual outfit, she could have been any young mother in the area. But she wasn't. She was a Jamieson, something he knew to his cost. She quickly turned away, then hurried up her front walk. Seeing him with his arms around another woman was probably as much a shock for her as having Tamara ring his doorbell had been for him. Christy reached her front porch. She unlocked the door without looking his way again and went inside.

As the door closed, a little bit of himself closed too. He eased away from Tamara to smile down at her. "Where are my manners? Will you come inside?"

She gave him a relieved smile and said, "I hoped you'd ask." Her voice wavered, as if she was uncertain of her welcome. Why? They'd been as close as two people could be and had still been consumed by passion for each other when she had apparently been killed. Why wouldn't he want to talk to her, find out what had happened, the details of where she'd been for these past three years? Any normal man would. But Quinn was also a journalist. The reporter in him knew her experiences would make a story, a big juicy story.

Inside, he directed her up the half staircase to the living room, then his hand at her waist, he said, "My dad's in the kitchen. Let me introduce you."

She hesitated, frowning. "How is he doing?" Quinn decided he must have looked confused, for she colored and added, "The last time I saw you, you were worried about him."

His expression cleared as he remembered. "When my mom was sick."

She nodded.

It was his turn to hesitate, then he shrugged mentally. His family's tragedy was not hers. "She died not long after you ... disappeared. Dad was pretty torn up. That's why I came home. Why I'm living here. That and—" He let the sentence hang unfinished, because he couldn't bring himself to refer directly to the horrific scene that had caused him and others to believe she was dead.

Tamara reached out and put her hand on his arm. "Oh, I'm so sorry, Quinn!"

"Thanks." The word came out too gruff. He cleared his throat and said, "Dad's doing better now. We both are. Come and meet him."

She nodded and let him guide her into the kitchen.

His father looked up from the laptop screen as they entered. Quinn knew him well enough to figure that meant he'd been listening in on the conversation with Tamara, but Roy didn't acknowledge he'd overheard anything. He simply raised his eyebrows and said, "Hello."

Quinn tried to see his father from Tamara's point of view. Roy Armstrong was a man who followed his own path. He wrote successful novels, protested government decisions that didn't fit well with his worldview, and always looked at what was behind words or actions. He dressed in casual, front button shirts, soft, faded blue jeans and he wore his greying black hair long and tied in a tail at the back of his neck. When he was writing, as he had been this afternoon, he ran his fingers through his hair, freeing some strands, while causing others, still bound in the tail, to bunch up into odd lumps and angles. The process could make him appear both scruffy and demented.

Tamara didn't seem bothered by his appearance, though, which was a positive for Quinn. She smiled as he said, "Tamara, this is my father, Roy Armstrong. Dad, this is Tamara Ahern."

As soon as Quinn said her first name, Roy stated to frown. By the time he had finished the introduction, Roy's eyebrows were reaching for his hair. "*The* Tamara Ahern?"

Quinn nodded. Tamara stuck out her hand. "Hi, Mr. Armstrong. I'm pleased to meet you."

Roy might be free spirited and independent, but he had manners and knew how to use them. He stood up and smiled broadly as he took her hand, clasping it warmly. "The pleasure is all mine, Tamara. I'm delighted you're here. Please call me Roy."

Tamara smiled, again looking relieved. "Thank you, Roy."

The introductions over, Roy folded down the top of his laptop and picked it up. "I'll leave you two to talk. Nice to meet you, Tamara." He smiled as he headed out of the kitchen.

Part of Quinn was urging him to call his father back, as if this unexpected meeting with Tamara would somehow be impersonal, the visit of an old friend with whom he no longer had a lot in common, if the three of them sat down together to chat. "Dad ... "

Roy was almost out of the kitchen now. He waved his hand vaguely and didn't turn around. "Have fun, you two," he said and moved into the living room, disappearing from sight. Moments later, Quinn heard his footsteps on the stairs and realized he was headed outside.

Quinn turned back to Tamara. "I'm sorry, Quinn," she said as they heard the front door close. "I've disrupted your day and your father's." She looked dismayed. "That wasn't my intention."

Quinn studied her, again thinking that this was not the Tamara he knew. That Tamara wore her dark blonde hair cropped close to her head, the bangs that fell over her forehead only concession to her femininity in the style. Her clothes were practical, medical scrubs during the day, jeans and a shirt in the evening. She'd never been overt in her sexuality, but it had always been there, in the way she moved, in the tilt of her head, or the promise in a glance from her beautiful dark eyes. The woman in front of him had longer hair, scraped back from her forehead and tied in a bun. Her clothes were shapeless and she seemed to be hunched into herself, as if she was hoping not to be noticed.

Whatever had happened to her during her captivity, she was now insecure and tentative. The old Tamara would have accepted Roy's departure at face value and moved on, pursuing her goal with a straightforward determination. He realized he wanted the old Tamara back and he'd do whatever it took to help her get there.

He reached out and took her hand. "Dad doesn't mind, Tamara. He can work wherever he is. I swear, if an earthquake happened and the house fell down around him, trapping him under the table, he'd be writing while he waited to be rescued."

She laughed as he hoped she would, and her expression relaxed.

"Why don't we go into the living room and you can tell me how you came to be here today." Tamara nodded in agreement. Quinn shepherded her out of the kitchen. When they were seated, he offered refreshments, which Tamara refused.

There was a sudden, uncomfortable silence. Tamara had never been one to dance around issues, using polite nothings to smooth the way, but today she didn't seem able to state the reason she'd come to visit. He thought about asking her outright how she'd survived that horrific slaughter in the barren village in the middle of Africa, but she seemed so fragile, so unlike the woman he'd known, that he couldn't. Instead, he said, "How have you been?"

What he really meant was *where* have you been.

She fidgeted, her fingers plucking at the fabric of the trousers she wore with a simple cotton shirt. "It's been tough," she said. Her gaze slid away from his, lowered as if she was fascinated by whatever her fingers were playing with on her pant leg. "The terrorists who kidnapped me that day in Africa needed a doctor. Their leader had been wounded in a skirmish a few days before. Once I'd tended him, and the wounds were healed, he decided I was useful to have around. They kept me with them until a suitable ransom was offered. The negotiations took a long time to finalize."

Quinn was quite sure Tamara had left a lot out of that brief explanation and his mind was going to places that made his gut clench. The man in him didn't want to know what Tamara had suffered. The reporter in him needed details. "I saw your body," he said, more bluntly than he'd intended.

She paled at his words. "You saw—" Leaning forward, she took his hands. "Oh, Quinn, I'm so sorry! I had no idea. I thought you'd been notified I was alive, like my family was." She stopped, drew a deep breath. "That wasn't me. It was Ruth Ives. CMSA had just sent her in and her personal stuff hadn't arrived yet. I loaned her some clothes that morning." Tears leaked from her eyes. "She said something the terrorists didn't like and they killed her. In front of me."

Quinn sucked in his breath and wished he could be swallowed up by the floor. CMSA—Canadian Medical Services Abroad—was a private organization, funded through donations and some government grants, that sent personnel to fragile, poverty-stricken areas in need of medical help. Sometimes that meant working in villages or rural areas helping to cure illness and teaching better health practices, but too often doctors like Tamara were needed in war zones.

"I'm sorry," he said. "I didn't mean to be insensitive."

She was shaking her head even before he'd finished speaking. "No, it's not you. Or what you said. I've been back for a few months, trying to ... readjust." Her lips quirked up into a rueful half-smile. "The shrinks have been telling me I need to be open about my experiences, to normalize them and accept that they are part of what now makes me, me. My parents have been great, but they're used to it. I forget other people aren't."

"Your parents are still in Toronto?" Quinn was relieved to be able to ask a normal question, but felt absurd at the same time.

"They are." She eyed him in what Quinn thought was a speculative way. "Parents are part of the reason I'm here in Vancouver."

That caught his interest. "Part of the reason?"

She said carefully, "Officially, I'm here to meet one of my sponsors."

CMSA received some government grants, but most of their funding was through donations. These were personalized by linking the donor to one of the medical personal serving abroad. The doctor, nurse, or medical technician wrote a monthly newsletter, outlining the conditions they were working in, the people healed, the progress they had made in the area. The newsletters linked the donor to the person being funded and created a bond that kept donors loyal to the organization.

"I'm meeting her tomorrow," Tamara said. She drew a deep breath. "I was hoping you would come with me."

Quinn stared at her. He hadn't seen her request coming and he didn't know how to respond. "Tamara, I—"

"Please, Quinn. There are things I need to ask her and ... " She hesitated, shrugged, swallowed hard. Her beautiful brown eyes were wide and pleading, digging deep into his soul. "I need back up," she said.

Back up? That was odd. "Why?"

She looked away.

His gut clenched and he thought again how much she had changed. "Tamara, I'll come with you to meet the sponsor, if that's what you want. But you know me, I like details and I want to know the background before I get into any situation. So what's up with this one?"

She bit her lip, then sighed. "I'm hoping she will help me find out who my birth parents are."

That was not the answer he was expecting. "Your birth parents? But ... " He hesitated. This was another new facet to Tamara. "You always said the people who raised you were your parents."

"They are. And they always will be, but ... When I was a captive it was hard to keep a sense of myself. I clung to memories. You. My parents. My work. But there were doubts too. Who am I really? My birth parents gave me up for adoption, but they set up a trust fund for me. Why? They had the money to support a baby. Was there something about me they didn't want? That bothered me, and the more I thought about it, the more it ate at me. I was terrified that I might die without ever knowing who I really am. Once I was back in Toronto and coping again, I asked my mom who my real parents were."

There was so much unsaid in this statement, Quinn wasn't sure how to respond. He opted to stick with the facts, for now. "A trust fund?" During their passionate liaison in Africa she'd never mentioned having a trust fund behind her. It struck him that he was surrounded by women who were the recipients of trust funds. How weird was that? "Where does that fit in?"

She looked down at their clasped hands. When she raised her eyes to his, they were shadowed. "Even though my parents weren't wealthy there was always money for extracurricular stuff—music lessons, swimming lessons, memberships in whatever clubs or orga-nizations I wanted. I was a kid. I didn't think about money or the cost of things. Then when I went to university I thought it was paid for by a full scholarship, because my parents sure couldn't afford to put me through med school."

"It wasn't."

"No. The trust fund paid for everything."

"When did you find out?"

"Just before I graduated. I was angry. I felt betrayed." She laughed without humor. "I probably would have done something stupid like dropping out if I'd found out sooner. Instead, I finished up the program, certified, then joined CMSA. I figured whoever my birth parents were, they had money and they probably had status and they wouldn't want a daughter who spent her life with the poor and underprivileged in a third world country."

He wondered how much of that anger had still fueled Tamara's passionate intensity when he'd first met her. Or if that anger had turned inward as she re-evaluated her life during captivity. "What makes you think your sponsor can help you find your birth parents?"

"Whoever created the trust fund took care to cover their tracks. The fund is managed by a law firm in Toronto and they can't tell me who the person or people behind it is. The information is buried under layers and layers of security." Tamara drew a deep breath. "My sponsor can cut through those layers. I just have to convince her to do it."

Warning bells were going off in Quinn's head. People who covered their tracks with the kind of precision Tamara's birth parents had were unlikely to take kindly to being revealed, even if the one doing the exposing was a child given up for adoption. Tamara was about to open up a wasps' nest and she hadn't a clue she might be swarmed the very angry inhabitants of that nest. "Who is this sponsor, anyway?"

"Olivia Waters, the cyber security guru."

Olivia Waters. Well hell. Tamara was right. Waters had written the book on how to keep your information private in a cyber world. If anyone knew how to ferret out someone's identity, it would be Olivia Waters. "It's a big ask, Tamara. How well do you know her?"

"I don't. All I know is that she believed in me enough to spend a ton of her money and a lot of her influence to ensure I got home. I thought ... " She nibbled her lip again, evidently one of her new unconscious nervous tells. "I thought when we met I'd mention that

16

I'm searching for my birth parents. Maybe ask her if she has any ideas where or how I could find information on them."

"Olivia Waters is into security. She's probably has *loose lips sink ships* tattooed on her palm."

Tamara frowned. "Loose lips?"

"World War Two security motto." He smiled at her to lessen the impact of his next statement. "Listen, Tamara. Olivia Waters has the reputation of being tough and unbending. She's a rules person. In an interview, she once described herself and her company as the ultimate shield. Nothing would get past the defenses she put in place. You're not going to be able to coax information out of this woman."

"See?" Tamara squeezed his hands. She didn't look at all put out by his warning. She actually seemed to be pleased. "That's why I need you there. You know about people and how they work. You can help me convince Olivia Waters that she wants to find my birth parents for me."

"Tamara ... "

She must have heard the doubt in his voice for she opened her eyes wide. "Please, Quinn," she whispered.

Hell. No matter how bad an idea he thought this was, he knew there was only one option.

He caved.

CHAPTER 3

"So where am I taking you?" Quinn asked as Tamara slipped into the car. She was wearing what he thought of as quiet clothes—jeans, a simple blouse that was a pale cream color and a slate gray all weather coat over top. The kind of clothes that didn't stand out. The kind that helped a person fade into a crowd. Those clothes upset him as much as her self-effacing manners did. They were so not the Tamara he remembered.

He drove out of the shelter of her downtown hotel's breezeway into a quiet downtown street. His wipers thumped back and forth regularly, fighting the steady rain and losing. Tamara consulted a piece of paper she pulled from her purse. "Olivia said to come to her office at English Bay University. She's a professor there." She glanced over at Quinn. "Do you know it?"

Oh, yeah, he knew EBU. He and Christy had investigated the murders of an EBU grad student and her faculty advisor. He pushed back memories of Christy and told himself to focus on the woman beside him instead. He gave Tamara a quick smile. "Not my alma mater, but yeah, I'm familiar with the campus."

"She said to come at two. She has a meeting at three, though."

"Shouldn't be a problem," Quinn said. "If the traffic cooperates, we can be there with time to spare."

"Oh, good," Tamara said, with a small sigh and an apologetic smile.

She lapsed into silence while he maneuvered through traffic, heading south, then turning onto Broadway, which would take him directly out to the EBU campus. Traffic moved quickly, without a lot of problems, despite the rain. Tamara sat quietly, staring out the window, observing the mix of commercial, then residential buildings that lined the street. There weren't a lot of landmarks Quinn could describe for her, leaving him free to indulge in more memories of Christy.

The last time he'd been out to EBU had been in November last year when he and Christy had been searching for the murderer of Brittany Day. They had just gotten together and every day he found himself sliding more and more deeply under her spell. He remembered the fearless way she'd confronted the predatory grad student, Lorne Cossi, and how she charmed Brittany's unfortunate faculty advisor, Jacob Peiling. The thoughts warmed him and made him ache at the same time. It didn't seem right that he was now headed out to the university with another woman.

Eventually, Tamara interrupted his brooding with a question, and rescued him from his painful, unproductive thoughts. He answered her, then deliberately kept the conversation going until they reached the edges of the EBU campus. After that it was easy to focus on the moment as he searched for a parking spot.

EBU was a large campus with lots of open space between the buildings, but on this rainy afternoon that was more of a problem than a benefit, since parking was on the outskirts and the buildings weren't interconnected. As soon as she was out of the car, Tamara reached into her bag and pulled out a collapsible umbrella. She huddled under it, offering to shelter Quinn too. He smiled, but shook his head. The spring rain was warm and he was used to walking in it without an umbrella.

They had no problem finding the building. It was one of the

university's newer structures, a streamlined infill in the modern style, set between two old grey stone buildings. Olivia Waters' office was on the third floor. When they found it, they were fifteen minutes early. Tamara knocked on her door anyway.

"Come in," a low, husky voice called. Quinn watched Tamara take a deep breath, gather her courage, and shove open the door.

The woman inside had blonde hair, cut short at the sides, with a side part that had a lock of hair crossing her forehead. Her pale skin was flawless, her cheekbones high, and her nose and chin both had a determined jut. Large blue eyes, fringed with thick, dark lashes studied Tamara critically as she entered. After a minute, Olivia smiled. In repose, her expression was formidable, but when she smiled her whole face lit up, expressing pleasure, mischief and delight. When you were at the receiving end of that smile you knew you were welcomed, without reservation.

Quinn frowned to himself, as something nagged at him. He shook off the feeling as Tamara introduced them both.

Olivia jumped up from her chair and came round the desk that dominated the center of the office. She was of average height, slender and lithe in her movements. She opened her arms and enveloped Tamara in a heartfelt hug. "My dear, I am so glad to finally meet you!" She stepped back, silently studying Tamara's face, before the turned to Quinn. "Mr. Armstrong, I've watched your broadcasts and read most of your work over the years. It is a pleasure to be introduced."

Quinn smiled back at her. Olivia Waters had a reputation of being something of a tyrant, but he was seeing nothing of that aspect of her personality right now. He wondered if she'd be open for an interview, but decided now was not the moment to ask. Instead, he said, "I'm delighted to meet you, Ms. Waters. You're a legend in the computer field."

She snorted as she pointed to a sofa set against one wall, indicating they should sit down. "Legend! That just means I've been around for a while and am getting old. You must both call me Olivia."

Laughter leapt into her eyes as she spoke and the smile on her lips hinted at mischief. She certainly didn't look old. Though Quinn knew she was in her fifties, with her vibrancy and the perfect skin with its lack of obvious wrinkles, she could have been ten or more years younger. Now she was a striking woman. In her twenties, she must have been a heart-stopping combination of refined, intelligent features and vibrant personality. Just like—

No. Couldn't be.

The sofa was flanked by two chairs. Quinn chose one of the chairs, while Tamara took the sofa. She cleared her throat and said in a low voice, "I know it's not usual protocol for donors to meet with the CMSA person they sponsor, so I want to thank you for seeing me. I hope I'm not intruding or causing any ... difficulty for you."

The laughter died in Olivia's eyes and was replaced by concern. She sank down onto the sofa beside Tamara, her gaze intent, her expression absorbed. Quinn had seen that look before, but not on the face of Olivia Waters.

She clasped both of Tamara's hands in her own. "Nonsense, my dear. If you hadn't come to me, I would have gone to Toronto to meet you. I was waiting until you were ... stronger before intruding on your recovery." She smiled again, but this time there was worry in her blue eyes. "But now you are here and we can talk. Tell me how you are feeling, what your plans are. How long you are able to stay on the West Coast." She flicked a mischievous glance Quinn's way. "How you came to meet the famous Quinn Armstrong."

Quinn cleared his throat, embarrassed. Tamara laughed, which he suspected was Olivia's intention all along.

"I met Quinn in North Africa, a few weeks before I was kidnapped." She glanced at him, the amusement still in her eyes, reminding him of the old Tamara. "We clicked right from the first." She looked back at Olivia. "I asked him to come with me today because I want to ask you a question. And, well, I felt I needed support." She paused, gathering herself.

Olivia frowned. Quinn wondered if she had any idea what was coming and how she would react when Tamara dropped her bomb.

"I ... You know I'm adopted." As Olivia's frown deepened, Tamara grimaced. "Or maybe you don't. Probably you don't. Well, I am."

Olivia sat very still. Her gaze didn't waver, and the frown hid whatever what reaction she might be having to Tamara's words.

"I never worried about who my birth parents were until I was kidnapped. Then I wondered whether they ever thought about me. Whether or not they would care if I never came back and we never met. It became an obsession with me, I'm afraid, a way to pass long hours alone. I decided if I did regain my freedom, I would find out who they were and I'd ... well, I'd meet them."

"How—" Now it was Olivia's turn to pause. She cleared her throat. "How does this concern me?"

Tamara leaned forward. Her expression was eager, her gaze hopeful, trusting. She had no idea who she was talking to. "My adoption was a private one and the names of my birth parents were carefully hidden, but I think they must have cared about me, because they set up a trust fund for me. The lawyer who administers it says he can't tell me who they are, because their identities are buried deep behind layers and layers of protection. You're an expert in cyber security. I was hoping that you'd help me peel back those layers and find them."

Olivia didn't say anything; she just stared. The frown etched on her features made her expression one of formidable disapproval. Tamara faltered and leaned back, pulling her hands from Olivia's for the first time. An ugly red flush darkened her cheeks. She lowered her eyes and bit her lip.

Quinn looked from Tamara to Olivia. "You should tell her," he said, his voice rougher than he intended. It had clearly taken a lot for Tamara to openly express these private thoughts. He wasn't going to let Olivia Waters hide behind pretense when she had the power to soothe and heal.

His comment shattered Olivia's composure. The frown dissolved, leaving behind naked vulnerability. "I did plan to, but not this way. Not today. Later, once we got to know each other a little bit."

"What ... what are you talking about?" Tamara's gaze flicked from Olivia to Quinn and back. "Tell me!"

"There's no need to dig through the trust fund's security to find your birth parents, Tamara. You've already found them." Tamara frowned. Olivia drew a deep breath. "I'm your mother."

"My mother?" Tamara whispered. The red in her cheeks leached away, leaving her pale.

Olivia nodded.

Tamara turned on Quinn. There was hurt and growing anger in dark eyes that dominated her colorless face. "Did you know before and not tell me?"

Quinn reflected that this was the way the old Tamara would have reacted, with angry fire that ignored the boundaries of socially correct behavior.

"Tamara!" Olivia said, using the disapproving tone of a mother censuring her misbehaving child.

Quinn shook his head. He didn't need Olivia's interference. He was glad to see Tamara let her passion loose again and he was up to the challenge of easing her fears. "I had no idea until you opened the door and I saw Olivia. I began to wonder then, but it wasn't until we started to talk that I realized."

"How?" Olivia asked. She sounded genuinely puzzled.

"Yes, how? When I had absolutely no idea," Tamara said.

A rueful smile quirked up one side of Quinn's mouth. "I've seen the expressions on Olivia's face before. It took me a while to figure out where, but once I did, I started to notice features you had in common. I was pretty sure I was right."

Tamara frowned at her mother, who frowned back. Quinn laughed. They were mirror expressions. Tamara's hair was a darker blonde than her mother's, her chin more rounded, her nose much less commanding, while her eyes were brown. Like Olivia, her cheekbones were high in a narrow face and her mouth had the same full, passionate lower lip.

"Why ... why did you give me up?" Tamara's voice shook, reminding Quinn that this had to be hard for her, even if finding a birth parent had been her ultimate goal.

Olivia sighed. "I was twenty, still at university, when I met your father. I was an intern in his department. We worked closely together and I fell for him. For a wonderful summer, I believed I was the most important person in his life." She shrugged. "Then the summer came to an end. I got pregnant with you and he broke it off. It was an old story. He was married and had two kids who were still toddlers. He said he already had a family and wasn't looking for a new one. He assumed I'd have an abortion, but I couldn't. I also wasn't ready to bring up a child. Over the years, I wished—"

Her expression hardened. "No excuses. Excuses aren't fair to either of us. I chose logic, not emotion, to make my decision. I interviewed single moms with kids of all ages, then I analyzed the data. It told me that placing you with a solid, loving family would provide you with a more stable home and a better financial future than you would have if you stayed with me. I took a year off school while I was pregnant and got a job at a small law firm. The lawyer I worked for found the Aherns and arranged the adoption before you were even born."

Tamara had been pale before, but hearing the stark reality of her birth put so bluntly, had her eyes wide and dark. She pulled her arms closer to her body, her hands in her lap. Quinn reached over, took one and held it. "Are you okay?"

"I don't know how to feel," she said, her voice small and tremulous, as if she was on the verge of tears.

"You'll have more questions," Olivia said. Her tone was brisk. There was no evidence of softer emotions in her expression. "I understand and I'll try to answer them, all of them." She took Tamara's other hand and rubbed it between both of hers. "I want to get to know you, Tamara, the woman you've become, your dreams and fears. I hope we can be friends."

"I'm not sure," Tamara whispered. Her eyes searched Olivia's face, her expression vulnerable.

Olivia nodded without expression, covering whatever emotions her daughter's dismay roused. "I understand."

"You said ... " Tamara took a deep breath and visibly calmed herself. "You said my father had children. That means I have siblings?"

"A brother and a sister." Olivia hesitated, then she said gently, "I doubt they know anything about you."

Tamara nodded as if she expected this. She glanced at Quinn for reassurance, before turning back to Olivia. "I want to meet him," she said.

Olivia was silent.

"My birth father," Tamara said, in case Olivia didn't understand. "I want to know who he is."

Olivia pressed her lips together. "I can't tell you his name until I speak to him. He needs to give me confirmation he's okay with it."

An alarm went off in Quinn's brain. If Tamara's father was the electrician down the street, or the manager of the local grocery store, Olivia would have popped out his identity without a second's hesitation. No, he must be someone of importance, a man with name recognition. A wealthy man, perhaps even a powerful one.

He looked thoughtfully at Olivia. "You stayed in touch, then. Even though he refused to acknowledge your baby."

Olivia colored, but she said coolly enough, "I'm a prominent person, Quinn, and there are times when Tamara's father and I connect."

Definitely a mover and shaker, then. He wondered who the man was.

"When I found out you were coming, Tamara, I knew it was time to reveal the truth. I told your father you would want to meet him," Olivia said briskly. "He didn't refuse to see you, but, Tamara, I must warn you." Her voice softened. "He didn't express excitement or indicate pleasure at the thought of meeting you. Now that the moment has come he may refuse outright. Please don't take it personally."

"How can I not?" Tamara said. Her voice was stronger, enriched with underlying anger, as she rebounded from the shock of all she'd learned.

Olivia sighed, looking down and away.

"When will you know if he's willing to meet Tamara?" Quinn asked into the tense silence that followed.

Olivia roused herself. "I'll call him this afternoon." She glanced at

Tamara. "I'll see if he's available soon. Tomorrow, perhaps? For dinner?"

After glancing at Quinn, Tamara said, "Fine, but I want Quinn there too."

"Oh, but—"

Her eyes narrowed, Tamara said, "I want to know who my father is, yes. His name, what he looks like. Even more, I want to *know* him, the kind of man he is. But I'll do it on my terms, not his. And my terms include Quinn."

Olivia stared back at her, then suddenly she tilted her head back and laughed. "His daughter is tougher than her mother was. All right, Tamara, Quinn comes to the meeting." She glanced at a clock high on the plain white wall. "Blast, it's five to three. I have to go, though I don't want to."

They all stood. Olivia hugged Tamara again, though this time Tamara stood more stiffly in her embrace than she had earlier. Olivia shook Quinn's hand, and as she walked them to the door, she said, "I'll call you tonight and let you know what's happening." When Tamara nodded, Olivia's gaze softened and she added, "I am so pleased you came today. So glad we have had this chance to meet each other properly."

Tamara's smile was just a faint curve of her lips. "Me, too," she said.

Quinn wondered exactly how true either of those statements were.

CHAPTER 4

"I have a bad feeling about this, Dad," Quinn said, as he paused in the kitchen to let his father know he was leaving. True to her word Olivia Waters had arranged a meeting with Tamara's birth father. She hadn't told Tamara who the man was, though, and that only added to Quinn's earlier sense of problems brewing.

Added to the lack of identification was the time and location of the dinner meeting—seven-thirty at Connoisseur, one of Vancouver's premier fine dining restaurants. A fashionable location and a fashionable hour, both of which raised questions in Quinn's mind. For a man who had shown no interest in acknowledging Tamara, her birth father was awfully keen on being seen with her at the kind of restaurant where who dined there was noticed.

Roy scrutinized him. "Figure you'll get stiffed with a four-figure bill?"

He tugged at the blue tie that he'd worn with a white dress suit and dark suit. You didn't go to Connoisseur dressed in jeans and a tee. Still, he felt as if he was about to meet his future father-in-law, which only added to his gut feeling that something was off.

"No, that's not ... " he began, then realized his father was teasing. "It's the mystery man. If he's an average guy, Olivia would have chosen a different venue for what will probably be a very emotional meeting. He must be someone with money, or status. Or both. Olivia Waters wouldn't invite him to Connoisseur otherwise."

"She might if she harbors a grudge for his desertion all those years ago," Roy said.

"You mean she knows he won't be comfortable and she's trying to embarrass him?" Quinn considered the suggestion and felt moderately better. His father was good at digging into people's motivations and he was probably right about this situation. People did all kinds of nasty things to each other after a breakup. His experience with Christy—who had never said a bad word against him since they split —couldn't be used as a benchmark. But then Christy hadn't been in love with him, and maybe Olivia Waters had been head over heels for her mystery man.

Thinking about Christy and what wasn't to be eliminated his burgeoning good cheer. "I suppose the only way to know is to go and meet the man. I'll see you later."

"Okay. Oh, I almost forgot. We're doing a barbeque tomorrow. Spur of the moment thing. Why don't you ask Tamara to come along?"

He looked at his father through narrowed eyes. "What are you up to, Dad?"

"Nothing!" Roy said. "Three mentioned that Sledge is stressing about this new manager situation so I thought he could use day with a completely different bunch of people than he usually hangs with."

His father looked sincere. Quinn knew from experience that didn't necessarily mean he was. "Right. You're worried about Sledge."

"I'm not. Three is." Three was Roy's name for his old friend, Trevor McCullagh, Sledge's father. "I thought a home-cooked meal might be a good way for Tamara to get to know us and for us to get to know her." He managed to look innocent, though his eyes twinkled as he spread his hands wide. "Two birds, you know?"

It was possible. "Okay. I'll ask her. She might not want to come, though."

"Sure she will. You'll convince her," Roy said.

28

The twinkle was more pronounced now. Quinn decided he'd better leave before his father suggested he invite Olivia Waters and the mystery dad as well.

He picked up Tamara at her hotel as he had the previous day. He'd warned her about the venue and suggested she wear a dress for the dinner. She had chosen a simple cotton frock with a high neck-line and three-quarter sleeves. The skirt reached to her knees and she wore flat sandals. The dress wasn't ill-fitting, but it did nothing to enhance her thin figure.

As Tamara rushed out to the car, Quinn thought about how the dress would look on Christy, her curves filling out all the extra fabric, and how she'd walk with her head high and confidence in every stride. By contrast, Tamara's movements were sharp and hurried and she moved with her head down. It made him realize that she wasn't comfortable in the dress, which had him wondering why she wore it. That thought was swiftly followed by one that it might not be the dress that made her uncomfortable, but her own skin, which made him ashamed for comparing Tamara to Christy at all.

They arrived at Connoisseur five minutes early. The restaurant was minimalist chic with snowy white walls decorated with abstract paintings in jewel tones. The tables were covered by starched white linen and the cutlery was designed with clean lines, but was heavy in the hand. The centerpiece was a crystal sculpture, different on every table, set on a platform that shone light through the crystal, making the statue glitter with embedded color.

The maître d' guided them to a private room at the back of the restaurant. It was decorated in the same understated way as the main dining room, but the windows that made up one wall provided a spectacular view across False Creek. Olivia was standing by those windows holding a wine glass when Tamara and Quinn arrived. The table, Quinn noted, was set for five.

For five? What the hell?

Olivia was dressed in a silk creation that flattered her figure and shouted out that she was an individual of stature, even as it empha-sized that she was all woman. She offered them the choice of white or red from the already uncorked wine bottles on the table. Quinn chose red.

Tamara shook her head as she eyed her birth mother's outfit and seemed to sink a little deeper into her own discomfort. "I lived as a Muslim for almost three years. I no longer drink alcohol."

Olivia raised her eyebrows, but didn't press. As she poured Quinn's red, she said, "I asked you here a few minutes early so I could tell you a bit about your father, Tamara. I ... "

There was a stir in the outer dining room. Olivia's gaze snapped toward the door and the dining room beyond. Her eyes narrowed. Quinn looked in the same direction. From where he was standing, he could see an average-sized man with impossibly golden hair, dressed in a bespoke blue suit that fit his trim body perfectly, striding through the dining room.

Headed their way, his entourage trailing behind him.

That nasty feeling that this was not a good idea came back with a vengeance. He should know by now to listen to his gut.

The man paused in the entrance to the private room. Olivia's smile was warm, but there was an edge of annoyance in her voice when she said, "Fredrick, you're early."

Fredrick waved a hand in response to this as he walked into the room. Behind him, his entourage shook itself out into two muscled men who positioned themselves at a table just outside the room and a thin man with a harassed expression, who followed him inside.

Olivia turned to Tamara. "This is Fredrick Jarvis—"

Tamara's expression was shocked, disbelieving, horrified. "I know who he is."

Of course she did. Everyone did. Fredrick Jarvis was a Canadian politician who'd begun his career working in the oil industry, first in management, later as a spokesman debunking global warming, before he entered politics as a member of the Dogwood Party, the most right wing of Canadian right wing parties. He was a talented speaker and he had a way of making people listen to him and consider his arguments, even if what he was saying was far out of their comfort zone. The Dogwoods were the current party in power in British Columbia and Frederic Jarvis was a provincial minister.

He was also one of a dozen people vying for the leadership of the federal wing of the Dogwood Party. If he won, he could one day be prime minister of Canada.

This, then, was Tamara's father. Quinn was having a hard time visualizing Olivia Waters with Fredrick Jarvis. While she wasn't politically active, the causes she did involve herself in benefited those without influence or money. But maybe their personal and political differences were why they had split up all those years ago.

Fredrick Jarvis scrutinized Tamara for a minute, then he nodded. "She has the look of my father's family. She could be mine."

"What do you mean she could be?" Olivia was staring at him as if he had just grown horns and a tail. "She is yours, Fredrick."

Jarvis raised his brows, but he smiled at Olivia in a way that was almost caressing. "We talked about this all those years ago, Olivia. You promised me you would do the sensible thing and terminate the pregnancy."

Tamara made a little sound of pain. Quinn put his arm around her waist and pulled her close. Olivia glanced their way, then refocused on Jarvis. "I put her up for adoption, Frederick. Wasn't that enough?"

There was anguish in her voice and Jarvis responded to it. He raised his hand to cup her cheek. "Dear Olivia. Such a strong moral center." The murmured words were as tender as his touch.

It was a performance that was riveting, Quinn thought, as they all waited for Frederick's next move. Olivia Waters, the cyber guru whose brisk, no nonsense style was legendary, was looking up at him with a beseeching vulnerability that exposed raw emotions she couldn't control. It was clear to Quinn that she had never gotten over Frederick Jarvis. Even now, as she was introducing the child he had never wanted to him, she desired his approval.

"I'm a prominent man, Olivia," Jarvis said gently. "Women have been known to lie about this sort of thing to gain a foothold, so to speak."

She paled. "I'm not just any woman, Frederick."

His thumb stroked along her cheekbone. He moved slightly and Quinn thought he was going to lean in for a kiss. Instead, he hovered, tantalizing, promising without providing. "No," he murmured. "You are my special one, Olivia. My beautiful computer genius. You know I couldn't do without you."

Her expression said she loved hearing those words, that Frederick Jarvis' approval was important to her, but she didn't get a chance to reply.

Tamara said loudly, "Stop!" Then more quietly, "Please."

Jarvis looked over, his brows raised. Twin patches of red blazed on Olivia's pale skin.

Tamara looked at her father. "Why did you agree to meet me?"

His hand fell away from Olivia's cheek. She reached up and put her hand to his face, as if touching him would bring his focus back to her. It didn't. He ignored the touch and Olivia's hand drifted away as he walked over to Tamara, moving with a sinuous grace that was as mesmerizing as his smooth, mellow voice.

He stopped a few feet away from her. After a quick assessing glance at Quinn, he focused on his daughter. He smiled in a tender way that was completely parental. "I didn't know about you before Olivia called."

She nodded jerkily, but didn't say anything. Waiting.

"I had Cowan ... " He turned his head to half look at the thin man with the harassed expression who had followed him into the room. "Mr. Cowan is my chief of staff. I don't know what I'd do without his brilliant ability to strategize."

Cowan perked up, buoyed by the praise.

"Cowan did some research for me," Jarvis continued. He was focused on Tamara now, watching her reactions. Assessing her response. "You have a fine reputation in medical circles."

Tamara stared up into his eyes. Her expression didn't change, but Quinn could see that she was completely fixated on Jarvis, drinking in every word he said.

"The work that you do in war zones, helping those who have done nothing but be born in the wrong place at the wrong time, shows not only a remarkable courage, but a compassion that is noteworthy. I applaud you."

"Thank you," Tamara said hoarsely.

"Your captivity. It must have been horrible."

"It was." She didn't elaborate.

Jarvis smiled. There was a world-weary understanding of the crimes people do to one another in that smile. A sadness for what his daughter had endured. "I am sorry," he said gently. The smile was gone, replaced by studied seriousness.

She nodded jerkily and said again, "Thank you."

He smiled in response to that, but this time the smile held hope, had a flare of optimism. "Of course, good can come out of tragedy. Cowan's research showed that your rescue and return is trending very nicely on social media."

Quinn was so deeply involved in the emotional intensity of the scene that it took him a few moments to process that statement. Trending nicely? What the hell?

Tamara was frowning, her eyes searching her father's face. "I'm afraid I don't understand."

"Frederick, no! Not now." Olivia sounded anguished.

Tamara glanced at her, then back at Jarvis. Her brows were raised in question. Quinn was very much afraid he knew where this conversation was going. His gut clenched as he anticipated Tamara's pain, and anger bloomed.

Jarvis shot Olivia a direct, steady look. "Don't interfere." He turned back to Tamara, his gaze warm again. "Your timing is excellent, my dear. With your approval rating, acknowledging you as my daughter will give my campaign the kind of push it needs to send me into the lead and leave my competitors in the dust."

"That's why you wanted to meet me?" Tamara said. There was no inflection in her voice. Her expression was frozen. Her gaze remained locked with her father's. But Quinn could feel the tremors wracking her body. Jarvis had dealt her an agonizing blow and she was feeling it, even if she wasn't showing her pain.

"I wanted to meet my daughter, of course," Frederick said. "To see if she was all her reputation proclaimed." The warmth of his smile invited Tamara to smile back. She didn't. There was the briefest of hesitations, then tenderness shone in that smile. He said, "And she is."

Tamara's expression didn't change, but Olivia looked relieved. Quinn could still feel Tamara shaking in the shelter of his arm and outrage seared through him at the way these two people who had made her were treating her. "Her name is Tamara, and she's your daughter, Jarvis, not a campaign ornament."

Jarvis blinked and frowned as he refocused on Quinn. "And you are?"

Quinn savored the moment. He figured Frederick Jarvis was about to go ballistic. He was going to enjoy the show. "I'm Quinn Armstrong."

It took a moment for Jarvis to place him, but Quinn knew the instant he did. Fury leapt into the man's eyes, then he turned on Olivia, his action the swift dart of a predator. "You invited a reporter to this meeting?"

She flared back. "I didn't. He's Tamara's friend. Besides, you love reporters. What's the harm in this one?"

"What's the harm? This isn't just any reporter, it's an Armstrong!"

Yes, Quinn thought. An Armstrong. The Armstrongs and Fredrick Jarvis went back a ways, and the relationship wasn't a good one.

"He's Roy Armstrong's son!"

Olivia's eyes opened wide. "Roy Armstrong, the author? The crazy guy who led the protests against the oil pipeline to the coast?"

"Yes! The man who almost cost me my career!"

Olivia put a hand to her lips. Her eyes were wide, her expression stricken. "I'm sorry. I didn't know."

Jarvis drew himself up, pulling back and putting a lid on his anger in a way that was almost visible. "Too late now," he said. His tone was harsh, the words clipped. His gaze swept the room and settled on Tamara. "He will have to go."

Her gaze locked with her father's. "No."

"No?" He sounded amused, as if her response was just a silly attempt at rebellion.

Tamara bit her lip, then she dragged her gaze away from her father and turned so she could look up into Quinn's face.

What he saw in her eyes chilled him. There was betrayal, desolation, despair.

"Quinn," she said. "Can we leave?"

"Sure." He slipped his arm from her waist and took her hand protectively.

"You can't go yet," Mr. Cowan, the campaign strategist, said suddenly. He'd positioned himself just inside the doorway, an observer of the scene, not a participant. "The press is waiting outside. If they see her coming out without Mr. Jarvis, they'll get the wrong impression."

"You notified the press?" Olivia said. Shock and dismay had her voice winging upwards as she finished.

"Of course," Cowan said. He nodded, apparently not at all disturbed by the emotions zinging through the room. "The check I did shows that people sympathize with her. They see her as a heroine, victimized by irrational and violent thugs. That's why we're at this meeting tonight. The public is sentimental, you know. What could be more touching than having a man discover his long-lost daughter, especially a daughter who has lived a nightmare, but who is now able to return to her loving family?"

"I'm not his daughter," Tamara said suddenly. Her hand tightened in Quinn's.

"But I thought ... " Cowan turned to Jarvis. "If the girl is correct, we'll look like fools. The press will have a field day."

"You're not?" Frowning, Jarvis looked from Tamara to Olivia. "What is going on, Olivia? You swore to me that this girl was mine." His expression hardened. "Are you trying to undercut my campaign? I expected better of you. I thought you were on my side."

"Of course she's your daughter, Fredrick! And I don't give a damn about your campaign."

Tamara's voice cut through the argument that threatened to turn

35

into a battle. "You may have donated the sperm that created me, but you are not my father, Mr. Jarvis. My father is Todd Ahern and he is a good man who has spent his life selflessly caring for others. He's a man I respect and a man I love. He is not you and he never will be."

"That's right. He's a clergyman, isn't he?" Jarvis said. At Tamara's outburst, he had shifted gears. Now he sounded remarkably mellow, as if this was just normal get-to-know-you chitchat. He turned to his assistant. "You checked him out, didn't you?"

Cowan nodded. He fiddled with this phone, then said, "He's a United Church minister with a congregation in downtown Toronto. No record, but he's protested a time or two over perceived mistreatment of the poor and destitute. He's also volunteered for his local MP, who is a Liberal."

"You made up a dossier on my father?" Tamara's voice was low. It shook with emotion, anger at the forefront. There were two spots of color on her cheeks. She dropped Quinn's hand and advanced on Jarvis, her eyes blazing.

Cowan hurried away from his post by the door and managed to slip between them. A big man, dressed in chef whites, surged into the opening. He was smiling. "Good evening, Minister Jarvis! It is a pleasure to have your patronage this evening. As per Ms. Waters instruction, I've prepared a special menu for your party. Antoine, my head server, will be caring for you tonight." His voice tapered off as he absorbed the charged scene before him. "Is everything all right?"

"No, it's not!" Tamara snapped.

"Everything is fine," Frederick said. He raised his eyebrows and smiled. "You're Jackson Vining, aren't you?"

Vining nodded. The owner of Connoisseur, he was a chef with international reputation for excellence. He looked around, clearly wondering if the emotional scene would somehow rebound against him and his restaurant.

"I'm sorry to interrupt, sir." The new voice came from the doorway. One of the security detail was standing there and his expression was impassive.

"Yes, what is it, Beck?" Jarvis said. The phrase was clipped, impatient.

"Your voices can be heard in the restaurant. People are taking notice."

Olivia rolled her eyes. "Now you've done it, Fredrick. You didn't have to notify the press to show up. We'll be all over the news before we even sit down to dinner."

"Not quite," Quinn said. "Chef, do you have a backdoor Dr. Ahern and I could use?"

Vining looked from him, to Tamara, to the others, then he nodded. "Come with me."

"You can't go! We have to sort this out," Cowan said. He sounded distraught, as if his world was collapsing around him.

Jarvis scrutinized Tamara's features. After a minute he said quietly, "Let her go. This has been a lot to take in. She needs time."

Quinn edged Tamara toward the doorway.

Cowan tapped his phone. "Perhaps she isn't worth cultivating. It was a long time."

"What are you talking about, you stupid little man?" Olivia demanded, sounding fraught.

Cowan looked up. Blinked. Said loudly, "Her captivity. She was held by radical terrorists for almost three years. In addition, she was brought up by a family with left leaning beliefs. She could have been turned." He shrugged. "She's probably some kind of fundamentalist spy."

Tamara stiffened. She turned toward her father, her eyes seeking his reaction. Jarvis looked thoughtful, apparently considering his strategist's comment.

It was not the right response. Fury blossomed in Tamara's eyes. Quinn decided he'd better get her out of there before she did or said something she'd later regret. He took her hand and led her to the door. Chef Vining, who had been watching this with an impassive expression, but narrowed, cautious eyes, indicated that they follow him.

As they hurried through the restaurant toward the kitchen and the rear exit, it was clear to Quinn that most of the diners had heard at least parts of the uncomfortable little scene. The press was going to be all over this. He needed to get Tamara away, now.

This was bad. Very bad.

He should have trusted his gut.

CHAPTER 5

"Welcome," Roy said as he opened his front door. "Glad you could make it on such short notice."

Olivia Waters was standing on the other side and she frowned at him. "Your invitation said this was a 'family' barbeque and a way to get to know Tamara."

She made quote marks with her fingers as she said family and her expression was ... not quite hostile, but not friendly either. Roy cocked an eyebrow. If that was the way she wanted to play this, well, so be it.

When Quinn told him that Tamara's birth mother was Olivia Waters and that both women seemed to be very positive about reconnecting, he'd called up Olivia and invited her to the barbeque. It would be, he reasoned, a non-threatening way for them to get to know each other. Besides, he wanted to know what kind of woman Olivia was. After all, if things didn't go right, she might one day be Quinn's mother-in-law and he'd have to deal with her at other 'family' events.

Then the dinner happened, Tamara discovered her father was Frederick Jarvis, and everything fell apart. He didn't like how Jarvis treated Tamara. Hell, he didn't like Jarvis anyway. He regretted the decision to invite Olivia, but by then it was too late. The offer had been made and she'd accepted.

So if she wanted to be grouchy, it was fine with him. He smiled at her slowly, in a way that he hoped would really irritate her, and said, "My Quinn and Tamara had a relationship before her kidnapping. Now she's back and I want to get to know her. She wants to get to know you. Seemed like a good fit."

"All friends together, then," Olivia said, ungraciously, he thought. She raised her brows when he didn't step back and tilted her chin in a way that suggested she didn't have a lot of time for empty social pursuits like friendship.

"You got it." He ignored her unfathomable hostility—it was Jarvis who'd been smarmy to Tamara, not the other way around—and gave her a big grin, designed to annoy. "So why don't we give it a try? The party's out back. Down the stairs and through Quinn's office."

Olivia looked around as they descended to the ground floor of the townhouse. "Nice space," she said in an offhand way. Then she added, in the same tone, "You're Roy Armstrong, the author, aren't you?"

Roy glanced at her. "I thought you didn't realize."

Olivia frowned. "Why wouldn't I? The press loves you and since this Jamieson affair last fall, your social media profile has shot way up. Your picture is everywhere. I've even read one of your books."

"Magnanimous of you."

"It was boring. That's your fault, not mine," she said, as if she was stating a truth, not an opinion.

Roy took a moment to decide if he was annoyed or amused. By that time they were through Quinn's office and at the sliding doors to the patio. He flung them open at the same time as he decided he was mainly amused, but also a little stung by her words. He'd take this opportunity to give her a verbal poke, then they'd be even.

Four heads turned toward the doors as they opened. Roy stepped out onto the small concrete pad that held the barbecue, a table with chairs, and a couple of loungers. "Hey, everyone, this is Olivia Waters. She's Tamara's mom, birth mom. Olivia, the two guys are Trevor and Rob McCullagh and the ladies are Christy and Ellen Jamieson. The cat is Stormy. Christy's daughter, Noelle is around somewhere. Or she was when I went to answer the door."

"She's off to get Mary Petrofsky," Christy said.

Why did you invite this old broad? Bad enough you've brought this Tamara chick into our circle.

Trevor shot a daggers look at the cat. Sledge raised his eyebrows.

Christy said, "Stop it." Her voice sounded raw, as if she was having a hard time with her emotions. Roy felt an uneasy guilt, but it was momentary. The players in his son's romance needed to step up. And if that meant taking a few hits—well, it happened.

Ellen glanced from Christy to Olivia then to the cat. "You will apologize."

Roy cocked his head and looked down at Stormy. The cat yawned.

There was no apology from Frank, but Olivia said indignantly, "For what? I've only just got here and I've done nothing."

Roy said hastily, "Quinn's picking up Tamara. He should be here any time."

I'm off then. I'd rather go talk to my daughter.

Ellen colored, pursed her lips, then studiously ignored the cat. Christy smiled at Olivia and said, "Don't mind us. You unfortunately came in at the end of a conversation."

Roy offered Olivia a glass of wine, which she sipped while she scrutinized the group. "Which one of you needs to apologize?"

Ellen sucked in her breath, as Christy flushed. Sledge gifted Olivia with his rock-star grin and said, "Guilty!" He shook his head, pretending to be abashed, but looking unrepentant. "I was talking back to my dad. Ellen ... " He winked. "Doesn't like it."

Trevor flubbed his cue and looked astonished at this statement. Olivia narrowed her eyes. "There's something going here. What are you hiding?"

"Should the question be what? Or should it be who?" Roy asked.

When Olivia looked at him, he raised his brows and indicated Sledge with a jut of his chin.

Olivia followed his gaze, but there was no enlightenment on her face as she looked at Sledge. "You?"

Roy concluded she wasn't a rock fan. He grinned at her, feeling mischievous. "We don't want the neighbors to know he's here."

She leveled a disbelieving look at Sledge, then turned back to Roy. "I know about you. You're a disruptor. You like to shake people up, make them question ordinary things, ask if there isn't a better way."

Trevor snorted. "That he does."

"What's wrong with that?" Roy asked, pulling another beer from the cooler under the table, then handing it to Sledge.

"If you had any computer skills you'd be a hacker," Olivia said, as if this explained everything.

Which maybe it did. Olivia was a cyber security expert. She'd think in metaphors relating to computers. Hackers caused problems in the cyber world. He caused problems in the real one. He figured she pretty much had him nailed. No need, then to be annoyed. "Good thing my computer skills are limited. Though it would be nice if I could figure out track changes," he added wistfully.

Olivia stared at him, her expression incredulous. "Track changes? What are you talking about?"

"My editor uses track changes, but even though I deal with all of the little balloons, my document is never clean after I'm finished. Every time I open afterwards the changes keep coming back."

"That's easy enough to fix," Olivia said.

"Really?"

"Of course."

"Show me," Roy said, galvanized by this information.

"Now?" Olivia sounded aghast.

"Why not?" Roy lifted his glass and made an onwards motion with his arm. "Bring your wine."

"But ... "

"We'll be back in a few minutes," he said to the rest, then headed inside. Looking uncertain, Olivia trailed behind.

As their footsteps sounded on the stairs, Sledge stretched out his legs and laughed. "Maybe explaining track changes will make Ms. Waters less grumpy."

"God bless track changes, then," Trevor said, and Sledge chuckled.

The strained atmosphere eased. Christy said, "Harry Endicott, the forensic auditor, wants to meet with me about the trust embezzlement. Ellen will be there as well, but I wonder if you would be able to attend, Trevor. I'd like someone with a legal background there, and I value your input."

Trevor looked surprised and pleased. "Of course. When?"

She was giving him the details when they heard footsteps coming down the stairs, Roy and Olivia apparently having solved the track changes issue. As they were about to come through the sliding glass doors onto the patio, the front door opened. Olivia stepped outside. Roy paused to shout, "We're out back, Quinn. Come on through."

Trevor pulled out his phone to enter the meeting details into his calendar. He was about to put it away when Quinn and Tamara reached the sliding glass doors.

The phone pinged. Trevor stared. "My God," he muttered.

Christy frowned at him. "Trevor? What's the matter?"

He looked up, glancing at all of them. His expression was horrified. "Fredrick Jarvis is dead, in what the police are calling suspicious circumstances. It looks like he was murdered."

"MURDERED?" That was Ellen and she sounded shocked. "Are you sure, Trevor?"

Trevor was scanning his phone, frowning as he read the news bulletin. He nodded. "Apparently, it happened earlier this afternoon. The police aren't giving out any details, but they are admitting his death was not from natural causes."

Christy heard Ellen and Trevor's conversation, but her focus wasn't on the news bulletin, or the death of a politician she didn't know and had no connection to. She was staring at Quinn and Tamara as they paused in the doorway, immobilized by Trevor's shocking news. Quinn had his hand on Tamara's back as if he had been about to introduce her to the group, but now he was bending toward her protectively. The expression on his face was filled with concern and, she thought sadly, affection.

She'd pushed him away and he'd moved on. She'd suspected it was true when she saw Quinn hug Tamara, but until this moment, she hadn't quite believed it. Accepting Roy's invitation had been a calculated risk, but Roy and the others had become a family to her over the past year, and she wanted to prove to herself she could be part of Roy's eclectic band even if she was not with Quinn.

She was so fixated on Quinn and Tamara she didn't notice Sledge was no longer sitting beside his father until he settled in next to her. She looked at him, surprised, and he flashed his bone-melting rock-star grin and took her hand in his. She looked down at their linked fingers, then back up to his face. The rock-star grin toned down to something softer, kinder. She realized that he understood what she was feeling and had joined her to help her through this initial meeting with Quinn's former and now new love. A burst of gratitude had her smiling back at him in a silent thank you.

Olivia said, "Frederick is dead? How is this possible?" Her voice rose on 'dead,' then cracked with emotion in the next sentence.

Christy looked away from Sledge, now able to join into the conversation. Olivia's expression was stricken, her eyes wide, her lips slightly parted. She'd lifted her hand to her throat in a classic gesture of vulnerability. Christy didn't know her, but she recognized the shock of death, those moments when the mind understood, but couldn't accept the horror of what had happened. It was a time when a person needed other people to help her through. Olivia was standing near to her. Impulsively, she reached out with her free hand to touch the other woman's. "Olivia, I am so sorry. We all are. Roy, why don't you help Olivia over to that chair and let her sit down?"

44

Roy shot Christy an appreciative glance. His gaze lingered on her hand linked with Sledge's and sharpened, then he said, "Good idea. Olivia, can I top up your wine?"

The offer of wine seemed to restore Olivia. She shot Roy a bemused look and said, "I'd prefer a shot of rye whisky, straight up, if you have it." She sat rather heavily on the chair Roy had guided her to.

Initial surprise was replaced by approval in Roy's expression. "The liquor stash is upstairs," he said. "I'll be back in a minute."

He disappeared into the house. Quinn said to Tamara, "You should sit beside Olivia."

His voice pulled everybody's attention from Olivia to Tamara. Christy thought she should offer her condolences to Tamara too, but there was no evidence that the woman was in any way affected by Frederick Jarvis's death.

"I won't say I'm glad he's dead, but I don't really care that he is," Tamara said, looking at Quinn. He was frowning, his concern obvious. Her expression was calm, almost peaceful.

Her comment was too much for Olivia. "How can you say that? He was your father. Without him you wouldn't be here!"

"He may have been my biological father, but he wasn't part of my life. In fact, he didn't want you to have me at all, so it's you and your decision not to abort me that is the reason I'm here, more than his sperm contribution."

She said this in an unemotional tone that Christy found quite chilling. She glanced at the others. Ellen's brows were raised in a disapproving way, while Trevor was frowning. Sledge was frowning too as he swirled his beer bottle around absentmindedly.

Olivia's eyes narrowed, anger clearly coming to life. She looked about to say something when Roy reappeared with a bottle of rye and a glass. He'd missed the whole conversation, but he must have picked up on the atmosphere, because he shot a frowning glance at the others as he handed Olivia the glass. The liquor sloshed as he poured her a generous serving, the only sound in the silence that had followed Tamara's remarks.

Olivia lifted the glass to her lips and drank deep, draining it. She held the glass out. Roy refilled it. Quinn got Tamara settled in a chair, the one on the other side of Sledge, and far too close to her, in Christy's opinion. She fought down resentment as Quinn sat beside Tamara. He could have taken the chair beside Sledge and put Tamara closer to Olivia. Even if they were currently at odds, Olivia was her mother. They needed to deal with this if they were ever to build a working relationship.

Olivia swirled the amber liquid in her glass and glared at her daughter. "That's a dreadful thing to say!"

Tamara shrugged.

Olivia's voice was strident as she continued. "Fredrick Jarvis had good values and he was dedicated to making this a better world. No man is perfect—"

"No person," Roy said.

Olivia turned hostile eyes on him. "I beg your pardon?"

Roy had succeeded in diverting the conversation and a little of the tension eased. He didn't appear at all put out by the snotty tone in Olivia's voice because he smiled and said, "It's more common to use the neutral term for the generic these days. Person reflects both sexes, where man is gender specific."

Olivia downed the shot of rye. Roy poured her another. "I was being gender specific. In my opinion, men are rarely perfect."

"You sound as if you still cared for him, Olivia," Ellen said, helping Roy keep the focus away from Tamara.

Some of the fight went out of Olivia. She shifted her glass back and forth and watched the whisky swirl as the glass moved. "Frederick Jarvis was a complex man. He used people, but somehow he kept them as friends and allies." She looked up suddenly. "His wife knew about me, that he and I were lovers. I thought she'd be furious. That she'd walk out on him. But she stayed with him. She forgave him. She ... she accepted that what he'd done had nothing to do with their relationship."

Tamara tilted her head to one side. "She might have changed her mind if she knew her kids had a half-sister."

Christy thought she saw hurt in the depths of Tamara's eyes, but she couldn't be sure. Tamara still seemed very calm, shrugging off the death of the man who was her biological father in an almost clinical way, making comments that were more analytical than emotional.

"Perhaps," Olivia said slowly. "Or she might have accepted you into their lives." She hesitated then added, "I was never sure I'd done the right thing giving you up. Keeping your existence from Frederick."

"You did!" Tamara said. The passion in her voice was shocking, coming so suddenly after her previous cool. "I have a great family. I didn't need his."

Olivia nodded, but she sighed.

"You sound like you were still in love with Jarvis," Trevor said to Olivia.

She shook her head. "I wasn't, but ... We were friends. He made opportunities for me. Came to me for advice on cyber security issues. Only last week we talked about a concern he had that his communications were being hacked. He thought some of his campaign plans were being leaked to his competitors and he wanted to know how to stop it."

"Is that a fact?" Trevor said. He rubbed his chin thoughtfully. "Sounds like his killing may have had a political motive."

"Oh! I hadn't thought of that," Olivia said.

"Not our problem this time," Christy said lightly. Her wine glass was empty. Sledge let go of her hand so he could refill it. She shot a sideways glance at Quinn to see if he noticed Sledge's warmth toward her. Quinn's gaze was fixed on Tamara's face. Her heart sank.

"Thank heavens!" Ellen said with heartfelt relief. "I have a casual acquaintance with Leticia Jarvis and I believe you know her daughter, Christy. Candis Blais. She was on the parents advisory committee at Noelle's old school when you were the chair." Christy nodded as Ellen continued on. "Even though there is a relationship, I see no reason to investigate the man's death."

Sledge laughed, but Tamara and Olivia both looked puzzled. In the rush to explain how Christy, Quinn, and the others had investigated three murders, personal talk of Frederick Jarvis faded away. The arrival of Noelle, with Mary Petrofsky and the cat in tow, ensured it didn't return. Instead, Christy spent the rest of the barbeque flirting with Sledge while Quinn smiled at Tamara.

CHAPTER 6

"I expect to see a substantial portion of the funds returned to the Trust by the end of summer."

Christy stared at the broad, beaming face of Harry Endicott. He was a bulky man, with thinning hair, unpretentious and careful. To say she was blindsided by his announcement was putting it mildly. When he'd asked her and Ellen to come to his office for a meeting, she thought he planned to tell them that the Jamieson fortune was gone forever. That the embezzlers had squirreled the money away so efficiently that those searching for it might guess where it had ended up, but would never be able to retrieve it. Now Harry was clearly waiting for a response, and from the look on his face he was expecting praise.

She drew a deep breath. Life was about to change, and all of the people seated on the simple wooden visitor chairs in Harry Endicott's cramped, airless office knew it. Beside her, Ellen was staring intently at Endicott, her expression giving nothing away. Ellen was the only trustee not currently in custody or serving a sentence, so this news was as important to her as it was to Christy. Beside Ellen was Trevor. He was there to provide legal advice should they need it. He was listening, an observer rather than an active participant. On Christy's other side was Detective Patterson. The Frank Jamieson murder case was still hers. Although charges had been laid, the trials had not yet happened. Christy supposed Harry's findings would become part of the evidence that would be produced in court.

The only other person in the room was the awful Samuel Macklin, a former trustee, who had plea bargained his way into a light sentence that included helping Harry Endicott recover the Jamieson funds and unraveling the twisted accounts of Homeless Help, a non-profit organization that Patterson was also investigating.

Part of Christy wanted to shout with joy at the news, but another part was worried. Yes, the financial concerns of the past year would ease, but there would be new problems. Somehow, she would have to blend the high-profile Jamieson world into the new, more comfortable lifestyle she'd created in the simple Burnaby Mountain townhouse complex. At this moment, she didn't know how she would do that. So, she fell back on what had worked in the past and summoned her Jamieson princess persona. Let everyone think this came as no surprise to her. "This is welcome news, Harry." She smiled and raised her brows in an enquiring way, a woman in perfect control. "How did you discover the location of the funds?"

Her question allowed Endicott to launch into an enthusiastic, and very detailed, explanation of his process. Beside her, Christy sensed Detective Patterson was listening carefully.

Christy knew this meeting was bringing back difficult memories for Ellen, and she was glad that Trevor was seated beside her. She'd noticed him patting Ellen's hand a couple of times, particularly when Macklin had been speaking. Ellen had come a long way since she had shared responsibility for Frank's fortune with Macklin and the other trustees. Back then, she'd let the others provide the direction and allowed herself to be the Jamieson figurehead in the organization. She'd been naive and come to regret it. The exposure of the embezzlement had shocked her and caused her to reevaluate her position as a trustee, and indeed, her life. It was clear she resented Macklin's presence here, as Christy herself did.

When Harry finished his dissertation, Patterson said, "Eve Fisher refuses to admit that any of the Jamieson money was laundered through Fisher Disposal. She's adamant that her husband is innocent of the charges against him. We know he used some of the money to buy Fisher Disposal shares, but we suspect there's more. We need the details before he comes to trial."

"Retrieving all of it won't be easy, but the money is there," Macklin said. "I wasn't the one who moved the cash, so I don't know the details of how it was done. I'll keep digging. We'll find it all, eventually."

Ellen's features froze into a pinched expression that had her lips tight and her jaw set. She stared straight ahead, not looking at Macklin, who was glancing around at the others in the meeting as if he was one of them, a victim of the embezzlement scam. Christy saw Trevor squeeze Ellen's hand and was again glad he'd come. Like Ellen, she didn't acknowledge Macklin's comment. Instead, she turned to Patterson and said, "What do you need me to do, Detective? Ellen and I want to help in any way we can."

A slow smile lifted the corner of Patterson's mouth. Apart from a scar that marred one side of her face, running down her jaw, she was a beautiful woman, even though she downplayed her looks. Now a rueful amusement warmed dark eyes, rimmed with lush black lashes. "You'll have to testify against the trustees, but you already knew that. Otherwise, hang on to your fortune this time, Mrs. Jamieson."

Christy nodded. Her stomach twisted at the reminder. She wasn't looking forward to taking the stand.

"Harry will need to keep meticulous records of what he and Mr. Macklin find, but then he always does," Patterson's smile widened as she tipped her head in Endicott's direction. "He'll write a detailed report hundreds of pages long, but so clear that defense counsel will have a hard time refuting it."

"We'll have to reconstruct the Trust," Ellen said. There was no emotion in her voice, nor did she look at Macklin. She turned to Christy. "We should do it before the money is returned."

"Good idea," Patterson said. She didn't add that they should choose the new trustees carefully. She didn't have to. Christy felt the burden without hearing the words. Since the embezzlement had been revealed, the Trust's office manager had been managing the money that remained, but the amount was small—a nest egg rather a fortune. On Trevor's advice, Ellen had petitioned the courts to have the trustees who had participated in the embezzlement removed from office, leaving Ellen the sole remaining trustee. She had often said how relieved she was that she didn't have to manage vast sums that made up the Jamieson fortune. Christy was willing to help, but as a secondary recipient of the Trust—first as Frank's wife, now as Noelle's mother—she wasn't sure if the terms of the Trust would allow her to become one of the trustees.

Harry beamed and nodded. "I will be happy to offer any assistance I can, Mrs. Jamieson. Do not hesitate to call me at any time."

She smiled at the accountant, and nodded, but she couldn't think of a single question to ask. She was still reeling from the scope of his news. "Thank you, Mr. Endicott. I'll be in touch."

Endicott nodded and stood. He stretched out his hand. "It has been a pleasure, Mrs. Jamieson. As always."

Christy stood and took his hand. The others rose as well and Harry went through the same ritual with each of them. She expected Patterson to stay and confer further with Endicott and Macklin while she, Ellen, and Trevor left. To her surprise, the detective followed them out of the small office.

She closed the door firmly behind her and said, "Mrs. Jamieson, if I might have a word?"

Christy paused in the middle of the hallway and half turned toward her.

Ellen said, "Trevor and I will meet you at the car."

Christy frowned, but she nodded and turned back to the detective.

Patterson waited until Ellen and Trevor were at the elevators and well out of earshot before she spoke. "You've heard about the murder of Fredrick Jarvis?"

Warning bells went off in Christy's head. She nodded cautiously.

"It was the topic of a discussion at a recent social gathering I was at."
A fancy way to describe one of the Armstrongs' backyard barbeques,
but she was still in her Jamieson princess persona. Fancy was the
norm, not the exception. "Is it one of your cases?"

Patterson nodded, then surprisingly her expression twisted into
one of derision and she shrugged.

Christy raised her brows. This was certainly odd behavior for the
usually impassive and professional cop.

Patterson made an effort to pull herself back into control. "It is
and it isn't, Mrs. Jamieson." There was annoyance in the words and in
her tone of voice. "Fredrick Jarvis was a national figure. His death is
being considered in the context of his position as a member of the
provincial government and his current campaign for the national
leadership of his party."

Christy nodded. "The news broadcasts are full of speculation on
who might have killed him. I've heard some reports that he was
murdered by an international terror group. Others suggest it was one
of the other leadership candidates. Even the possibility of a disgrun-
tled constituent has been mentioned."

"All of those options have been raised. A joint taskforce made up
of federal and city police has been appointed." Patterson hesitated
and Christy thought she was choosing her words carefully. "With the
assumption that Mr. Jarvis' death was politically motivated, the inves-
tigator leading the taskforce is Inspector Fortier from Ottawa."

"I see," Christy said. Though she didn't, not really. Patterson was
clearly annoyed that the feds were guiding the taskforce, not
someone from the Vancouver police department, but why had she
deliberately chosen to talk to Christy?

Patterson nodded. Again, she hesitated. "Fortier is focused on Mr.
Jarvis' public life. He's looking at anyone who has ever disagreed with
him politically, the people who protested his policies, his competitors
in the current leadership campaign, anyone with international
connections."

Christy stared at Patterson. She heard Roy's voice reminiscing
about the protests he'd participated in while Jarvis was minister of

the environment and his still-firm view that Jarvis was dead wrong in his policies. She thought about Tamara, held captive by radicals, and so newly returned to Canada.

And Quinn, Tamara's former, and possibly current, lover. A journalist who spent years in war zones, interviewing friends—and when he could arrange it—foes, alike.

The cold of stark fear washed over her. "Everyone?"

Patterson raised her brows as she nodded. "I don't believe Mr. Jarvis was killed by an international terrorist. I think he was murdered for one of the usual reasons—money, revenge, jealousy, fear. I think his killer is close to home. But I'm a lone voice."

Which meant that Roy and Quinn, possibly even Trevor, were in danger. "I wish she had never come here," Christy said fiercely.

Patterson knew exactly who Christy meant. She nodded. "Dr. Ahern is certainly a suspect. Do you know why she chose this moment to visit Vancouver?"

"She claims it was to find her birth parents."

"And she'd never shown any interest in them before?"

Christy decided she didn't mind sacrificing Tamara if it meant taking the heat off Quinn and Roy. "Not from what I've heard."

"You can see why the taskforce is focusing on her actions."

Christy nodded. She felt sick inside, devastated by the turn the conversation had taken.

Patterson watched her carefully. "If Dr. Ahern was planning an assassination, she'd need a local contact. Someone she could trust."

Anger ripped through Christy. Patterson had conned her, drawing her out, getting her to say what she didn't mean. She wrapped her Jamieson manner around her like a protective cloak, and said, "If you're implying Quinn Armstrong is that person, Detective, you're wrong. He would never participate in a killing, for either political or personal reasons."

Amusement gleamed in Patterson's eyes, though her features remained impassive. "Bravo, Mrs. Jamieson. I like your style."

"I meant what I said, Detective," she snapped. "Quinn is guilty of nothing but being a good friend to a woman who has been through three years of hell."

"I think you're right, Mrs. Jamieson. I've heard rumors that Fredrick Jarvis had enemies. The personal kind, not political ones."

"Well then?"

"Jarvis was killed by a precision gunshot to the head. Fortier thinks it was a sniper shot done by a professional assassin."

"What does that mean?" That hollow sense of fear was building again, because, although she'd asked the question, Christy already knew the answer.

"It means I don't have the time or manpower to dig deep into the lives of the people in Frederick Jarvis's personal life, because Fortier has the taskforce focused on the national and international connection." Patterson's expression hardened and there was an edge of threat in her voice. "He'll put Dr. Ahern's life under a spotlight. It will shine on everyone around her. The glare will be intense."

Christy knew all about that public spotlight. She knew how it could distort even the most innocent of actions. She'd lived with it for months after her husband disappeared. "And if Fortier is wrong? If it isn't Tamara?"

Patterson shrugged. Her jaw was set. "There's a lot of pressure to find Mr. Jarvis' murderer."

"If you believe Jarvis was killed for personal reasons, why don't you investigate that angle?"

"Like I said, Mrs. Jamieson, the taskforce is focused. And I am part of it. Everyone involved is working flat out to sift through a mountain of data. I had to get special permission to come to the meeting this afternoon."

Christy frowned. "You came to warn me Quinn might be under investigation?"

Patterson didn't immediately reply. Again, Christy had the sense that she was wrestling with herself. Finally, she said, "Mr. Jarvis moved in the kind of social circles the Jamiesons play in. I'm sure you, or your aunt, know his wife and children. You might even be on a first name basis with them."

"His daughter was on one of the committees I belonged to before Frank died, but—" Horrified realization dawned. "You want me to investigate Fred Jarvis' family?"

"Ears, eyes and feet, Mrs. Jamieson. You can go where I cannot."

Patterson wanted her to be a confidential informant, someone who could get close to a suspect, gather information, then report back. "Detective, this is a big request. I'm not sure ... "

Patterson's gaze was steady on hers, but she didn't speak. She just let Christy stew about spotlights, and consequences, and danger to those she loved.

"All right," Christy said at last. "Give me the names on your suspect list."

CHAPTER 7

"I cannot remain as a trustee," Ellen said, for the umpteenth time.

She, Trevor, and Christy had talked about how to restructure the Trust on the way home from Harry Endicott's stuffy little downtown office. They had identified the kind of skills the new trustees should have, but not the names. The discussion provided Christy with time to assess the disturbing conversation she'd had with Patterson. She knew Ellen and Trevor were both curious about what the detective wanted, but they assumed it had to do with the Trust, so they didn't push. Then Ellen had dropped the bombshell about resigning her position, and she had to focus on this new crisis.

The discussion turned into an argument that didn't abate until Christy turned into the townhouse driveway, and then only to bid good-bye to Trevor, who took the opportunity to bow out by heading over to the Armstrong house.

Ellen now sat stiffly on one corner of the sofa in Christy's living room, determined, inflexible. Her face still wore the frown she'd had through most of the meeting at Harry Endicott's office. She was not going to budge.

Seated on the other end of the couch, Christy picked up the antique silver urn resting on the coffee table and poured coffee into a fragile cup from the Jamieson bone china service. She rarely used the delicate china, preferring more practical stoneware, but with the news that the Jamieson fortune was to be restored, it seemed appropriate. "Since Frank wasn't at the meeting or in the van coming home, explain again why you are so adamant that you should not remain as one of the trustees." She handed the cup to Ellen as she finished speaking.

Ellen accepted the coffee, but didn't seem to notice the cup, although she stared at it while she stirred in cream and sugar. "I am not qualified."

Stormy was perched between them on the sofa, his tail curled around his front paws in his usual neat and tidy way. *Of course you're qualified! You've been a trustee since my parents died.*

"Exactly," Ellen said. She sipped her coffee, still refusing to look at Christy or the cat.

Regrets, Aunt Ellen?

Her hand shook and she put the cup onto the coffee table in front of her. "You have always been able to pinpoint my weaknesses. Yes, Frank, I have regrets and far too many of them."

"Ellen," Christy said gently. She thought that at last they were getting to the heart of the problem.

Ellen shook her head, then leaned over and put her hand on Christy's. "These past months have shown me how little faith I had in my own nephew, a man I raised. I chose strangers over family. I believed when the other trustees said Frank was beyond help. Beyond hope. I assumed you didn't love Frank, that you married him for his money and the Jamieson name. I accepted that because Gerry Fisher told me it was true. Gerry was wrong. I know that now. I didn't ask the kind of questions I should have. So, yes, I regret those years and the hurt I caused."

Ellen's voice shook with emotion barely restrained and Christy found herself responding. When Ellen had turned up on her doorstep eight months ago she would never have believed she would hear Frank's aunt utter these words, but in the subsequent months, Ellen had settled into the little household and become Christy's partner in raising Noelle.

Part of Christy wanted to take the easy way out and simply say everything was okay now, then move on. Another part realized that Ellen needed to cleanse the wound before she could go forward. She drew a deep breath. "I was lonely a lot of the time. Frank ... Frank was often not there for me."

Stormy tensed, then hunkered down into a crouch. His tail lashed back and forth. Frank didn't speak.

"I could have used your support then. I admit it," Christy said. "But I don't bear a grudge. In the past months, you've made up for those years and I think we've become friends."

Ellen nodded. "Yes."

"I think we should put the past where it belongs. Behind us."

Ellen put her hand to her throat. Her fingers fiddled with the rope of natural pearls she wore. After a moment, she nodded and opened her mouth. But it wasn't Ellen who spoke, but Frank. *I can't.*

Both women looked at the cat, still hunched down on his part of the sofa.

I promised you I would always look after you, Chris, and I failed.

"You were murdered, Frank."

You're right. I wasn't there for you. I want to be there now.

Christy stared at the cat. Stormy's head was up now, staring at her, big green eyes unblinking, body crouched, muscles tense. Was this why Frank was still here, camping in Stormy's body? Because he needed to atone for the sins of his past? "Frank—"

"Frank is quite right," Ellen said briskly. "The Jamieson family has treated you quite disgracefully, Christy. You deserve to have our support while you create your new role as the senior Jamieson."

"The senior Jamieson? Wait. What?" Christy wasn't going to say it, because age was always a dicey subject, but Ellen had thirty years on her, and that made Ellen the senior Jamieson, didn't it?

"You are the mother of the Jamieson heir, Christy, which means you are the senior Jamieson. I know Trevor said that makes you ineligible to be one of the new trustees—"

Why? The demand had the impact of a slap and stopped Ellen cold.

"As your wife, Frank, as Noelle's mother, I benefit from the Trust, even though I am not the direct heir. In legal terms, as a secondary beneficiary of the Trust, I am precluded from making decisions on how the money is invested or distributed."

"You can be an employee of the Trust, however," Ellen said. She spoke crisply, once more in control of herself. "As the senior Jamieson, you would represent the Trust and the family. The Jamiesons have been part of the fabric of this city and this province for three generations. It's time for the new generation to take its place. Frank can't do it and Noelle is too young."

"Which leaves me," Christy said. There was a horrible logic to Ellen's position. But to be the senior Jamieson? It was not a job she wanted.

She's right, said Frank. *We'll help you learn what you need know. I'll be there for you, this time.*

"What would you expect me to do?"

"In addition to being the face of the Jamiesons?"

The face of the Jamiesons. That meant attending events, accepting board positions on appropriate charities, being visible. Christy swallowed hard.

Ellen continued on. "I think you should be the CEO of the Trust. Isabel Pascoe is a good office manager, and she has been fine managing the funds that remained after the embezzlement, but she was never the representative of the Trust. As CEO, you would be able to ensure that the Jamieson name once again means something in this city."

However little she wanted the position, Christy had the sinking feeling there was no way out. Still, if she was going to be pushed into a situation she hadn't sought, she wasn't about to go alone. "I may regret this, but all right. I'll do it."

"Good," said Ellen. Stormy rose from his crouch and stretched.

"Provided," Christy said, spinning out the word, "that you stay on as a trustee, Ellen."

Ellen's hand fluttered to her throat again. "I can't—"

"I need you with me on this, Ellen. Please."

She hesitated, fiddled with the pearls, then finally said, "All right. Thank you."

Christy smiled and squeezed her hand. "Start thinking about candidates for the other trustees. We don't have to talk about it now," she added hastily. Not with all of the fraught emotions swirling around them. "But I think we should prepare new operating rules for the trust before the funds are returned and I'd like to have the input from the new trustees for it."

"Very sensible," Ellen said.

Stormy began to purr. *See? You've already got the hang of the job. This is why you'll make a good CEO.*

Ellen retrieved her cup, sipped the coffee, then wrinkled her nose.

"Is it cold?" Christy asked. She reached for the coffee urn and held it up. "Would you like a top up?"

Ellen nodded. As she watched Christy pour, she said, "Is the future of the Trust what that dreadful Detective Patterson wanted to talk to you about after the meeting broke up?"

Christy thought about the detective's request as she finished pouring for Ellen, then added to her own cup. Had Patterson meant their conversation to be confidential? Probably not. "Patterson wants me to look for Fred Jarvis' killer."

Ellen froze, her saucer in one hand, her cup halfway to her mouth in the other.

The cat stared, green eyes wide. *You're kidding, right?*

Christy laughed and shook her head.

"There's a whole taskforce looking into his death," Ellen said. "Why would she need your assistance?"

"I'm a Jamieson."

"Of course you are, but that doesn't make any sense."

"The taskforce is assuming a political motive for the murder. Patterson thinks the killer is closer to home. Hence the need for Jamieson involvement."

"She wants you to use your social connections?"

Christy nodded. "Yes." Then she sighed. "Though I don't really have any connections to Fred Jarvis or his wife. I know his daughter from the parent council at Noelle's old school, but that's all."

"I've met Letitia Jarvis a number of times, but she's a political wife and she tends to move in different circles than I do." Ellen hesitated, then added, "Gerry Fisher used to schmooze with Fred and Letitia. On behalf of the Trust, I used to think, but probably to feather his own nest."

I don't know them either. I went to the same high school as Colin Jarvis, their kid, but he was a couple of years ahead of me. He's intense and just as political as his old man. Not my kind of guy. We weren't close.

Ellen was frowning again. "Why did you agree to take this on?" Her expression said she knew there had to be more to Christy's agreement than simply doing the detective a favor.

Christy sipped her coffee before she said, "Apparently, the taskforce is investigating everyone who has ever had a political disagreement with Fred Jarvis. Even more than that, they are focused on individuals with exposure to international crisis situations."

Ellen sucked in her breath. "Roy and Quinn."

Christy looked at the cat, then feeling a little like a traitor, she said, "Exactly."

Stormy sat on his haunches and shot out a hind leg, which he proceeded to clean with considerable enthusiasm.

Looks like we're all about to get close to the Jarvis family.

CHAPTER 8

The Inspector watched Quinn with flat, emotionless brown eyes. "I must ask you again, Monsieur Armstrong, what was your exact location on the afternoon Minister Jarvis was killed?"

"I was in my car, driving downtown to meet Tamara Ahern at her hotel," Quinn said for what must be the fifth time since the taskforce, in the person of its chief officer, Bernard Fortier, came to call.

"Please provide me with the precise route, Monsieur Armstrong," Fortier said.

Quinn assessed him coolly, mainly as a way to beat back the feelings of anger, annoyance, and fear, which were churning in his gut in equal measures. In appearance, Fortier was dressed in an off-the-rack charcoal gray suit, which he'd combined with a white shirt and a dark blue tie. Black shoes and dark socks completed the look of respectful sobriety. His bearing, just short of military, had him sitting ramrod straight in the deeply padded chair Quinn's dad usually slouched comfortably in. The military look continued in Fortier's short cropped black hair, though his round face sported a bushy black mustache. Fortier looked what he was and Quinn had pegged him for a cop from the moment he opened the front door and saw the man standing there.

"Monsieur Armstrong? Is there a problem?"

"No," Quinn snapped. Fortier liked to drop words from his native French into his speech, and for some reason it annoyed him. "I just resent repeating the same information over and over again."

"I wish to be clear, Monsieur Armstrong," Fortier said, blandly without the hint of an expression crossing his face or gleaming in his eyes.

"I was clear," Quinn said. He kept his voice even, but he could feel emotions building, gathering strength, the energy searching for an outlet.

"Your route, Monsieur, if you please."

He and Fortier were in the living room. Fortier's sergeant was in the kitchen interrogating his father. Quinn could hear the sergeant's rather nasal voice demanding Roy explain exactly what he was doing between the hours of two and five on the fateful day Frederick Jarvis was killed. Quinn couldn't see his father, but he hoped Roy was handling the questioning better than he was.

"I took the highway to Hastings—"

"From the beginning please, Monsieur, with correct street and route names."

Fortier wasn't a local cop. He'd been imported from Ottawa where he apparently worked in some special national security unit. If Patterson had been handling the case, she'd have known exactly what Quinn was talking about and realized with considerable precision how long it would take to get from Burnaby Mountain to downtown Vancouver. But this guy, Fortier, apparently wasn't interested in using the skills of a local expert like Patterson. Patterson was a murder cop. She specialized in normal killings—the ones motivated by greed, lust, jealousy and all the other powerful emotions that made human beings tick. Fortier's focus was political, a world away from Patterson's.

"Monsieur Armstrong, you are stalling. That makes me wonder why you would do so. Do you have something you wish to hide from me?"

Quinn contemplated telling this officious prig that he was irritating, obnoxious and stupid with it. Instead he said, "Why don't you have any Vancouver cops working with you? Someone like Detective Patterson of the VPD could translate our local jargon so you wouldn't have to waste your time coaxing out ridiculous details that don't really matter."

"Detective Patterson is on my taskforce," Fortier said, his voice holding just the hint of annoyance, though his expression remained bland. "She is working on other leads at the moment."

"Other leads," Quinn said. He raised his brows. "You mean you actually have suspects other than Tamara Ahern and me?"

"Your route, Monsieur Armstrong, if you please."

"I told you my route. An hour ago. I included stop lights and traffic patterns. What more do you want?"

"I want to know why it took you so long to reach Dr. Ahern's hotel, which is so conveniently close to the murder site." Fortier's voice hardened. "I want to know what you were really doing."

He'd pulled over on to a side street half way there and thought about Christy and Tamara and what the hell he was going to do with two women he cared about in different ways. He was not about to mention Christy's name to Fortier, though. The bastard would probably hurry next door to interrogate her. She'd already had enough wrongful accusations to last a lifetime. He didn't plan to add to her total through an inadvisable comment.

He raised his eyebrows and said with the muted scorn of a local, "You're new to Vancouver traffic, Inspector. It can bunch up for no apparent reason and suddenly you're crawling along, going nowhere fast."

"Every city has traffic problems, Monsieur. Please do not insult my intelligence with such a trivial diversion. Who did you stop to see on your way to meet with Dr. Ahern?"

"No one!" In the kitchen, Quinn heard his father's laugh, joined with a chuckle that must have come from the sergeant. His father was probably picking the cop's brain for his new mystery series, which had grown out of the story he'd written last year when they'd been investigating Frank Jamieson's murder. He now had a cop—loosely modeled on Patterson, but different enough that she wouldn't see herself in the role—and a sleuth who was a combination of Christy and Quinn himself, as ongoing characters. He claimed that writing mysteries was a lot more fun than the heavy social commentary he used to do, and his agent was already talking movie deals.

Fortier's expression darkened into a frown as he looked toward the kitchen, apparently alerted by the cheerful sounds emanating from it. Quinn wanted to laugh at that annoyed look, but all he allowed himself was a small amused smile. He figured Fortier would go ballistic over a laugh, and the fallout wouldn't be pretty.

Fortier's eyes flickered when he noticed Quinn's smile, but after a moment his expressionless mask was back in place. "Then you must have met Dr. Ahern earlier than you claim. Why? Were you arriving at the meeting place in advance in order to set up your sniper position?"

Quinn stared, shocked. This was the first time Fortier had come out and suggested that he and Tamara were in on the murder. "Sniper position? What are you talking about?"

"Come, come, Monsieur Armstrong. We both know that Dr. Ahern was tasked with inserting herself into Minister Jarvis' life and that she was to ensure he was in a certain place at a certain time. We do not believe she is the shooter. She had an accomplice for that."

"And you think that person is me," Quinn said, spacing out the words.

Fortier's expression didn't change, nor did he confirm or deny. He simply stared out of cool brown eyes that expressed nothing.

Quinn drew a deep breath. "Time for you to leave, Fortier."

There was a burst of laughter from the kitchen. Not just laughter, but a full on gleeful chortle. A hand slapped the table and Quinn heard his father say, "Awesome idea. Oh man, I can use that."

Fortier didn't move, though his attention was now riveted on the action in the kitchen. Rage bubbled up in Quinn. This was his house, not an interrogation room in some cop shop. Fortier was on his premises, on his sufferance. If he wanted the bastard to leave, Fortier had to go.

He stood, looking down on the still seated inspector. "Now, Fortier." He paused, and in the silence they could both hear the cheerful tenor of the sergeant mixing with Roy's deeper baritone. Fortier looked like a terrier sighting a rat. His eyes were narrowed, his lips pinched together with annoyance. He wasn't making the least effort to move. Quinn had had enough. "Out. And take your chatty sergeant with you."

At that the inspector looked over and up. Quinn caught what he thought was a gleam of pleasure, which didn't make sense unless Fortier assumed Quinn's demand that he leave indicated guilt.

Well, it didn't. Fortier had nothing on him.

"Sit down, Mr. Armstrong. We're not finished here."

So the gleam was because Fortier thought he'd cracked Quinn's nerve and could now squeeze a confession out of him. *Think again, Fortier*, Quinn seethed silently to himself. He headed for the kitchen.

"If you surrender your weapon and explain the details of Dr. Ahern's plan, I can talk to the Crown Attorney about a plea bargain," Fortier said behind him.

This guy was unbelievable. "Dad," Quinn said when he reached the doorway into the kitchen.

Roy and the sergeant looked up. They both had mugs of coffee in their hands and it was Roy who was writing notes from their conversation, not the cop. It was a cozy little scene, one carefully engineered by his father, of that Quinn was quite certain.

Fortier came up behind him. He could feel the heat from the man's body and when he spoke, his breath tickled Quinn's ear. "Sergeant!"

Was he trying to see into the kitchen? Or was the bastard deliberately crowding him? If he was, Quinn was not about to give him the satisfaction of moving away.

Looking guilty, the sergeant stood. "It has been a pleasure meeting you, Mr. Armstrong," he said politely, as he reached out to shake hands.

"Always fun to talk to a fan," Roy said, in a deceptively good-natured way. In reality he was setting the poor sod up. He wasn't particularly fond of cops when they were targeting a member of his family or Roy himself for that matter.

"A fan?" said Fortier, sounding incensed.

"Mr. Armstrong was telling me about his new series," the sergeant said, stepping out into the abyss without apparent realization. "A new direction. Murder mysteries," he added helpfully.

Roy beamed. The sergeant must have caught sight of his inspector's furious expression, for he blanched.

"Fortier and his henchman are leaving," Quinn said, deliberately reducing the inspector to the level of a thug and his muscle.

"Fair enough," Roy said. He made ushering movement with his hands, herding the sergeant toward the doorway.

Quinn turned, ready to do his own bit of herding on Fortier.

The inspector stood his ground, his face inches away from Quinn's. "I will leave, Mr. Armstrong. For now. But make no mistake, I will be back."

"I suggest you call and make an appointment this time," Quinn said, refusing to back down. The bastard wanted to intimidate him? Force a confession? Not in this lifetime. "I won't speak to you again without counsel present."

Fortier's upper lip curled. "This is a national security issue, Mr. Armstrong. My rights are extensive. Yours are not."

Fury ripped through Quinn. He'd spent his career exposing corrupt organizations that allowed petty tyrants like Fortier to proliferate. He damn well was not about to let one in his own country intimidate him. "Out. Now." He drawled the last word with satisfying menace.

Fortier turned on his heel and headed for the stairs. The sergeant followed, shooting Quinn a wary glance as he passed. Together, Quinn and his father chivvied the two men down the stairs and out the door. They stood on the front porch and watched Fortier's black SUV muscle its way up the steep road, then disappear around the corner.

"Fortier will be back," Quinn said.

"I expect so," Roy said.

"The neighbors will be upset."

Roy frowned thoughtfully. "Not so much upset, as entertained. Life's pretty quiet up here."

Quinn sighed. "It's only a matter of time. I need to back up my desktop onto a portable drive." He turned to his father. "You should too. They'll confiscate both of our computers to search for their damned conspiracy. I want proof of what's on my drive now, while I still have it in my possession."

"Good plan, but if they want to insert incriminating files onto the hard drive once they have the computer in their possession, who is to say that you simply didn't copy those documents?"

Quinn frowned at him. "An interesting point."

Roy thought for a minute, then he grinned. "How's this? We'll get Three to have one of the lawyers in his firm do the copying. That person can certify that he or she cloned the whole drive and, at the same time, can take the backup drive to McCullagh, McCullagh, and Walker for safekeeping."

Quinn looked at his father with considerable admiration and laughed. "I was thinking of mailing the copied drive to my editor, but yours is a much better idea." He shook his head. "Helps to have a novelist in the family."

Roy beamed. "Backing up hard drives will take quite some time. Best to get started." He headed back into the house.

Quinn took one last look around the quiet neighborhood, then followed.

CHAPTER 9

"They're going to railroad him. I can feel it in my bones." Sunk deep in gloom, Roy crossed one ankle over the other knee and stared fiercely at the sole of his Birkenstock sandal. The sole was worn, but still serviceable though he'd had the sandals for years.

Trevor frowned. "Not if I can help it."

"What if you can't? They're looking at Quinn for a political killing, for God's sake! They could take him away one day for questioning and make sure he never reappears again."

Trevor's mouth turned down as he frowned. "No, they can't."

Roy grunted. Canada's law provided the national security services with considerable power to investigate and detain individuals who were suspected of terrorist acts or sympathies. Charges didn't have to be laid or proof of wrong doing supplied. Trevor had been a card-carrying member of the legal system when personal freedom and innocent until proven guilty was still a cornerstone. He'd been retired for years now and the system had mutated into a one that often chose to see a bogyman behind the mask of a simple clown.

Not that Quinn was a clown. Bad analogy. Still, Roy decided, the meaning behind his thought was valid. Quinn was in danger simply because he was who he was and his friendship with a woman who had survived an ordeal that was unimaginable to most people. Trevor was being naïve and putting too much stock in a flawed system.

The silence lengthened. Roy knew he was brooding, but he couldn't help it. He wasn't going to let his son be trampled on by the state gone wild. He just needed to figure out a way to subvert the minions of a Fasci—

Ellen's on her way.

Frank's voice was in his mind even before Stormy's lithe body bounded across the grassy area that connected the backyards of the row of townhouses.

Trevor brightened and he stood, moving so that he could see past the ten-foot fences that partitioned the green space and gave each townhouse some privacy. "Ellen!" he said as he peered around the whitewashed wood. His smile could have lit a dozen Christmas trees.

Roy heard her say, "Trevor! I didn't expect to see you here." Then she reached the fence and entered his field of vision. She was smiling as brightly as Trevor. The apparent pleasure his old friend and new one were taking in each other should have improved his mood. Instead it just sank him deeper into the dismals.

He ruminated glumly while Trevor and Ellen enjoyed some light social chitchat. Then he heard Ellen say, "She's gone down to the Trust offices to meet with Isabelle Pascoe, the manager. I expect she'll be spending a lot of time down there from now on. At least, she will once she's finished this assignment for Patterson," which brought him abruptly out of his dark deliberations.

"She?"

Ellen and Trevor both looked at him, Trevor with raised brows, Ellen blinking with surprise. "Christy, of course," she said.

Why Christy would be spending more time at the Trust would have to wait. "What's this about an assignment for Patterson? I thought the detective was part of this nasty taskforce that's looking into the death of Fred Jarvis."

"She is. Inspector Fortier believes there is a political motivation behind Fred Jarvis' murder. Patterson isn't so sure."

Detective Patterson's intelligence rose a few notches in Roy's mind. Still, he wasn't ready to believe Fortier and his taskforce would actually evaluate any new information in a fair and unbiased way. They'd picked their targets—Tamara and Quinn—and they wouldn't let up until they found the proof they needed. "Why would Patterson want Christy involved?"

Because she's a Jamieson, of course.

There was pride in the voice and perhaps a little derision, as if the speaker was somehow superior. Roy's usually amiable temper, already stressed by the threat to his son, unraveled further. "It may be obvious to you, Frank, but it isn't to me. Clarify or let the people do the talking."

There was a shocked, uneasy silence, then the cat arched his back, fluffed his tail, and pounced. He landed on Roy's foot and bit his bare toe.

"Ow! What was that for?"

I don't like your tone.

"Well, you can just—"

"Patterson wants Christy to approach the members of Jarvis' family and find out if any of them had a motive to murder him," Ellen said, intervening hastily.

And she's doing it because of your son! The voice was furious. The cat's tail lashed back and forth. His green eyes were hard.

"Is she putting herself in danger?" Trevor asked.

Probably. She is a Jamieson.

Ellen sat down on one of the webbed deck chairs. "I'm going to help her."

"This sounds inadvisable," Trevor, the lawyer, said.

"Christy can't do this on her own," Ellen said. She sounded determined. Clearly, she'd already made the decision. "Patterson is not in charge of this investigation, so she can't change the direction unless she has a solid lead that will result in evidence and a conviction. That's what she wants Christy to do. Look for leads, like motive. Find discrepancies in people's stories."

Roy brightened. It sounded as if Christy would be doing exactly what he planned to do—redirect the focus of the taskforce away from Quinn and Tamara. "I like the sound of that."

Of course you do.

The cat still glowered at him. The voice was contemptuous.

Ellen looked from the cat and to the two men. The tiny lines between her brows indicated she was disturbed by the hostility between them. "Patterson told Christy that the taskforce saw Tamara as their prime suspect, with Quinn involved as well."

Trevor rubbed his jaw. "They've interviewed all of us. Quinn is in the most trouble, because he was alone in his car when the shooting happened, but Roy's alibi is shaky too. He was seen here before the time they've pinpointed, then sometime later he was seen as well. The travel time between Burnaby and Yaletown where murder occurred means it is unlikely he could have been the shooter. But I'm sure they're examining every detail of his story to see if they can pick it apart and perhaps find a loophole."

"And I hope they do," Roy said fiercely.

Ellen's eyes opened wide. "Do you even know how to fire a gun, Roy?"

He shot her a brooding look from under his brows. "Of course I do. Anyone can."

"This was a sharpshooter shot," Trevor said.

"So?" Roy snapped, hostile.

"So you're not likely to be the killer," Ellen said.

"You don't even own a gun," Trevor said. "If they were stupid enough to charge you, I could get you off in an instant."

"Not if I give them more evidence to prove my motivation."

You want *the taskforce to arrest you?*

Roy glared at the cat. "Don't sound so surprised, Frank. They already like me for it. Fred Jarvis and I have been at odds for years. He wants—wanted!—to rape our environment. Cut down old growth forests to feed sawmills or ship logs to China. Build houses and office buildings on the habitats of endangered species. Pave over the most fertile farmland in the province just because it is located close to this city. The man was a slave to corporate interests. He—"

We got it. Your motive is better than Quinn's.

"Perhaps not," Ellen said. Her tone was gentle, her eyes sad. "The best motives are the emotional ones and I understand Quinn is deeply attached to Tamara. If she's guilty, they can certainly make a case against Quinn as well."

Roy nodded. "That's why I need to get them to look at me, instead. I can't let them take Quinn down."

"Roy." There was disapproval in Trevor's voice, but there was compassion too.

"Christy won't let that happen," Ellen said. She leaned over and patted Roy's knee. "And neither will I." Sitting back, she looked at each man in turn. "Now, gentlemen. We are going to help Christy find the killer and we need a plan. Let's get started."

CHRISTY STOOD in the hallway outside the door marked with the name Jamieson Trust. She drew a deep breath, gathering her defenses, drawing the cloak of her Jamieson princess persona around her. She reached out, took the handle and turned it. Then she walked inside, head high, expression calm.

The offices of the Jamieson Trust were the same as they had been when Frank was alive and his fortune intact. In those days, Christy rarely visited—if a trustee needed to talk to Frank, he came to the mansion, Frank didn't go to him. Christy's most memorable visit had been the day when the four trustees had told her to stop searching for Frank. Events had spun out of control after that, resulting in her being reported to child services as a poor parent. An investigation and ongoing home inspections by the child services agent Joan Shively followed. To say that Christy had an aversion to the space was putting it mildly.

The reception area was quietly opulent. The walls were painted the rich dark green of BC jade above a crisp white chair rail. Below, thick mahogany paneling gave the room a traditional look and hinted at wealth tastefully restrained. The deep pile carpet was off white, complimenting the colors in the room. It confirmed the impression of wealth—who else, but people used to unlimited funds, would choose a floor covering that would so easily capture dirt and grime for a professional office?

A sofa and two chairs lined the walls to allow the occasional visitor to sit. At the end of the room a door opened into what Christy knew was the hallway that lead to the offices. The door was guarded by a receptionist seated at an elegant mahogany desk that glowed with the same vibrant red gold as the wall paneling. The receptionist was young, and pretty. She was also new and Christy had never met her. Still, the woman jumped to her feet as Christy entered.

"Mrs. Jamieson, welcome!" She came round the desk, mincing in a tight skirt and sky-high heels, her hips swaying. Her smile was a mixture of rampant curiosity, bright-eyed enthusiasm, and cool sophistication. The result made her seem impossibly young.

Christy hadn't expected this level of effusiveness, though she probably should have. With confirmation that a large part of the Jamieson fortune would be restored, the Trust would once again become a power in the Vancouver scene. As its primary representative, Christy was now an important person in the life of this young woman. She would naturally want to make a good impression.

Christy smiled warmly and held out her hand. "Thank you. I'm afraid we haven't been introduced."

"Oh," the young woman said. She eyed Christy's hand, clearly not expecting the friendly gesture from her new boss. Then her smile returned, she grabbed Christy's hand and said, "I'm Bonnie King, Mrs. Jamieson. I'm so pleased to be working with you. Mrs. Pascoe asked that I bring you to the conference room as soon as you arrived."

"The conference room?" When the trustees bullied her into quitting her hunt for Frank they had called her into the conference room like a misbehaving teen summoned to the principal's office. The memory of that confrontation made her quite sure she didn't want to have the meeting where she was establishing her position as the head of the Jamieson Trust take place in that room. "No need to be so formal," she said to the enthusiastic Bonnie. "Why don't you direct me to Isabelle's office?"

Bonnie hesitated, concern at this breech in protocol clear in her expression. "Well ... "

"I'm sure she won't mind."

"Well," Bonnie said again, hovering indecisively.

Christy gave her a little wave and headed for the opening to the hallway.

Bonnie caved and led the way.

Isabelle Pascoe's office was located beside the corner office that was reserved for the use of the senior Trustee. It was a small cubical, more appropriate to a secretary than to the woman who did the day-to-day management of a financial empire. On the way, Christy and Bonnie had passed three large offices, originally used, Christy presumed, by the three other trustees, space for clerks—currently empty—a supply center that also housed the coffee maker and a refrigerator, and the despised conference room.

Isabelle's door was open and when Bonnie and Christy arrived, she stood hastily. She shot Bonnie an annoyed look, but smiled when she turned to Christy. "Mrs. Jamieson, a pleasure to see you again. Let's adjourn to the conference room. Bonnie will bring us coffee. Or would you prefer tea?"

"Coffee would be fine," Christy said as she walked into the office and stood by the lone visitor chair opposite the utilitarian steel single pedestal desk. "Bonnie has already suggested the conference room. I asked her to bring me here, Isabelle, because you and I will be working closely together and I don't think we need to begin our relationship with false formality." She smiled. "I'm new to this, but I want to secure my daughter's future, and for that I need your help."

The stiffness eased from Isabelle's posture and she smiled back. "You have it, Mrs. Jamieson." She gestured to the chair. "Please sit and make yourself comfortable. Bonnie, can you bring the coffee service here, please?"

"Of course, Mrs. Pascoe." Bonnie moved away, silent on the thick carpeting.

Isabelle waited until Christy sat, then she eased back into her simple swivel desk chair. Christy looked around the room. The walls were white and file cabinets took up much of the floor space that wasn't given over to the desk and chairs. The space was inappropriate, Christy decided. Isabelle deserved a larger office, but she put the thought aside for now. She'd act on it once she'd established her own position at the Jamieson Trust.

They talked about the upcoming return of the Jamieson funds, what Isabelle's role would be in the reconstituted Trust and Christy's, until Bonnie carried in a silver tray loaded with fragile bone china cups and saucers, a silver coffee urn and a plate of petite fours. "I can see why you suggested the conference room," Christy said wryly.

Isabelle shifted papers on her desk. Bonnie off loaded the contents of the tray. "It's fine," Isabelle said. Bonnie retreated, leaving Christy and Isabelle to get back to work.

"Will you be appointing a new group of trustees?" Isabelle asked. She sipped her coffee and watched Christy.

Christy nodded. "Ellen Jamieson and I have discussed this. She has agreed to remain as a trustee and will head the search for another three individuals to replace the men charged in the embezzlement of the Trust."

Isabelle nodded. "An accountant and a lawyer would be useful. Do you have anyone in mind?"

"Ellen has some ideas," Christy said, "but she's not ready to name them yet."

Isabelle nodded again and Christy took a deep breath. She was about to get into the tricky part of the conversation. "Ellen has asked me to take on the role as the family representative and has given me the title and authority of CEO of the Trust." Isabelle's expression didn't change. Christy couldn't tell if she was upset by the changes, relieved, or ambivalent. "You and I have been working well together for the past months and I hope that you will continue on in your present position and help me with the transition."

Isabelle sat back in her chair. Holding her teacup in both hands, she studied Christy over the rim. "And after the transition?"

"I hope you will continue on at the Trust." Christy smiled warmly. "As I see it, Isabelle, my main job in the Jamieson world is to raise my daughter to be the best woman she can be. My second focus is to represent the family within the community. I don't want to manage the day to day running of the Trust. That's your job. You do it very well and I want you to continue doing it."

"Thank you, Mrs. Jamieson." Isabelle sat forward and returned her cup to the saucer. Then she smiled. "I accept your offer and would be pleased to continue working with you."

Relief washed through Christy. "Excellent!"

Isabelle hesitated a moment, then said, "While we're on the subject of representing the family in the community, there's an event I think you should attend."

She stopped and Christy raised her brows in question, waiting silently for her to continue.

"Frederick Jarvis' funeral."

Taken aback, Christy said, "His funeral? I didn't know the man."

Isabelle hesitated again, then she said on a rush, "Mr. Fisher always made sure the Trust was represented at important events."

"Galas and fundraisers, yes. But a funeral?"

"He said it was important to be involved in the community, even if that meant showing our respects when a prominent person passed."

"Still," Christy murmured. She didn't want to attend Fred Jarvis' funeral, on her own or as the representative of the Trust. She'd feel like an interloper, gate crashing a solemn, intensely personal event. She couldn't do it.

Then she thought about Detective Patterson's request that she investigate the people in Fred Jarvis' personal life. The funeral would be a perfect venue to identify those people. Perhaps even to question them a little. When would she have that opportunity again?

With a silent groan, she surrendered. "Yes, all right, I'll attend."

Isabelle drew a deep breath, her expression relieved. "Excellent. I gather the arrangements are quite complex. There's a great deal of security, given who he was and the way he died. I'll let his office know and they'll put you on the guest list. I'll send you the details once I receive them."

Christy frowned at her. "I haven't heard anything about the service. Do you know if it will be here or in Victoria?" Though Fred Jarvis represented one of the Vancouver area ridings and had a house in Lion's Bay just up the coast, political funerals were often held in Victoria, the provincial capital.

"They're holding it here, right downtown." Isabelle leaned forward. "It's not a state funeral, but I hear it's pretty close. The Premier wants to attend so they had to make the timing fit with his schedule. That's why it's next week, not this."

Great. A high-profile funeral. Crushing security. People she didn't know. What a way to initiate her position as the Jamieson representative. The idea of it made her want to turn tail and run.

She wouldn't run, of course, but that didn't mean she had to endure this alone. "Isabelle, I'm sure that Ellen would like to pay her respects to Mr. Jarvis as well. Arrange for both of us to attend."

Isabelle nodded. "Of course, Mrs. Jamieson."

CHAPTER 10

Quinn glared at his father, who glared back.

"It's not a good idea," Roy said.

"There's no other option," Quinn retorted. There was a snap to his voice that was perilously close to a snarl. He knew he was reacting badly, but he was desperate.

"There are always other options." That was Trevor, using his most soothing tone of voice. Beside him, Sledge sprawled on the sofa, one arm flung over the back, his ankle resting on his knee. He looked relaxed, but his eyes glittered with interest as he watched and listened.

Quinn knew that look. He hadn't seen it in a while. It told him that Sledge was bored. The search for a new manager for his band, SledgeHammer, had stalled. Hammer, the other permanent member of the band, had taken off to China with his girlfriend, Jahlina Wong, to search for her roots. Before this whole mess with Fred Jarvis had started, Sledge had admitted that he hadn't written words or music in weeks. His creativity was being sucked out of him by the emotional aftermath of their manager, Vince's, murder, and the grinding frustration of the manager search. He needed an outlet. Quinn suspected he'd found it in the current craziness.

Quinn refocused on Trevor. "In this case there aren't," he said crisply. "Tamara is besieged by legitimate media as well as the paparazzi. She can't go outside without causing a sensation so she's stuck in her room. All day. All night. It's like a prison." He thought about telling them that she was having flashbacks to her captivity, but decided that was her business ... and his.

"If you bring her here you'll only draw the media to our front door." Roy shot him a baleful look. "Think of what that means to everybody around here."

He was talking about Christy, though he wasn't using her name. Quinn knew how much she valued her privacy. If the media descended on his house because he'd brought Tamara here, they'd inevitably find out that Christy Jamieson, the wife of the late Frank Jamieson whose murder had created a sensation and whose body had not yet been found, lived two doors down. Once that secret was out she'd never have any peace.

He swallowed hard. He hated the idea of bringing trouble to Christy, but Tamara's situation was desperate. "The hotel is getting complaints from their other guests. They want Tamara gone. I've phoned around, tried to book her another room, but as soon as they find out who will be registering, they are suddenly full. I'm out of options."

Sledge stirred. "What about my place? I have plenty of room." He lived in a sprawling house on the shoulders of Cypress Mountain in West Vancouver. The house had both space and privacy. It was the perfect option.

On the surface. "Tamara doesn't know you."

Sledge raised his brows. "Sure she does. We met at your barbeque, remember? What's the problem?"

"She's—" Quinn hesitated, still reluctant to be specific about the reason for her current state of high anxiety. "Everything that's happened since she came to Vancouver is freaking her out. She's frightened."

"Not surprising," Sledge said. His gaze was steady on Quinn's. He had a point to make and Quinn knew he wasn't going to let it go.

"A murder tends to be a pretty emotional situation," Sledge said, and suddenly his expression hardened and his jaw tensed. "I've got experience, I know."

"She's insecure. She wants people she knows around her," Quinn countered. It sounded lame, because Sledge had a point. He had emotional context Quinn didn't have. He'd dealt with the devastating shock of having a murder committed on his own property, with the victim being a trusted ally and friend.

But Sledge had not known Tamara before she was kidnapped, before her birth father had been murdered, before she became a suspect in his murder. Quinn had. He knew the real Tamara, the one who dove into danger with a careless *joie de vivre* that was intoxicating. That Tamara was in hiding. It was Quinn's job to coax her back to the light.

If it took bringing her to this townhouse in Burnaby, then so be it.

Roy sat up. He'd been glowering through the whole conversation to this moment. Now he brightened. "Why doesn't she stay with that Olivia Waters woman? She's snotty enough to make mincemeat out of the paparazzi, so Tamara would be safe with her. Added bonus, they could get to know each other."

Though his father's suggestion was also a good one, he'd already discussed the idea with Tamara when she told him that the hotel was evicting her. She hadn't ruled out the possibility, but was hesitant. Her relationship with Olivia was only beginning. She didn't want to put the fragile bond they'd formed to the test. "Long-term, staying with Olivia would be the best option, but I thought Tamara could stay here for a couple of days while we worked out something with Olivia."

"You mean Tamara refuses to stay with Olivia and you're buying into it," Roy said, glaring.

Quinn drew a deep breath to keep from saying something he'd regret. "I mean that Olivia is going to Jarvis' funeral. That will result in a lot of media attention on her. Tamara will be as much a prisoner at Olivia's home as she is in the hotel."

"So?" said Roy, his chin jutting out aggressively. "When the paparazzi find her here, the same thing will happen, only other people will be hurt in the process."

Quinn set his jaw and glared back at his father. "I talked to Christy. She's okay with it."

"Really?" said Trevor, frowning.

"Yes, really." He'd caught her as she was returning from some kind of business meeting. She was wearing a simple dress, whose elegant lines shouted expensive sophistication. She'd topped it with a short jacket that gave the garment an added edge of authority. Shoes with four-inch heels did great things for her long legs and she carried a leather clutch purse under her arm. In that outfit, she was all Jamieson. Then she'd smiled at him and she was his Christy again.

Well, not his, precisely. He'd told her about Tamara, the media scrum she had to face every time she left her room, and her feelings of claustrophobia and fear. Christy had understood immediately and told him he should bring Tamara out to Burnaby.

He'd known she would react that way. She was generous and caring. He hadn't expected her to act any differently.

Sledge shifted in his seat again. "When's the funeral?"

"Wednesday, next week," Roy said.

Quinn frowned at his father. Roy had answered awfully quickly. He wouldn't put it past him to be planning something.

Sledge rubbed his chin. "So, you want to stash Tamara here until it's over then send her to Olivia's place? That's it?"

"That's the plan." Plans could go awry, of course, but he really did think that moving Tamara to Olivia's after the funeral would be the best option.

"I still don't like it," Roy said.

The house was as much his father's as it was Quinn's. If Roy refused to have Tamara stay, then he would have to take Sledge up on his suggestion that she hide out with him. Quinn wasn't sure he was comfortable with that.

There was no option but to tell his father the whole. "Tamara has PTSD," he said, feeling grim. "She's been having flashbacks. During her captivity, she was kept in a room, alone, for long periods of time.

Her only visitors would be her captors and the visits weren't ... " He hesitated, uncomfortably aware that this was Tamara's private hell and sure she wouldn't want the others to know all the details. "Pleasant. She needs people around her. People she can trust. People she's comfortable with."

"You," Sledge said.

Quinn nodded. "Me."

"Hell," Roy muttered.

Sledge sat up. He leaned forward, rubbing his hands together. The gleam was back in his eyes and the smile on his face was full of daredevil mischief. "So, we need to extract Tamara without the media noticing."

Trevor looked at his son. The expression on his face was wary, as was the tone of his voice. "A good suggestion. How?"

"Fortunately, I'm an expert in attracting the media as well as avoiding it. What we need is a diversion." Sledge's grin widened. "This is what I suggest."

CHAPTER 11

They critiqued his idea, of course. Sledge had expected that, given who he was plotting with. Roy Armstrong had never met an idea that couldn't be tweaked and his father—well, Trevor McCullagh was in the business of looking for the weakness in any argument and designing a successful media hoodwink was no exception.

And Quinn? He was getting squeamish in his old age, that's all Sledge could think. Either that or he wasn't as over Christy Jamieson as he pretended to be.

Sledge guided the scarlet Lamborghini down the quiet side street. Despite Quinn's objections, Christy Jamieson was sitting on the passenger seat beside him.

She was currently staring at her phone, reviewing texts. "They're not ready yet."

"Idiots," Sledge muttered under his breath. Louder, he said, "We're coming up on the hotel. Look sharp. We're supposed to be arguing." He took his eyes off the road, which only had light traffic at this early Saturday morning hour—thankfully—and lifted both hands off the wheel as if gesturing in an impassioned way. Christy shrieked out his name, as he hoped she would, and lifted her own hands emotionally.

They passed the hotel. Sledge grasped the wheel again and looked out his rearview mirror. "Excellent. They noticed us."

"For God's sake, Sledge! Of course they noticed us. You almost drove a red muscle car into a pedestrian. How could they not notice?"

While it was true there were lots of people wandering the sidewalks in this part of downtown, the sidewalk had been free of stray pedestrians when he'd released the wheel. "I wasn't going fast enough to hit anything," he said cheerfully. Another glance out the rearview just before they reached the intersection showed him that there was now a little cluster of interested media members peering down the street at the flashy red car. "How are Quinn and Roy doing? Are they in place yet?"

"Not yet," Christy said, scanning the messages.

"Shit. I can only circle the block so many times in this beast." The Lamborghini was a showoff car, from the ever-present grumble of the powerful engine through the sleek lines and bright flashy color. He drove it when he was Sledge, making appearances, doing interviews. It was part of his rocker image, wild, racy, untamable. When he was Rob McCullagh and wanted to get from place-to-place without fanfare he drove an easy-on-the-gas serviceable Ford subcompact that kept him under the radar.

"I know, I know," Christy muttered, typing vigorously into her cell. They were halfway through the circle when she said, "At last! Quinn's at the entrance to the alley, so they're in place."

"Showtime." Sledge was surprised to feel butterflies take flight in his stomach. Ridiculous. It wasn't as if he was about to go on stage before thousands in a packed arena.

No. He was about to put on a show for a couple of dozen cynical media types so his best friend could rescue his girlfriend—or whatever Tamara Ahern was to Quinn Armstrong. He suspected this was a much tougher audience. Not only that, but the consequences were inestimably higher.

Beside him, Christy drew a deep breath as they turned back onto the quiet street Tamara's hotel was located on. She typed out another text, sent it, then typed in a second.

The first, Sledge knew, would let Roy, who was riding shotgun for Quinn, know that they were almost at the hotel. Christy would hold the one not sent until the reporters guarding the rear of the hotel had joined their brethren at the front, leaving the back free of observers when Quinn and Roy drove by.

Sledge shot a quick look at Christy. "Ready?"

She nodded.

"Okay. Let's argue." He revved the engine, then pulled the powerful car into the breezeway that divided the hotel into two distinct buildings and stopped with a squeal of tires.

The lobby was located in the south side of the complex, while the hotel's well-known restaurant was in the northern building. Both were on ground level with the breezeway separating them. A cluster of media types—reporters, TV camera crews, paparazzi—were huddled in front of the double glass doors that opened into the lobby. Sledge's theatrical entrance had drawn all eyes and now he was parked in the middle of the hotel's drop off, blocking the only vehicle access to the parking garage entrance located in the alley beyond.

Most of the reporters and paparazzi trying to catch Tamara for an interview or a photo were hanging out in front of the lobby area, but an earlier reconnaissance had shown that some were staked out in the alley, lurking around the dumpster there and watching the garage entry for vehicles attempting to smuggle Tamara out of the hotel. For their plan to work, Sledge and Christy were going to have to capture the attention of not just the lobby lurkers, but also the alley observers.

Sledge cut the motor. In the sudden silence, Christy shouted, "You're nuts!" and shook her fist at him.

He grinned at her, then leaned in, threaded the fingers of one hand through her hair, and kissed her.

She wasn't prepared for that, which was exactly why he'd done it. She'd be furious when he released her, and all of her reactions would be natural and much more believable than a carefully staged argument. Besides, Christy Jamieson was a gorgeous woman; he wanted to know if there was any spark between them.

Though his eyes were closed, he could feel the flash of the cameras and he heard footsteps and the sound of voices coming near.

"That's Sledge!"

"Who's the broad with him?"

Clicks, whirs, and running footsteps now. Some of the guys from the back alley, Sledge thought. The plan was working. He drew back from the kiss and opened his eyes.

Christy's were already open and they flashed with temper. "That was low!" she hissed. Then she shifted in a fluid way, opened her door and exited with way more grace than should have been possible from the low-slung car.

Sledge rolled out of his side and when he heard the door slam behind Christy, he turned to face her over the long, elegant hood. He shot her his I'm-a-cocky-rock-star grin and watched her eyes smolder with temper.

They'd attracted quite a little crowd. The media types had surrounded the front of the car in a semi-circle that looked out toward the street. Because he'd parked so the flashy car was pointed toward the alley, he and Christy were the only ones looking in that direction. As he watched, a couple of men bearing fancy DSLR cameras emerged from the alley into the breezeway and headed their way.

"I told you people would notice," Christy said, loudly. She glared at him. "There's no parking here. See the sign?" She waved her hand at the crowd. "We're creating a scene. All for a stupid sandwich!"

"Montreal smoked meat isn't stupid," he said. "It's Canadian ambrosia. And this is the best place in town to find it."

Cameras clicked. Someone said, "Hey! It's that actress from that TV show, the one with the creepy aliens. With Sledge. What a coup." A camera clicked while another voice shouted, "Hey, Sledge! Look this way."

Sledge did, while Christy half turned to keep her face in shadow, so she wouldn't be easily identified if she was in the photographs. At the end of the breezeway he saw one of the reporters pause, step back into alley and put a hand to his mouth. He heard the shout. "Sledge and his new girlfriend! Heading for the restaurant!" Having done his duty and alerted his fellows, the photographer loped down the breezeway to join the crowd. Behind him two more cameramen rolled into the breezeway, running hard, determined to get a picture.

Sledge guessed they were the last of the men guarding the garage entry. He winked at Christy, then softened his expression to one of his 'come hither' smiles. It should attract the focus of the photographers, and it did.

The wink and smile were also a pre-arranged signal. Christy hunched her shoulders as she shoved her hands into her pockets where she'd stashed the phone. Then she tossed her head, another signal that told him she'd sent the text alerting Quinn and Roy the way was clear. Moments later, he saw Quinn's little car bolt past the breezeway.

He came round the hood until he was beside Christy. His position gave him a good view of the alley. He leaned against the fender and smiled at her. The cameras clicked, and the crowd of photographers were focused exactly where he wanted them to be. "Come on, beautiful. Let's go eat."

She looked up at him, a melting look from under her lashes. More clicks. Some obnoxious brutes shouted demands Christy and Sledge look their way. "What about the car?" she asked. She sounded sulky and sexy at the same time.

He shrugged. "What about it?"

The sexy look turned into a frown. "We can't leave it here."

He smiled down at her, putting on his best rock star swagger. The look that turned most of his female fans to mush. "Sure we can."

Christy shook her head and she glared at him. For real. No mush here. "No, we cannot. You've parked the damn car in the middle of the breezeway. No one registering at the hotel can come in."

He shrugged, silently indicating that the needs of unknown hotel guests were not his problem.

Christy made a little growl in her throat and all but stamped her foot. Cameras clicked. "Hey, Sledge," someone shouted. "How're you going to get out of this one?"

At the other end of the breezeway, Quinn's car zipped past at breakneck speed.

"I'm going to give the keys to that nice hotel employee there," Sledge said. He winked as he tossed the keys to a concierge who had been gawking at the back of the crowd. The woman reached up, cupping her hands, and caught the keys. "And the nice lady is going to take very good care of my car when she parks it." He grinned at her. "Isn't she?"

The woman clutched the keys, swallowed hard, and nodded.

It was nice to know he hadn't lost his touch. Sledge raised his brows as he surveyed the reporters and paparazzi, still snapping pictures. "Now I'm going to take my good friend to lunch."

He tugged Christy's hand. Lunch was an improvisation. He wanted to give Quinn plenty of time to get away. But honestly? Christy deserved a reward after participating in this stunt.

The least he could do was treat her to a meal out.

CHAPTER 12

"Mary and her mom just got home," Noelle said. Her eyes were bright and she fairly vibrated with excitement. She and Christy were sitting on the steps of their front porch. "Can I go up and see her, Mom? Please?"

It was Tuesday, one of Rebecca Petrofsky's work days, so Mary had been in after school care. Normally, Noelle would have been doing her homework at this point in the afternoon, but with school ending in a couple of weeks even the tough Mrs. Morton, Noelle's teacher, had given up on sending homework home. Christy had come out with Noelle to play hopscotch and savor a little mom and daughter time.

Now she resisted the urge to laugh at her daughter's big-eyed, innocent expression. Instead, she said sternly, "You can, but no coaxing an invitation to dinner from Mrs. Petrofsky. You were over at their house last night."

"I wouldn't!" Noelle said, a horrified tone added to the still innocent expression.

"Of course you wouldn't," Christy said.

Noelle giggled, then headed up the street, skipping as she went. At the Petrofsky's, Mary barreled out of the car and ran toward

Noelle. The two of them met closer to Mary's than Noelle's and hugged like they hadn't seen each other in months, when they'd actually been together in their classroom at school only a few hours before.

Rebecca Petrofsky waved and shouted, "I've got them."

"Thanks!" Christy called back. "She can stay till dinner time, but don't let her con you into providing another meal."

"Got it," Rebecca said. "Come on, girls, you can help me put the groceries away."

Noelle and Mary each picked up a small bag, while Rebecca hefted the larger ones, and they all disappeared into the Petrofsky house. Christy thought she should go into her own house and start dinner prep, but instead she sat and brooded over her last few days.

She'd agreed to Sledge's crazy hotel stunt because she had a sneaking empathy for what Tamara Ahern was dealing with. Her memories of the media camped outside the Jamieson mansion after Frank disappeared were vivid and painful. She had felt besieged, at times terrified, overwhelmed by the unwanted attention. As the pressure from the media attention increased, she'd also started to question her own innocence. Oh, she'd known she hadn't embezzled from the Jamieson Trust, but she second-guessed every action, wondered if she'd somehow precipitated Frank's decision to steal away his fortune. When Detective Patterson questioned her, she'd found it difficult to stand behind her innocence and defend herself. She'd done it, but it had been hard.

Her situation had been uncomfortable, even lonely, but it was nowhere near as precarious as Tamara's was. The crime she was being investigated for was murder. Even worse, it was the murder of a prominent government official. If Tamara crumbled under the pressure, she could be in a danger that far surpassed anything Christy had faced.

So she'd agreed to participate in the scheme so Quinn could get Tamara out of the glare of the media. It had worked beautifully. The press had focused on Christy and Sledge, while Quinn rescued

Tamara and brought her here to Burnaby, without any of them being the wiser.

And Christy and Sledge ended up on the front page of the newspaper, with the caption, *Sledge's New Woman?*

She sighed and put her chin on her hand.

Stormy the Cat emerged from the bushes on the other side of the street and trotted over to her. He came to an abrupt stop at the bottom of the stairs, then sat primly, tail curled around his paws. *Where's Noelle?*

"Mary's house." Christy straightened. "I should go in and start dinner."

Who's that?

Two large, black SUVs had turned onto the street and were slowly rolling their way down the hill with a ponderous menace that had Christy's nerve endings tingling with primitive fear. "What the hell?"

She stood up. To get a better view, the cat leapt up onto the flower box that separated her walk from her next-door neighbor's. The SUVs kept coming, passing every house on the street, until only the final block of townhouses was left.

The first vehicle stopped in front of the Armstrong's walk. The second parked in front of their driveway, effectively cutting off access to the house. Doors opened and men emerged.

The cops, Frank said. Stormy's back arched, his tail fluffed, and he danced to one side, the picture of an upset cat. *Wonder what they're up to.*

"I expect they're here to interrogate Tamara," Christy muttered.

At the sound of her voice one of the cops, dressed in a dark blue suit and wearing a white shirt with a blue tie, glanced her way. "You should be inside, Madame."

This must be Fortier, the head of the taskforce. Christy hadn't met the man, but Quinn had mentioned he had an accent, which was very much in evidence today. She made a swift review of the police contingent, searching for Patterson in the hopes the Vancouver cop would be able to enlighten her as to what was going on, but she wasn't there. Instead, Fortier had brought another detective in plain clothes and several uniforms wearing Kevlar vests and armed with lethal looking weapons.

A SWAT team. This was bad. Very bad.

Frank decided to do his part to make it worse. Stormy, still arched and fluffed, hissed and flattened his ears. *Who does this bozo think he is?*

Fortier's gaze shifted to Stormy. "And take the cat with you."

"What are you doing here?" Christy asked.

Fortier's eyes narrowed and his mouth pursed. "That is none of your business, Madame."

She swallowed hard as his eyes skewered her, but she didn't like the menace of the Kevlar-clad assault team. It wasn't needed. No one was armed and dangerous in this neighborhood. "Sure it is. I'm part of the Neighborhood Watch."

Fortier's eyebrows rose.

Seriously, Chris? Neighborhood Watch? This guy is about to storm Roy's house and that's the best you've got?

"Oh, shut up, Frank!"

Fortier's expression morphed in an instant from patronizing to dangerous. His eyes narrowed as he frowned. "Who are you talking to, Madame?"

He impaled her with a look that had Christy's heart pounding and butterflies leaping in her stomach.

Stormy hissed again. Relieved, Christy said with complete honesty, "The cat."

Fortier shot Stormy a disdainful look and turned away.

While Fortier was accosting Christy, the second plainclothes cop mounted the stairs to the Armstrongs' front door and rang the bell. The door opened. Trevor McCullagh stood in the opening.

"We are here for Tamara Ahern," the cop said.

"I am Dr. Ahern's representative," Trevor replied, not moving from his position. He looked out at the SWAT team, weapons raised and at the ready. His expression didn't change, but he widened his stance and settled more firmly in place. "Dr. Ahern is willing to speak to a detective, but the bully brigade will have to stay outside."

Fortier abandoned Christy to stroll up the Armstrong front walk to the stairs. There was a hush of expectation as he made his unhurried, deliberate way.

Stormy deserted his lookout on the flower box and followed.

"Frank!" Christy hissed.

Everyone ignored her except Trevor, who caught sight of the cat sliding between the legs of one of the armed men. A grim smile touched his lips.

"Surrender Dr. Ahern, or we will storm the premises," Fortier said. He sounded like he enjoyed the idea of wreaking havoc on this quiet suburban townhouse.

There was an ominous ripping sound. One of the armed cops shouted, "What the hell?" and Stormy bolted for the stairs.

Fortier was quick. As the cat passed, he reached down, caught him by the scruff of the neck and hauled him up so that he was eye-to-eye with the cat.

"Put him down!" Christy shrieked. Without pausing to think, she dove to the rescue.

She got as far as the SUVs. As she tried to get to Fortier, one of the armed cops caught her around the waist and anchored her to his body with a muscular arm that felt like iron and stopped her cold. She struggled, but the guy's hold was unbreakable. All she could do was shout, "Don't hurt him!"

"Why not, Madame? He has torn my officer's trousers." He shook the cat. "Deliberately, I think, eh, *petit chat*?"

Stormy hissed and Frank said, *F-off*.

It was a good thing Fortier seemed to be immune to Frank's thought speak, Christy reflected, but then one of the Kevlar-clad cops looked around with a frown and said, "Who said that?"

There was action in the doorway as Trevor stepped forward, out onto the porch. Quinn pushed past him and ran lightly down the stairs. Sledge had moved out behind Quinn. Now he stood beside his father, feet planted widely, hands in the pockets of his jeans, but thumbs out, a bad boy glower on his face. Just inside the house,

Christy could see Roy standing, with Tamara hovering by his shoulder.

"Let her go and drop the damned cat," Quinn said as he reached the walk, a couple of feet away from Fortier.

Apparently tired of being held like a wet, unpleasant rag, Stormy chose that moment to attempt an escape, writhing in Fortier's hold. When that wasn't effective, he emitted a wail of pure tomcat fury.

Quinn made a dive for the cat, weapons were raised, and Christy screamed, "Stop!"

Surprisingly, everyone did.

She took a deep breath and said, "Detective Fortier—"

"Inspector, Madame, if you please."

"Okay. Inspector. My daughter loves our cat and she'll be devastated if he's hurt. Please tell your officer to let me go. Then give me the cat and I'll return to my house and take him inside." Her voice shook, but only a little. She was proud of that. She didn't like the idea of the inspector knowing how scared she really was.

Fortier made a quick head gesture and the cop holding Christy let her go. She walked toward Fortier cautiously, making certain not to make any sudden moves. When she reached him, she held out her hands for the cat.

Stormy howled again and Fortier opened his fingers and dropped him into Christy's hands as if he was disposing of a sodden rag into a garbage can.

Show some respect, you arrogant piece of—

"Thank you," Christy said. "Time to go home, Frank. There's nothing we can do here."

"Are you okay?" Quinn asked, the tension in his body echoing in his voice.

She met his eyes and saw anger smoldering there, as well as fear. He knew what could have happened, and what probably would happen in a few minutes, and he was mad as hell about it, particularly because he knew there was little he could do to stop it. "Yes. We're both fine."

He nodded abruptly and turned his focus back to Fortier.

Christy did too. "Inspector, this is a quiet neighborhood. Law abiding families with kids live here. Please have your men put their guns away. Make an arrest if you must, but do it peacefully."

Fortier raised his brows. "You speak for the local Neighborhood Watch, I suppose, Madame?"

Stormy began to wiggle in Christy's arms. She tightened her grip. He hissed.

Watch your tone, you unspeakable braggart.

"Is that *the cat* talking?" the cop who apparently was able to hear Frank's mind-speak said incredulously.

There was a moment of stunned silence, then elation brightened Quinn's eyes and he grabbed the opportunity. "And so says a man who is carrying a lethal weapon." He shook his head and allowed contempt to curl his lips. "You choose your storm troopers well, Fortier." The cop who had burst out with the comment turned a dark red.

Annoyed, the inspector said, "Madame, take your animal and be gone." He looked past Quinn to where Trevor and Sledge stood on the porch. "As soon as Monsieur SledgeHammer and the old man make way and surrender Dr. Ahern, I will have my men lower their weapons."

Christy eased to one side, clutching Stormy. This was not going to end well unless someone did something to diffuse the situation. "The cat thinks he's part of the Neighborhood Watch too. He doesn't like violence and guns frighten him. He's just reacting to the situation."

Sledge laughed. Quinn shook his head and sighed. "See, Fortier, even the bystanders have to make excuses for your bozos."

Fortier's expression morphed from annoyance to impatience. "Dr. Ahern, surrender yourself, if you please."

"Come into the house—alone—and we can discuss this," Trevor said.

"He won't do that," Quinn said. His tone was deliberately provocative. "He doesn't have anything on Tamara, and without his posse of thugs he doesn't have any clout."

Fortier's brows rose. "Do I not, Monsieur Armstrong?" He turned to the cop who apparently could hear Frank speak. "Arrest him."

"With pleasure," the cop said. He advanced on Quinn.

Trevor stepped forward, breaking ranks with Sledge. "On what charges?" he demanded. From his tone of voice, Fortier's order had caught him unawares.

"I don't like his attitude," Fortier said, briskly.

Roy rushed out from the house and pushed past Trevor. "You have no right!" He ran down the porch steps, heading for his son.

The cop reached Quinn and pulled out a set of handcuffs. He grabbed Quinn's arm, ready to snap them on. Quinn didn't resist. He looked at Fortier and said, "You'll regret this, Fortier."

Fortier shook his head. "I do not think I will. Doucet, now."

The other plainclothes cop, the one who had knocked on the door, had been standing quietly to one side of Trevor, largely forgotten in the midst of the action. At his boss' command, he moved quickly, slipping in behind Trevor. Grabbing Tamara's wrist, he hauled her out of the house.

She screamed. Sledge nudged his father aside and pounced on Doucet, freeing Tamara. The detective went down with Sledge's six foot plus on top of him. Trevor staggered across the porch and almost lost his balance at the top of the steps.

It was a con! Damn it, the whole thing was one big con.

About to snap the handcuffs on Quinn, the cop who could hear Frank hesitated. He peered at the cat, his expression suspicious. Quinn took advantage of the cop's moment of distraction to put his shoulder against the guy's chest and shove. The cop stumbled backward just as Roy reached him. They collided and both men went down. Quinn leapt over their squirming bodies and bounded up the stairs, passing Trevor, who had righted himself, on his way to Tamara, who was cringing in the doorway. She huddled there, shaking, her arms wrapped around her chest, her shoulders hunched, her whole attitude one of abject terror. Quinn pulled her into his arms and held her tightly.

"Enough!" Fortier roared. His squad members raised their weapons.

Everyone else froze.

In the silence that followed, the sound of a door opening, then closing, followed by the click of a woman's high heels on the wooden surface of a front porch, echoed loudly.

As Christy turned to stare, Stormy quieted in her arms. *Aunt Ellen?*

Dressed in an elegant sheath that had cost thousands and was accessorized with a necklace of real diamonds, Ellen Jamieson stood straight and regal. She eyed the group at the Armstrongs' with considerable disapproval. "I will have you know that I've phoned the police to report a home invasion in progress. A patrol car is on the way here and confirm they expect to arrive within three minutes. You." She pointed at Fortier. "Leave now, or suffer the consequences."

Fortier goggled at her. "*Mon Dieu!*" he said to no one in particular. "I am surrounded by madmen!"

CHAPTER 13

"What the hell is going on?"

Christy rarely swore. It was a measure of the impotent anger, well mixed with fear, that had kept her on edge since the task-force had taken Quinn and Tamara away for questioning.

"There's not a lot I can tell you, Mrs. Jamieson," Detective Patterson said. She paused to lean against the chain link fence that edged the cliffs on the north side of Burnaby Mountain Park where she and Christy had agreed to meet.

Christy noted that Patterson was staring out at the gorgeous view of Indian Arm, rimmed by the lofty green North Shore Mountains and framed by a deep blue sky as she spoke. Was it a deliberate attempt to avoid meeting her gaze? Probably. The thought added fuel to her already smoldering temper. She planted herself beside Patterson, her side against the fence, facing the other woman. She was in Patterson's space, determined to force her to make eye contact.

"Two hours ago, I watched a good man hustled into a black SUV by a bunch of gun toting cops because he did nothing more than demand that a woman he cares for be treated with respect and given her legal rights. I'm not in the mood to play word games, Detective Patterson."

As Ellen had predicted, a cop car had arrived at the townhouse within a few minutes. The patrolmen had hovered at the edge of the fray, outranked by Fortier and the taskforce, badgered by an imperious Ellen. Those neighbors who were not at work emerged from their houses to watch the action. There were a lot of raised voices and some swearing, but somehow the addition of lots of civilians and a couple of patrolmen to the mix defused the dangerous tension. The SWAT team stood down, the arrests were made. The taskforce members loaded their prisoners into separate SUVs, piled in after them, then slowly, with proper decorum, drove away.

Leaving Christy shaken and furious.

So she glared at Patterson and waited for the detective to respond. She didn't.

Christy drew a deep breath. Patterson's silence and her refusal to meet Christy's eyes added unease to her anger. "You asked me to be involved, Detective Patterson."

At that, Patterson finally dragged her gaze away from the dramatic vista of tree-clad mountains bisected by the silver gleam of the ocean fiord. Her expression was troubled as she met Christy's eyes. "Things have been moving quickly."

"Too quickly," Christy snapped. She stopped. She pursed her lips in an effort to control her emotions, to give herself time to think. "You asked me to look for suspects in Fred Jarvis' personal life. I can do that, but I need time. I'm scheduled to go to the man's funeral tomorrow. His family will be there. That's how I'll start."

"The funeral is generating a lot of media interest, and that is putting pressure on Fortier," Patterson said. "He wants a suspect in custody before the funeral so Jarvis can be buried in peace."

The implication of that ratcheted Christy's temper up another notch. "So he's railroading a good man and a vulnerable woman?"

"He believes the murder is politically motivated."

Patterson sounded defensive. Well she should. Fortier might outrank her, but this was her home turf and she was a respected officer. She could make her voice heard. "Olivia Waters was Fred Jarvis' mistress thirty years ago. Maybe he's had others since. Olivia plans to attend his funeral. Perhaps the others will be there too, even if they've been dumped. A scorned woman can be a very angry woman."

Patterson shook her head. "This wasn't an act of passion. Jarvis was deliberately targeted. He was shot through the head. A precision shot by an expert."

Christy raised her brows. "You've come round to the taskforce's way of thinking."

Patterson's lips parted as if to reply, then she firmed her mouth into a straight line. Looking away, she stared again at the glorious vista before them. "The evidence doesn't lie."

Christy turned. Like Patterson she looked out across the Burrard Inlet to the mountains beyond. "I don't suppose it does. The interpretation of it might, though."

"What do you mean?"

She felt Patterson's quick, sharp glance and shifted to meet it. "Experts can be hired if you have the money to spend."

"Money, not fanaticism," Patterson murmured.

"Quinn had a handgun. You took it away from him when he shot at my attacker last year. When he *missed* my attacker."

Patterson smiled faintly.

Encouraged, Christy said, "Quite apart from the fact that I don't think he has it in him to shoot someone in cold blood, he never replaced the gun."

"So he says."

Christy nodded. "Yeah, he says. You'll check that out, but you won't find a gun, because there isn't one."

"Okay. Fortier over stepped. He shouldn't have taken Quinn Armstrong in for interrogation. Tamara Ahern, on the other hand? There is ample evidence that she's been turned."

"Like what?"

Patterson shook her head. "I can't say."

Christy had gotten a lot further than she expected and her anger was now at a simmer, not a boil. She smiled thinly at Patterson and said, "I can guess. How's this? Tamara spent almost three years in the hands of terrorists. She has PTSD. The father she never knew and was desperate to find turned out to be a total jerk who wanted to use her to further his political ends." She hardened her voice and narrowed her eyes. "This is the kind of proof Trevor McCullagh would call circumstantial."

"Perhaps, but you've outlined some pretty good motives for murder, Mrs. Jamieson," Patterson said. A muscle twitched in her jaw. "She also had opportunity."

"Yeah. She was alone at the time of his death."

"Don't sound so scornful. She says she was walking in Stanley Park. She has no one who can place her there."

Christy lifted her chin in challenge. "Did she have the means to do the murder? Is she a crack shot? Does she own the same kind of gun as the murder weapon?" When Patterson was silent, she said, "I'm sure you've searched her hotel room and the one she used at the Armstrong's house. Did you find a weapon?"

"The murder weapon hasn't been found yet," Patterson said. She bit the words out. Her expression was annoyed. "All right, you've made your point. Go to the funeral. Dig up what you can on Jarvis' friends and family."

"Quinn is innocent," Christy said, sending her a level stare.

"I'll do what I can to spring him, but Fortier thinks Ahern was working with someone and he likes Armstrong for it."

Indignation merged with annoyance and chose her words as Christy said, "Has this idiot man actually looked into the actions of anyone other than Quinn and Tamara?"

Patterson laughed. "His job is national security. It's natural that he'd search for political reasons first."

"And he found them."

"Yeah, he did." Patterson pulled away from the fence and started to walk, back toward the parking lot. "Look, Mrs. Jamieson, he's managed a thorough investigation. Jarvis' political and office staff have been investigated and they all have alibis."

"How big was his staff?" Christy asked. They were walking slowly, finishing up a conversation that hadn't—in her opinion, anyway—been particularly useful.

"The key players are his campaign manager, Harold Cowan, his secretary, Teresa Atkinson, his communications manager, Joyce Crothers, and his event planner, Phoebe Beck. Her husband, Russell Beck, was one of Jarvis' security detail. Cowan and Crothers were with Jarvis at his Yaletown office, working on campaign details on that Saturday afternoon. The Becks were at a party in the same area. Teresa Atkinson was at home, hosting a family get together which included her in-laws. Who have never liked her, she says." Patterson shrugged. "They confirm her statement, which makes it pretty solid."

They had reached the parking lot. At her car, Patterson stopped and faced Christy. "You'll be in touch."

Christy allowed herself a small, tight smile. "You bet I will."

Patterson nodded and slipped into the car. Christy stood beside her van and watched while the detective drove away.

Solving this mystery was up to the amateurs now, Christy and the little band of friends she'd made since moving into her Burnaby townhouse.

There was no way Quinn and his Tamara were going to be convicted of this crime.

Not if she could help it.

CHAPTER 14

W hile she watched Patterson drive away she put out a call to Ellen, Trevor, and Roy, asking them to meet for a strategy session after dinner. Ellen was downtown, at her condo, where she'd gone to pick up a dress for the funeral the next day, but she was planning to return to Burnaby for dinner anyway. Trevor and Roy were also out—at the police station where Trevor was trying to force Fortier to let him speak to Quinn and Tamara, and Roy was doing his best to persuade the members of the taskforce that the power of the written word would produce a hideous backlash on them if Quinn was wrongfully charged.

Trevor sounded harassed when he talked to her. Christy got the impression that part of his mission was to keep Roy from doing something that would lead to his being arrested too. He promised to send Sledge to the meeting in his stead and rang off.

Another quick call, this time to Rebecca Petrofsky, ensured that Noelle could stay at the Petrofskys' until the meeting was over, relieving Christy's concern that her daughter shouldn't be listening-in on a conference on searching for a murderer. Then she headed home to prep.

Since it would only be her, Ellen and Sledge, she figured she might as well combine the meeting with supper. She was busy putting together a poor man's Stroganoff, made with hamburger instead of steak, when Stormy sauntered into the kitchen, yawning widely. *Hey, babe. Where were you?*

"I was up at Burnaby Mountain Park talking to Patterson about Fred Jarvis' death."

Stormy headed to his food dish and sniffed the empty bowl. He looked up and meowed at Christy.

"I'll feed you once I've got the meal organized," she said.

The cat's tail shivered with annoyance, but he turned his attention to his water bowl and began to lap.

The sound of a car outside had Christy heading to the window and peeking out. A taxi was parked in front of their walk. "Ellen's arrived. I wonder how long Sledge will be."

We're having a meeting?

Christy nodded as she moved away from the window.

About what?

"Fred Jarvis' murder. Fortier and his taskforce believe Tamara is the killer and Quinn is her accomplice."

Downstairs the front door opened and Ellen called, "I'm here. Where are you, Christy?"

"In the kitchen with Frank."

Ellen's footsteps sounded on the stairs. She appeared in the opening between the living room and the kitchen. She was holding a small suitcase. "I'll take this upstairs and hang up my clothes before we begin."

Christy nodded. "Trevor and Roy are down at the police station, but Sledge is coming. I'll call you when he arrives."

Ellen nodded and disappeared. Christy set about laying the table, then putting together a salad. She had just finished filling Stormy's food bowl when she heard the sound of a car engine again. It was rapidly followed by the doorbell.

Ellen poked her head through the kitchen doorway. "I'll get it." She sniffed. "Something smells good."

Sledge's expression was somber when he entered the kitchen. He came over to Christy, wrapped his arm around her shoulders in a quick hug and kissed her cheek. Christy smiled at him and ignored Ellen's speculative expression and raised brows. "Hi Sledge. Thanks for coming."

He nodded and released her. She offered him a plate and told the others to help themselves to noodles and stroganoff, then waited until they'd finished before serving herself.

"Dad's worried," Sledge said, as she sat down at the table.

"He should be," Christy said, giving her outrage a little taste of freedom. "Patterson says Fortier has decided the murder has international roots that implicate Tamara and because of her, Quinn."

Sledge scooped noodles and stroganoff onto his fork and ate. His eyes lit up. "What is this? It's really good."

"Thanks," Christy said. "It's an easy supper my mom makes." She smiled faintly. "A childhood favorite." Sobering, she said, "But getting back to the murder. Did Trevor say anything else?"

Sledge shook his head, even as he added more stroganoff to his fork. "Only that Fortier insists that Tamara is a person of interest and that he hasn't charged her yet."

"Not yet, but there's a good chance he will."

"What does Patterson have to say about Fortier's handling of the case?" Ellen asked. She raised her brows in a haughty way. "After all, she was the one who asked you to look into the family and friends aspect of it."

Christy pushed a mushroom to one side of her plate. "The task-force has investigated the alibis of the family members as well as Jarvis' staff, and they are all solid. She wants me to back off."

Stormy finished his meal and leapt up onto the last chair, the one opposite Christy. He sat down in his usual tidy position, body straight, tail wrapped around his paws. His nose, eyes, and ears were just visible over the edge of the tabletop.

Sledge frowned. "Does she think Tamara and Quinn are the perps?" He grinned suddenly, as if using Hollywood cop show slang gave him a little rush of fun.

Ellen shot him a disapproving look. She didn't like nicknames or shortened forms of perfectly good words.

"She isn't certain," Christy said. "I got the impression Fortier is persuasive, that people listen to him and accept what he thinks. Patterson may have her own suspicions, but she's keeping them to herself."

"Why doesn't she speak up?" Ellen asked. She pursed her lips and her nostrils flared in an expression of disdain. She'd never forgive the detective for once arresting her.

Christy shrugged. "Cop politics? Game playing? Fortier isn't listening because he's a misogynistic male or just a jealous one? Patterson was being very circumspect when we talked, so she didn't specify. Whatever the reason, Tamara and Quinn are being interrogated by cops intent on scoring a big arrest, and Roy is doing his best to make the taskforce pay attention to him so they'll stop focusing on his son. It's a mess."

Ellen nodded gloomily. Sledge shot Christy a compassionate look. Frank said nothing.

Christy drew a deep breath. She'd let her outrage slip, turning her explanation into something close to a rant. She needed to let it fuel her determination, give her an edge, but she had to keep it under control or she'd come across as another emotional female. "The investigation is now on us. If she can, Patterson will use anything we find, but she's not actively looking for new suspects." She paused to sip from the wine Sledge had poured her. "The funeral is tomorrow. I want to have a plan. Let's start with who we believe will be there and what we know about their relationship with Jarvis. Then we can move on to who might attend and do the same thing."

Ellen had brought her leather binder, stocked with fancy letterhead, to the kitchen. With it were the fountain pens filled with vivid colors she used to keep track of the information they discovered. She moved her plate to one side and nodded as she opened the binder. "Excellent idea." She made a note using a pen with aquamarine ink. "I'll start. As I mentioned when we first heard of the murder, I have a passing acquaintance with Letitia Jarvis, the victim's wife. She comes from an old establishment family and she is very much the politician's wife. She never worked—she didn't have to. Her father owns a manufacturing empire that supplies house brand products for hardware stores. She has two children with Jarvis. Colin, the boy, is the eldest. He and his father were always at odds when he was a teenager. Colin also has political interests, but he has never worked for his father, because of their personal differences. Their daughter is Candis. She married George Blais right out of university. She had a child nine months later."

"I didn't know that," Christy said. She made a face. "I would never have suspected Candis of taking a risk with her reputation. When I worked with her on the parent committee at Noelle's old school she was always so very prim and proper. Every rule enforced, unless it meant that her dear little daughter didn't get to be first at some activity." Christy paused and lifted a hand in a dismissive wave. "I think she had a pretty good relationship with her father, though. He was certainly interested in his granddaughter's education. I saw him around the school quite often." She laughed softly. "Hilda Toutov, the principal at RVA, and a total dragon, was always pleasant to him. Warm and friendly, in fact."

Sledge raised his eyebrows. "To the point of flirting with him?"

Christy frowned. "You think she was having an affair with him?"

"Why not?" He shrugged.

You obviously never met Hilda Toutov. She doesn't flirt. Chris says she is a dragon. I'd call her an iron maiden.

"It's an interesting thought, though," Ellen said. She played with her pen, moving it back and forth between her fingers. "We know he had an affair with Olivia Waters. Who is to say that was his only one?"

"Why would a woman with Letitia Jarvis' connections put up with a husband who constantly strayed?" Christy asked.

Ellen shot her a long look. "Her father had the reputation of being a player and her parents never divorced. If she was brought up to believe that marriage was an alliance rather than a partnership, she might be willing to overlook serial philandering."

"Until a child she'd never known about showed up," Christy said.

Ellen nodded. "That could be more than she was willing to accept."

"Okay, so we have a wife who might feel her position is being undercut, a son who was at odds with his father, and a daughter who —what? Does Candis have a motive?"

"You said Jarvis spent a lot of time at his granddaughter's school. Sounds like his relationship with Candis was close. Maybe she was jealous of a half-sister she'd never heard of before. Especially a half-sister who was something of a heroine."

Good one, Sledge!

Sledge shot the cat a bemused look. "Thanks."

"Any other family members we'll see there?" Christy asked, ignoring Frank's gushing comment. He was a long-time fan of Sledge-Hammer and he hadn't quite got over the excitement of knowing one of the band members personally.

"Letitia's family may attend. Her parents live back East, though, so I can't be sure," Ellen said. "Her sister will certainly be there as she lives in West Vancouver."

"That's Sharon Conroy, isn't it?" Ellen nodded and Christy continued. "Candis once let out that her father and aunt didn't speak. There's been some kind of family spat. It happened years ago, but the estrangement never healed."

"She kept in touch with Letitia, even if she refused to talk to Fred," Ellen said. "I've seen them having lunch together. I'm sure Sharon will be there to support Letitia."

"Anyone from the Jarvis side?"

"His brother and his family will probably attend. They live in Calgary, though, so they are unlikely suspects." Ellen added to the list she'd been busily compiling. "Still, I'll include them. You never know."

"The funeral is being held downtown. I've heard a big crowd is expected," Sledge said. "The premier and his cabinet are attending, as well as a bunch of other political figures."

"I don't think the Premier of the province of British Columbia did it," Ellen said. She wasn't writing anything down.

"No, but maybe one of the people Jarvis worked with every day, did," Sledge said. "You know, his office staff, campaign manager, those kind of people."

Christy shook her head. "They might be there, but there's no point investigating them. Patterson said that the taskforce already has and they all came up clean."

"Friends then."

Ellen nodded at Sledge's suggestion and wrote down *Friends?* Then she said, "Mistresses, too?" as she wrote down the word.

Sledge slouched back in his chair, holding his wineglass. His mouth quirked into a wry smile. "Pretty ballsy to show up at your lover's funeral."

Christy laughed. "Not really. All you have to do is pretend you're supposed to be there."

Sledge shifted forward. "Talking about being there, do you want me to escort you?"

The cat narrowed his eyes. *What do you mean?*

Sledge looked at the cat, his expression non-committal. "This is going to be tough for Christy. I want to know if she needs my support."

She's got mine!

Sledge raised his brows.

Stormy stood and placed his front paws on the table. *I'll be going with her.*

"Good grief," Ellen said. She put down her pen with careful precision. "I don't think that's a good idea, Frank."

If she showed up with Sledge, there'd be mass hysteria, Christy thought. "Thank you both. Frank, you're a cat. I'm wearing a dress and heels. I'm not bringing a tote I can carry you in. Besides, cats don't go to funerals. Sledge, you're a rock star. If I showed up with you, we'd make more news than Frederick Jarvis himself."

Sledge's eyes gleamed with mischief. "Exactly."

Christy laughed. "I think it's better if we stick with the plan and just Ellen and I attend."

Sledge sighed theatrically. "Okay."

The cat said nothing.

Christy shot him a determined look. "Frank?"

The cat blinked slowly. *Right. No tote. Sure, babe.*

Now why did his agreement fill her with concern?

CHAPTER 15

Frederick Jarvis' funeral took place at a venerable church located on the corner of two of Vancouver's main downtown streets. It was a very visible event, designed to highlight his position in the provincial government, as well as the national one he aspired to and might have achieved had his life not been cut short. Attendance was by invitation only, and the guest list was packed full of the great, the famous, and the wealthy.

Like any celebrity event, the media was out in full force, and security was tight. Crowds pressed against the barriers erected by the police to provide a safe perimeter for the guests to arrive and mingle. They cheered or clapped as people they recognized disembarked from chauffer driven cars or limousines that then moved off, out of the compound, as there was no parking allowed in the area.

The audience was not universally approving of the spectacle that was being presented. Amid the cheers were boos and a determined group of anti-Jarvis protesters had set themselves up in a prominent position on the corner of Burrard and West Georgia streets. They held up signs with slogans like "Funerals should be private not public" and "Jarvis just ordinary man. Grieve, don't deify." At their head was Roy Armstrong.

As Christy's town car slid through the mobs of people into the security area, she noticed him through the darkened window. He was carrying one of the "Funerals should be private not public" signs. As she watched, he lifted a megaphone to his mouth. She dimly heard him shout, "Fred Jarvis may have been a jerk in life, but he deserves better than this!"

Ellen, who was seated on the church side of the vehicle, leaned around Christy to look out her window. "Is that Roy over there with the sign?" She sounded incredulous.

Christy managed the ghost of a laugh over the panic that was tying knots in her stomach. "It is."

"What is the man thinking? This is a funeral."

Christy laughed again. "I think that's his point." Their car slid past Roy, who had put down the megaphone when a man with a microphone and a cameraman behind hustled over to him. Christy identified the man as a senior reporter from Canada's public broadcasting network and thought that Roy would be pleased by the attention he was generating.

"This is insane," Ellen murmured, shaking her head as she observed the masses of ordinary people who had come to view the event.

Christy said, "I don't know if I can do this," as she stared out the window. She waved her hand to indicate the chaos on the around them. "Be one of the celebrities all these people have come to see, I mean."

"Yes, you can." Ellen's tone was stern, her expression serious. "You were Frank's wife for ten years. You've been in situations like this before."

"Yes," Christy said quietly. "But then I had Frank to take the heat. People looked at him, not me. I just followed where he went."

Ellen was silent for a minute. She reached up and smoothed Christy's hair at her temple in an oddly tender, almost maternal, gesture. "And now people will look at you, even though you aren't comfortable with it. But you are the head of the family now. You decide how the Jamieson name will be perceived. You are an intelligent, capable woman who has come into her own. You lead, Christy. I'll follow and make sure you don't come to harm."

Her words were the closest thing to a statement of affection Ellen had ever uttered. Christy teared up and sniffed. "Thank you."

The car came to a stop. Christy had enough time to straighten the short spencer jacket that covered the bodice of the slim black silk dress she wore before the door opened and an usher leaned in, extending a hand to help first Ellen, and then Christy, alight.

Out on the street she surveyed the crowd. Mourners waiting to enter the church were gathered in a rough queue that was part line and part clumps of related people. The shouts of the mob behind the barricades caught her attention and she noticed Roy was now waving his sign with great energy. This was so very Roy-like that she had started to smile, when, to her complete horror, she noticed a small tabby striped cat slide through his legs, slip past the reporter filming him, and run toward the assembly area. "Ellen, look," she hissed as their car slid away to exit the compound.

Ellen peered where she indicated. "Is that Stormy?"

"Yes!"

"What's he doing here? How did he get here? I thought you told Frank he couldn't come to the funeral?"

More precisely, she'd said, 'Cats don't attend funerals,' but that was neither here nor there. "Frank must have convinced Roy to bring Stormy." They'd have a conversation about this when she got home, and neither Frank nor Roy would be happy about it.

"Or Stormy hitched a ride the way he did that day I came down to Homeless Help to talk to Sydney Haynes," Ellen said. Her tone was soothing. Her eyes tracked the fast-moving cat, who slid between human feet and idling cars with remarkable precision. By now, people in the watching crowd had noticed his progression. Arms were raised, fingers pointing. A buzz went up, containing equal measures of curiosity and amusement.

"Let's get into the church," Christy said. "Surely someone will keep the cat out." Frank seemed determined to make a scene. She was equally determined to avoid one.

As she and Ellen joined the line, Stormy changed direction to intercept them. The crowd of mourners was large and admission to the church was slow, though steady, as people had to pass through a security checkpoint before being allowed to enter. It was impossible for Christy and Ellen to move more quickly than the nimble cat, who went where he wanted.

Stormy reached Christy when the line had twisted so that she and Ellen were alone on the sidewalk, visible to the audience behind the barricades, as well as to the people waiting for entry. He twinned between her legs and she could feel his purr as it reverberated through his body.

Pat the poor guy, will you, Chris? He's here because I asked him to come and he's not keen on all these people. Give him some human reassurance, okay?

"Well," said Ellen. Christy thought she sounded choked, as if she was only just containing laughter. Ellen crouched down and patted Stormy. "Good kitty."

Christy sighed, but she crouched beside Ellen and patted Stormy, too. The cat arched his back and preened. His purr was a loud rumble of pleasure. A camera flashed and she looked up to see a photographer with a long lens taking pictures of the scene. Nearby, a cameraman from one of the national TV networks was filming the action. She'd be on the news tonight, a counterpart to Roy's protest. "Thanks, Frank," she said, rather grimly.

The person ahead of her in line turned to see what was happening. She was dressed in a practical skirt suit of cloth that was a dark blue, rather than deep mourning black. The matching jacket, with a pearl gray polyester shell underneath, gave Christy the sense that it was a serviceable office outfit, rather than something she'd bought for the funeral. Her brown hair was short, styled in an easy-to-care-for way. Probably one of Jarvis' staff, rather than a family member or a political associate, Christy thought.

"You brought your cat?" the woman asked, eyes wide. They were nice eyes, a warm blue, fringed with black lashes.

"No. I met the cat here," Christy said, avoiding the intent of the question, but sticking to the truth.

The woman smiled. "He likes you."

Until that smile, Christy had thought the woman was somewhere in her late thirties. The smile dazzled though, lightening her expression, eliminating years from her apparent age. The smile triggered something in Christy's mind, but she couldn't grasp it. Did she know the woman? But where would they have met? Though she tried, she couldn't place her.

Stormy twined and purred, making the woman's comment more a statement of the obvious than an acute observation. "I guess he does," Christy said. "But he needs to go away. This is no place for a cat."

"Oh, I don't know," the woman said. "Fred loved my cat, Cottontail." She smiled sadly. There was suspicious moisture in her eyes. "They used cuddle together. Cottontail is a Persian. Fred said stroking his long soft fur was soothing. It helped him so much whenever he had a tough decision to make." She sighed. "I should have brought Cottontail as a tribute to Fred."

Ellen and Christy shared an incredulous glance. Christy murmured something polite. The line moved and the woman turned forward to pay attention to her feet as she negotiated the steps up to the doorway.

Stormy bounded away. *See you inside, babe!*

Christy wanted to shout for Frank to stop, but she couldn't do it with the mourners and media looking on. "I'm going to kill him when I get home," she said to Ellen.

"Perhaps he won't make it through security," Ellen said. She didn't sound at all certain, though.

She was right. The cat slipped past the feet of the province's premier as the security detail was ushering him through. Though one officer shouted and apparently tried to grab the cat, Stormy changed direction suddenly and avoided the man's grasp. He bolted into the dim quiet of the church's gothic interior and disappeared from sight. The security detail refocused on admitting the human mourners.

The line moved slowly toward the heavy oaken double doors that gave entry into the quiet of the church. Apart from the sounds emitted from the ever-growing crowd behind the barriers, there wasn't much talking amongst the group wending its way into the church. That gave Christy lots of time to look around.

The church was an excellent venue to hold a public funeral of this kind. The walls were thick, gray stone, and there were few entry points, allowing security to control admittance. A Vancouver landmark for over a century, the Gothic-style building was dwarfed by the office towers that surrounded it. She let her gaze drift around, looking at those glass clad towers and wondering if there were policemen in some of the offices, staking out the crowd, watching for any untoward activity.

The line moved and she and Ellen climbed up another couple of steps. They were almost at the doorway now.

She noticed a movement in the crowd not far from where Roy was standing with his little band of protesters, and her gaze sharpened. A dark-haired woman, her long hair falling over her shoulders, was standing, watching the protesters. Her stance, her alert expression, made her standout from the people around her. A breeze teased a lock of hair across her face and she reached up to brush it away. The movement pushed her hair back and revealed a scar on her cheek.

Patterson, and she was watching Roy. That didn't bode well.

Christy was about to suggest Ellen take a look, when the line shifted again. This time they fetched up at the security checkpoint where they had to show their invitations and back it up with ID. By the time they were through into the church, the moment was lost.

A pretty young woman met them. Like the one whose Persian Jarvis had enjoyed patting, she was dressed in a dark, but not black, skirt suit. Her eyes were red and skin blotchy from crying. Even so, she was a spectacularly beautiful young woman, with even features and lush pink lips that quivered in the moments before she spoke. "Good afternoon. I'm Phoebe Beck. I worked with Mr. Jarvis, and it is my pleasure to guide you to your seat today."

Christy and Ellen gave her their names and murmured their thanks. Christy said, "Did you work closely with Mr. Jarvis?"

118

Phoebe smiled tremulously. "Very. I was his admin assistant. I organized his events—" Her voice cracked and she sniffed. "I organized this final one for him. I was part of his team. He was a wonderful man."

"I am so sorry for your loss," Christy said as the woman's quavering voice died away.

"Thank you," she whispered. She indicated stairs going up to the gallery and they all trooped up.

"You'll miss him," Christy said, when they reached the top.

Phoebe nodded, sniffing again. She led them to a pew not far from the gallery railing.

"You'll be unemployed," Ellen said, apparently unimpressed by the woman's distraught manner.

Phoebe's eyes widened. "The Party has asked me to stay on to close his office and to transition to the new minister."

"Of course," Christy said, shooting a quelling look at Ellen.

Ellen ignored her. "The Dogwood Party looks after its own, then," she said, nodding as if she considered this to be the only acceptable path.

Phoebe nodded back. "They do and I'm thankful for it. Of course, I don't really need the job." They'd reached their placement, which Phoebe indicated with a gesture of her hand.

"You don't?" Ellen asked as she waited for Christy to slide into the pew.

"No. Fred provided for me in his will. He wanted me to have a nest egg for the future." She nodded to each of them, then hurried away to guide her next group into the dim interior of the church.

Ellen and Christy settled into their assigned places. The gallery was at the back of the church, but it gave them a tremendous view of the glorious interior with its vaulted ceiling and vivid stained-glass windows. They watched the people still filing into the main floor seats through the long central aisle. The family were seated in the front rows, of course, but Christy could see the provincial premier a couple of rows behind, as well as other cabinet members Jarvis had worked with. Her eyes widened as she caught sight of a familiar profile directly behind a woman she recognized as Letitia Jarvis. "Ellen. Look at the woman behind the family row. Isn't that Olivia Waters?"

Ellen frowned as she peered where Christy had indicated. After a moment, she reached into her purse and pulled out opera glasses for a closer look. "Yes, you're right."

Christy looked at the opera glasses, but decided not to comment. "What is Olivia doing seated so close to the family?"

"What is that woman we were talking to while we waited to enter doing in the same row?" Ellen's brows were raised as she handed the glasses to Christy.

Christy looked. It was indeed the woman whose cat Fred Jarvis had liked to stroke when he was stressed. She handed the glasses back to Ellen. "You don't think she was one of Jarvis' women too, do you?"

"Anything is possible." Ellen put the glasses to her eyes again for another look. "Well, well, well. Look who's entering that row now." She handed the glasses to Christy again.

Christy wasn't sure what to expect, but it wasn't what she saw. "That's Archie Fleming and his wife Marian!"

"The competition," Ellen said, nodding.

Archie Fleming and Fred Jarvis had both been vying for the leadership of the national wing of the Dogwood Party. They were the acknowledged front runners. That meant Archie Fleming had been Fred's main competition. What was he doing sitting directly behind the family?

The stream of people was beginning to slow and a few minutes later Christy saw Phoebe Beck, followed by a large, good-looking man, slip into her pew.

The one right behind the family.

Wide-eyed, Christy turned to Ellen. "You don't think ... "

"That all those women in the row behind the family are Fred's mistresses?" Ellen's tone was cynical. Her expression was knowing. "There have been rumors for years, so yes, I wouldn't be at all surprised. We know Olivia was once his mistress. Why not the others?"

"Good point," Christy murmured. There was no chance for further discussion as the choir rose, and a string ensemble began to play. Together, they performed the Lacrimosa from Mozart's *Requiem* as the minister led the family into the church.

The service proceeded smoothly, well planned by the emotional Phoebe, except for one disruption when a tiger stripped tabby cat hopped up onto Letitia Jarvis's lap and proceeded to snuggle against her shoulder. The minister stopped preaching. The congregation held its collective breath.

"Frank!" Christy hissed, sotto voice.

Ellen raised her opera glasses. "He's licking her cheek. Collecting her tears, I think."

Then Letitia lifted her hand to stroke the cat's back. The minister began again and the congregation breathed a sigh of relief. The crisis, if there had ever been one, was averted.

"I don't care what he's doing," Christy said grimly. "I'm going to kill him."

CHAPTER 16

After the funeral, the guests retired to the Jarvis home in Lion's Bay, a village north of Vancouver on Howe Sound. Like the church service, the reception was by invitation only. Christy was surprised when Harold Cowan, Fred's campaign manager and chief of staff, invited them to the house, but Ellen shrugged and said, "It's the Trust, my dear, and the Jamieson name." As much as anything else that had happened in the last couple of weeks, this told Christy that her life had once again changed in a way far beyond her control.

Access to Lion's Bay was by the Sea to Sky Highway, a road carved into the slopes of the North Shore Mountains. In the summer, the Sea to Sky was a popular tourist excursion, known for its glorious views of Howe Sound and the mountains of the Sunshine Coast beyond. On this June day, the highway was a line of limousines and expensive private cars slowly making their way along the twisting road to the Jarvis house.

Named for the twin peaks called the Lions, one of Vancouver's North Shore landmarks, the houses in the village of Lion's Bay clung precariously to the unstable side of the towering mountains. There was little parking, certainly not enough to accommodate the fleet of cars bringing mourners to the Jarvis house, so the cars were being redirected to park at nearby Horseshoe Bay after dropping guests at the door.

"Good thing we decided not to drive ourselves," Christy said, as she watched their limo driver join the long line of vehicles drawing away from the Jarvis residence.

"It's always better to have a driver for an affair like this," Ellen said. She and Christy were standing outside the house waiting to gain entrance. It wasn't only the cars ensnared in a traffic snarl. As at the church, security was tight, names were being checked against a guest list, and ID was required to gain entrance. The result was that an informal reception was taking place out on the lawn while guests waited to go inside to join the family.

Waiters carrying round trays filled with glasses of red and white wine wandered through the crowd. As one passed, Christy snagged a red wine. Ellen chose white. They were sipping their drinks and watching the front door when Olivia Waters sauntered up to them.

"Quite a turnout," she said. She was drinking red wine, like Christy. Her cheeks wore a little flush of pink. This evidently wasn't her first glass.

"Yes, it is," Christy said. She eyed Olivia. "I saw you at the funeral. I was surprised you were sitting in the pew right behind the family."

Olivia shrugged. "That's because I am family." She lifted the glass and drank deep, almost half the contents deep.

Christy raised her brows. Olivia was more than a little drunk and apparently on her way to becoming more intoxicated. Ellen pursed her lips in disapproval. A well-bred woman did not over indulge at the reception following a funeral. It just was not done.

Olivia shot them a defiant glance, sober enough to acknowledge the disapproval. "Of a sort, anyway. Fred and I had our differences, but he was my daughter's father and for that I will always be bound to him." Tears started in her eyes and she raised her glass. "To Fred," she said.

"To Fred," Ellen murmured, her brows raised. Christy smiled faintly and followed suit. Though Olivia downed the rest of her glass, Christy and Ellen merely sipped from theirs.

Olivia wandered off to speak to another mourner. Christy said, "I did not expect this."

"Olivia's emotional response? Or her drunkenness?" Ellen was watching Olivia as she switched her empty glass for a full one.

"Both, I suppose. She was upset about his death, but now that Tamara is being treated as the chief suspect, I thought she'd be angry. Resentful, maybe."

"She may feel that way and be conflicted," Ellen said thoughtfully. "Or she may be living in the moment, letting herself grieve before she moves on."

"Maybe," Christy said. "But if it was my daughter who was the suspect, I'd be moving heaven and earth to discover who the real killer was."

That made Ellen smile. "Then it is lucky, is it not, that Tamara has Quinn—and you—and doesn't have to depend on Olivia for her future."

The knot of people ahead of Christy and Ellen untangled itself as individuals were admitted to the residence. Christy found herself being scrutinized by a cold-eyed security officer who reminded her uncomfortably of the taskforce head, Bernard Fortier. She gave her name and showed her ID, then he nodded her through into the house. She paused in the foyer to wait for Ellen.

The Jarvis residence was a modern construction, spacious, but not huge. The foyer opened up into a great room, which featured high ceilings and spectacular views of water and mountains. Or at least she thought the views would be spectacular. Right now, it was hard to catch more than a glimpse, because the open space was packed with people. Voices echoed from the cathedral ceiling as they shared memories and celebrated the life of Frederick Jarvis.

"Do you see Letitia? We should pay our respects," Christy said as Ellen came up beside her, still tucking her passport back into her purse. The crowd was so thick it was difficult to find any one person in the crush.

They scanned the room, then Ellen said, "There, by the table. She's talking to Archie and Marion Fleming."

"Fred Jarvis' main competition for the leadership of the Dogwood Party?" Christy said. She was still surprised that the Flemings had been positioned in that row behind the family.

Ellen nodded. "He and Archie joined the party together years ago. They were rivals, but friends as well, I think. I do know that Letitia and Marion Fleming have been friends for years."

"Perhaps that's the reason they were seated near the family," Christy said. "They were old friends." She made it sound like a statement, but in her mind, it was a question. Yes, Archie and Fred had been colleagues and their wives were friends, but to have his biggest political rival seated that close? And in the same row as at least one of Fred's mistresses? It was definitely odd. She made a mental note to dig deeper and tucked the thought away as she and Ellen moved through the crowd toward Letitia.

The Flemings had drifted away by the time she and Ellen reached Letitia. She was smiling, but close up Christy could see the bleakness in her eyes and marks of strain on her face. Warmth and pity flooded through Christy as she listened to Ellen express her condolences. Letitia Jarvis looked like she needed a hug and a shoulder to have a good long cry on. "I'm so sorry for your loss," she said, meaning the familiar words.

Letitia must have understood her sentiments were real for she relaxed a little and her smile became less fixed. "Thank you, Mrs. Jamieson. It was good of you to come to Fred's memorial."

"It was well attended," Ellen said.

"Yes. Fred would be pleased." Letitia laughed, a genuine sound that surprised Christy. "He was such a meticulous man. A planner to the core, even for his own funeral. He had a guest list, you know, and a seating plan. Every year he would update it and add a few more people in."

Letitia's eyes were sparkling with amusement now as she remembered her late husband's odd idiosyncrasy. Christy smiled back, pleased to see the sorrow lift from her expression, at least for a short time. "He'd add people in, but he didn't take any out?"

Letitia laughed again. "Never. Fred gathered people around him.

If you had an important part in his life, you stayed in his life. Even people like Olivia Waters." She paused and her expression darkened, then cleared again. "Their affair was a long time ago, but Olivia remained important to Fred after the lust was gone."

"We spoke to Olivia earlier," Ellen said. "She's devastated by his death, I think."

"Yes." Letitia took a moment to sip from a glass of white wine. "Over the years, she and I have become friends. We've had many conversations these last few days. Consoling each other, you know?"

"Talking helps," Christy said.

"Yes," Letitia said again as she nodded. "I know you understand, having lost your husband so recently."

She didn't wait for Christy to reply, which was a good thing because Christy hadn't a clue what to say. *My husband was at your husband's funeral today. He came and nuzzled your ear in the middle of the service.* Not a comment you could safely drop in polite company.

Letitia didn't notice her silence. "Of course, our conversations always came back to that poor, troubled girl."

"Tamara Ahern," Ellen said.

Letitia nodded. "Yes. If only she had the patience to get to know Fred, to understand his ways, she would never have done this terrible thing. She would have been like Olivia and the others—part of his extended family."

Christy was surprised by that absolute certainty in Letitia's voice. "You think Tamara killed your husband?"

Letitia raised her brows in surprise. "Of course. Inspector Fortier is confident she is the one." She sipped her wine again. "Mind you, he believes the crime was politically motivated, but in that I think he must be incorrect. This young woman simply didn't understand Fred's ways. She must have felt cheated of his affection, when, in fact, she merely had to allow herself time to become part of his life." She shook her head, then sighed. "Such a tragedy. For all of us, of course, but especially for her. She must have endured terrible treatment after she was kidnapped. It left scars, in her heart and her mind."

"I'm surprised you don't think your husband's death was politically motivated," Ellen said. "Surely, that would be easier to accept than to believe a family member did it."

Letitia's expression hardened and there was a cutting edge to her tone. "Not my family." She paused, gathered herself, replaced her social mask. She smiled, in control once more. "The women, his love child, they were Fred's—extended—family. My family is my sister and my two children. None of us would ever harm Fred. I can't speak for the others, though."

"Of course," Christy murmured. She glanced at Ellen, wondering if she found this conversation as odd as she did. Ellen's focus, though, was on a tall man coming their way. When Christy looked back at Letitia, she saw that the widow's face had lit up.

"Premier!" Letitia said, reaching out with both hands. "So good of you to come."

The head of the provincial government caught her hands in both of his and leaned forward to kiss her cheek. "I had to, Letitia. I'm so sorry about Fred. He's a great loss to my government, and the country as a whole."

Christy and Ellen murmured respectful greetings to the Premier, then eased away, leaving Letitia alone with him.

Having done their duty, Christy called their driver to pick them up, then they made their way through the press of bodies to the door. She was relieved that the ordeal of her first outing as the senior Jamieson was almost over. Leaving wasn't achieved as quickly as she would have liked, though. Ellen greeted friends, made introductions, paused to chat. The car was at the door waiting for them by the time they escaped.

They were settled inside, back on the Sea to Sky Highway when Ellen brought up the murder. "Letitia thinks Tamara did it."

"Because Fortier told her she was the culprit." Christy leaned back against her seat. "I think Letitia wants to believe Tamara is guilty, because she's afraid someone close to her organized Fred's shooting, even if they might not have pulled the trigger."

Ellen frowned. "You mean she suspects her sister or one of her children?"

Christy shrugged. "Why mention them so specifically?"

"Possibly. I wonder, though, if she was really as okay with her husband's collection of lovers as she seemed to be."

The road curved around the mountain, exposing the sheer drop off to the sea below on the other side. All that separated the speeding car from the edge of the cliff were a few meters of rocky verge and a row of low posts tied together by a ribbon of steel. The highway had a reputation of being dangerous. Reports of fatal accidents happened often and Christy was always on edge when she drove on it. Perhaps that was why Ellen's question had her stiffening uneasily. "You think Letitia arranged to have her own husband murdered?"

"Why not?" Ellen said. "Letitia is a power in her own right. She's on the boards of a half a dozen national charities, not to mention the ones in this province. She was an asset to Fred's political work in so many ways. And yet he expected her to acknowledge his mistresses." She shook her head. "That would be hard on a woman like Letitia."

Christy mulled that over. How would she have felt in Letitia's position? Frank had never, to her knowledge, had a mistress, but if he had, what would she have done? Leave him, taking Noelle with her? But would she have been able to?

Last year, when Frank was missing and believed to be living in Mexico with his girlfriend, she told the trustees that she would be seeking a divorce. Their reaction was to take steps to ensure that if she split with Frank, they would take custody of Noelle, the Jamieson heir. That had been a nightmare she would never forget—and one she could never accept. She'd do anything to keep her daughter safe and with her, including remaining married to a man who had disappeared from her life forever.

Was that what motivated Letitia Jarvis? The need to keep her kids safe and with her? She said, "So when the opportunity offers, in the form of Fred's love child, Tamara Ahern, arriving in Vancouver, Letitia takes action?"

Ellen nodded. "Tamara is the outlier, you see. She can be blamed and no one in Letitia's private circle will be suspected."

Christy thought about that for a moment. "I don't know. For this scenario to work, Letitia would have to have had a paid assassin on speed dial."

"Who's to say she didn't?" Ellen retorted calmly.

Christy laughed. "You're not serious?"

"I am."

"Okay. What about the taskforce? Hitmen aren't cheap. Surely, Fortier would have had bank accounts examined. He would have noticed a large sum of money being withdrawn from her account."

"If she had a hitman on speed dial, she may also have prepaid him. How far back do you think Fortier and his taskforce would go?"

Ellen's point was good. Fortier was determined to see the murder as a political one. He checked the alibis of family members, but wasn't digging deep. If Letitia Jarvis appeared to be innocent on the surface, he'd move on. "We need to put Letitia Jarvis on the suspect list."

Ellen nodded. "She has motive."

She did indeed. But was she ruthless enough to arrange the job?

CHAPTER 17

Christy rang the Armstrongs' doorbell and fumed as she waited. Frank and Stormy had made themselves scarce yesterday after the funeral. At dinnertime, the cat had slunk into kitchen while Noelle was in the room with her. She figured Frank knew that she wouldn't berate him while his daughter was present, and he was right. Stormy consumed his bowl of cat food with a kind of desperation, then disappeared to lie low in some dark corner where the cat could snooze and recoup his energy from his undoubtedly stressful afternoon. This morning, Stormy had rushed out the door when Christy was taking Noelle to school. She hadn't seen him since.

No one answered the bell, but the door was partially ajar, so Christy pushed it open. She could hear voices coming from the living room. She headed up the stairs.

"What possessed you to go to Fred Jarvis' funeral?" Trevor was saying as she reached the landing.

Trevor, Roy, Ellen, and the cat were seated in the Armstrong living room staring at the flat screen TV mounted above the fireplace. They were watching a clip of protesters straining against the barricades the police had erected to ensure the safety and security of all who attended the high-profile event.

"Hi," she said, deliberately calling attention to herself. The other four swung around at the sound of her voice. "I rang, but no one answered. The door was open so I came up."

"We left it open for Frank," Roy said. "He says Stormy gets bored watching too much TV."

"Don't we all," Trevor muttered. His expression was grim. He didn't look like he was in a particularly good mood.

Hey babe. Some reporter caught your arrival. You and Aunt Ellen looked awesome.

That clip also showed Roy standing by the barricades shouting slogans as the chauffeur driven cars of the political and social elite slid past to enter the protected arrival area. As Roy made play with his megaphone and protest sign, the camera caught Stormy slinking through his legs, then darting past the security detail, heading for the church. On the way, he paused to twine around Christy's silk clad ankles, before bolting again and avoiding the combined efforts of three policemen to capture him. The reporter commented that this was the cat that would later disrupt the service midway through.

"That clip is why I'm here," Christy said. "Frank, how could you? You knew I didn't want you to go to the funeral."

Stormy licked a front paw. *It's my job. I'm the senior Jamieson.*

"No. You. Are. Not," Christy said, drawing out the words. She sucked in a deep breath and let it out slowly as she worked on control. "Cats don't go to funerals, Frank. We had that discussion."

Stormy hopped off the couch where he was sitting between Ellen and Trevor, to twine around Christy's ankles. *I do.*

Knowing it would be impossible to get through to Frank in this mood, Christy turned her irritation on Roy. "I suppose he caught a ride with you."

Roy blinked a couple of times and managed to look innocent. "He did."

"Did he tell you why I wouldn't take him in the hired car?"

"You sound fierce, Christy," Ellen said. "Frank hitching a ride with Roy isn't the end of the world, you know. Stormy got home safely. Letitia Jarvis was charmed that a cat came up to her and purred in her ear in church. She said as much when she was interviewed this morning. 'The cat gave me great comfort,' were her exact words, I believe."

"I know," Christy said. She sat down on one of the stairs going up to the next level. Stormy hopped up onto her lap and she patted him absently. "The woman's a fruitcake. She knew her husband had an affair that resulted in a child, but it didn't seem bother her. She even thinks that his own daughter killed him. And that seems perfectly reasonable to her."

"Fred Jarvis always presented himself as a very ordinary man," Ellen said. Her expression was dubious. The individual being revealed since his death was far from ordinary.

"Fred Jarvis was a two-faced liar," Roy said with some heat. "If he couldn't charm you into agreeing with him, he'd lie about his intentions to achieve his goal. He'd do whatever was needed to get what he wanted."

"Is that why you protested at his funeral?" Christy wrinkled her forehead. "Seems a bit harsh. After all, the guy's dead. He can't do any more harm."

Roy hesitated, then he said, rather defiantly, "Yes."

Trevor said heavily, "He wanted the cops to notice him so they'd focus on him and not on Quinn."

Ellen turned wide eyes on him. "Is that true, Roy?"

Roy's expression was fierce. "That idiot inspector says he can hold Quinn indefinitely because he's a security risk. He needs to know that the only thing my Quinn is guilty of is caring for a vulnerable woman."

Trevor said briskly, "You holding a megaphone at the man's funeral and shouting demands that the barricades be lowered, isn't going to help Quinn."

"I was merely pointing out that funerals are private events and there was no reason to make such a spectacle of this one. Fred Jarvis was a politician. He wasn't the damned Prime Minister. He didn't deserve a state funeral."

"It wasn't a state funeral," Trevor said.

"Close enough," Roy retorted, thrusting out his chin. "Every major street in downtown Vancouver was shut down. On a weekday afternoon! Traffic was a nightmare. It wasn't right." His tone was ridiculously virtuous for a man whose goal was to disrupt a major event and cause as many problems as possible for the authorities.

"The only way we can help Quinn is to prove who killed Fred Jarvis," Christy said, breaking into what promised to become an epic argument between Trevor and Roy. "Which is another reason I'm here. Aunt Ellen, can you pick up Noelle from school this afternoon?" When Ellen nodded, Christy said, "Thanks. I've got an appointment to see Olivia Waters at three. I tried to arrange an earlier time, but she was having none of it." Christy's lips twitched. "I think she might be a bit hungover."

"She was certainly putting it away at the reception yesterday," Ellen said.

Christy nodded. "She was undoubtedly distraught by Jarvis' death. Which makes me wonder, what are her real feelings for her daughter? Tamara is her blood and the main suspect. Doesn't she care?"

"She's an irritating woman," Roy said. "Full of herself and too smart for her own good."

She's got your number, old man.

"Which is why I want you to come with me, Roy," Christy said, ignoring Frank.

"Not a good idea," Trevor said.

"Why?" Ellen asked.

"Olivia's daughter and Roy's son are prime suspects. If Fortier found out, he'd probably figure the three of you were brewing a conspiracy."

Trevor sounded impatient, although Christy couldn't tell if it was with laws that gave the Canadian government sweeping powers of arrest in terror motivated crimes, or with the actual individuals involved. She lifted Stormy from her lap and put him on the stair beside her. "I'm taking Roy with me because he and Olivia strike sparks off each other. If Inspector Fortier has an issue with our visit he can talk to Detective Patterson. After all, I'm working for her." She stood up. "Olivia lives in an apartment in Dundarave on the North Shore. If we're going to make it for three, we should get going."

"Lead the way," Roy said, rising to his feet.

I'll come too! Stormy leapt down to the floor, then darted down the stairs to the open front door.

Christy stared after him. Roy shot her an amused look, eyebrows raised. "Well?"

After a minute, she shrugged. "Why not? Frank and Stormy will either charm her into giving up her secrets or she'll be so annoyed I brought my cat she'll tell me what I want to know just to get rid of me. Either way I win."

Dundarave was an enclave in the larger district of West Vancouver. Olivia Waters lived in an unassuming low-rise apartment building in the quirky little village. The area was popular, but expensive. A few blocks in one direction was a sandy beach where families swam in the icy north Pacific during the summer, while in the other was Marine Drive with its collection of shops and galleries. Parking was at a premium, so it took Christy a few tries, but eventually she found a spot a couple of blocks away from Olivia's building.

Christy and Roy planned their strategy while they walked to their destination. Stormy poked his head out of Christy's tote and took in the smells of the ocean wafting up from the nearby seaside. Frank was silent.

The building proved to be a charming six-story heritage site, built not long after the Lion's Gate Bridge connected the holiday resorts on the North Shore to Vancouver proper and opened the area to development. Its Art Deco style featured rounded corners and lots of windows to take in the view. Inside the spacious lobby was a concierge, who looked disapprovingly at Stormy, but passed them through to the elevator without comment, since they were on his visitor's list.

"I wonder if there are any units for sale?" Christy said as the ultra-modern elevator doors slid closed. "This building looks like it's been updated fairly recently, but they've kept the ambience of the original. It might fit all of Aunt Ellen's exacting standards."

It's in West Van. She wants to live downtown.

"I know, but ... " The elevator doors slide open into a foyer of the single penthouse apartment. "I suppose she wouldn't want a unit on one of the lower floors anyway."

Roy rang the doorbell. Stormy squirmed in the tote and Christy lowered the bag and widened the opening so he could jump out. She was straightening when the door opened.

"Right on time," Olivia said. Her features were drawn and she looked tired, but she had dressed with some care in an expensive pair of slacks and a silk top. Though she raised her brows at Roy, she stepped to one side and waved her hand. "Come in."

"Thanks," Christy said. She and Roy stepped into the apartment. Stormy pranced behind, tail up and ears pricked.

Olivia's brows rose higher. "Not only do you bring my daughter's co-conspirator's father, but you bring your cat too?"

"He wanted to come," Roy said. His words were clipped, his tone hostile. He walked deeper into the apartment, heading for the plate glass windows and their exquisite view.

"I'm out on the terrace," Olivia said. She sounded annoyed. "It's a lovely day and my head aches. I want the sun and the sea air."

Hungover. You were right, babe.

The terrace was spacious, the size of a large room, and designed for three seasons, if not year-round use. On this warm, clear, June day the afternoon sun competed with a breeze off the water, resulting in a soothing warmth that Christy admitted would be a very pleasant atmosphere to ride out a hangover. Olivia waved them over to a padded sofa and offered them drinks. "Rye and water?" she said to

Roy. He nodded and settled at one end of the sofa. Olivia turned to Christy. "Wine? A cocktail?"

"I'm the driver, so I'll have water." She headed over to the waist high balustrade that enclosed the terrace. Stormy was strutting along its narrow top. She lifted him off and placed him on the floor. "Stormy stays off the railing and on the ground."

"An odd way of talking to your cat," Olivia said. She was watching Christy with a marked curiosity.

"He's an exceptional cat," Roy said. He still sounded grouchy.

Olivia cocked her head, shrugged, then went over to a sideboard on which were decanters, a tray holding a crystal jug filled with water, and a cocktail shaker. She poured a hefty slug of Rye from one of the decanters into a cut-glass tumbler and topped it up with water. She handed it to Roy, then poured Christy's water from the jug into a tall glass. After Christy accepted it, she poured herself a Martini from a cocktail shaker.

Stormy hopped up onto the sofa and settled in beside Roy. *Not nursing a hangover then, still working on one.*

"Hair of the dog?" Roy said, indicating her Martini.

"I'm grieving," Olivia said shortly. "I'm allowed."

Christy took her water and went back to stand by the balustrade. She leaned against it, her back to the glorious view of English Bay and the city of Vancouver beyond. "When we first met I got the impression you no longer had romantic feelings for Frederick Jarvis."

"I don't." She sat on the sofa, on the other side of the cat. "I'm grieving for opportunities lost and mistakes made."

"You're talking about Tamara." Christy said.

Olivia ran her finger around the rim of her glass. "Fred and I made Tamara together. She's as much his daughter as she is mine. And she killed him. Would she have done that if she'd grown up knowing him? Was I wrong to give her away all those years ago?" She lifted the glass and downed a hefty slug. "I was so pleased she came to Vancouver. I thought this would be my chance to build a relationship with her. Instead, I provided her with the perfect opportunity to murder a man who was my friend."

"You believe Tamara killed him?"

"Who else?"

"You," Roy said.

Olivia stared at him. She looked bewildered by his bluntness. "Me? Why would I kill Fred?"

"Because he wanted to use your daughter as a tool to get himself elected to the leadership of his party," Roy said. "Because he didn't want Tamara all those years ago and he didn't care about her now."

Olivia downed the last of her Martini, then stood up to get herself a refill. She tipped the cocktail shaker, but only a dribble came out. She set about making herself another batch. "I will admit that Fredrick Jarvis could be a manipulative bastard, but he had a charm that was hard to resist." Her hands shook as she measured vermouth and followed it with vodka. "Ask any of his mistresses. They will all tell you the same thing. When Fred wanted you, there was no resisting him." Her eyes were dreamy. Then she shook her head and put the top on the shaker.

Christy stared at her as she shook the beaker, mixing the drink. "How many mistresses did he have?"

"I'm not sure," Olivia said, pouring the mix into her glass and adding an olive. "I know about Marian Fleming, of course. She was one of his more important relationships. I think they were together for years. He moved on eventually, after Marian got pregnant. Fred was never very good with the complication of pregnancy." She paused, contemplated her cocktail. "That may have been Letitia. She was fine with Fred having a string of mistresses, but she didn't want any competition for her own brood."

"Was Marian's child Fred's or her husband, Archie's?" Christy wondered if Archie knew about his wife's liaison with a man he'd worked closely with for years.

"Archie's." Olivia laughed a little. "No denying that. The kid has Archie's beak of a nose and his icy blue eyes."

"So Fred didn't have to worry about an unwanted child," Christy said, watching Olivia as she took another deep swallow of her drink. "Yet he still broke up with Marian?"

Olivia shrugged. "It was his way. You accepted it and moved on to a new place in his life."

There was a decided clunk as Roy put his glass on the Plexiglas top of the coffee table. "Ever thought that Letitia might have killed her husband, then made it look like his bastard did it?"

Christy thought Roy was being deliberately harsh in his choice of words, but Olivia simply opened her eyes and shook her head. "She doesn't have it in her."

Frank made a derisive sound in Christy's mind and Roy said, "Everyone has violence in them if they're pushed too far."

"You don't understand!" Olivia said. "If you were with Fred you knew you were the most important woman in his life. He made you feel—" She shook her head as she searched for the right words. "Sexy. Sensual. Beautiful. Needed. Desired. Perfect. Yes, you knew that he had a wife, but that didn't matter. All that mattered was how vital he made you feel."

"And then he dumped you." Roy's eyes were hard. His expression said he didn't approve of Frederick Jarvis.

Olivia shook her head again. "No. Well, yes, at first it felt like being dumped. At least for me it did. And then, when I came back to Vancouver after Tamara was born, he ... " She hesitated, then she said deliberately, "He courted me. He drew me back into his life. Not as his lover, but as his friend. And that's what we've been ever since."

"Is that what he did with Marian Fleming?" Christy asked before Roy could say something caustic.

Olivia turned to her eagerly. "Yes. That was his pattern. He did that with all of his mistresses. Once the initial hurt was gone, he brought them into his extended family, as friends and allies. He was an extraordinarily complex man."

"He was a self-absorbed narcissist," Roy said with considerable hostility. "I can't believe you'd choose him over your own flesh and blood."

Olivia sipped her martini. Her eyes glistened with tears. "I don't know who Tamara is. Is she the dedicated doctor who went out into the world to help the most desperate? Or is she a woman who has been turned into a terrorist by her years in captivity?" She sipped again, then said in a low voice, "I don't know Tamara, but I do know her father. He's been part of my life for thirty years. How can I not choose him?"

CHAPTER 18

Ellen was standing by the planter at the end of the walk watching Noelle and Mary Petrofsky when Christy, Roy, and the cat returned. She was wearing a chic and expensive designer dress, handmade leather heels, and the diamond necklace she'd worn the day the taskforce arrested Quinn and Tamara. The outfit was a little odd for minding two kids at play, Christy thought, but quickly dismissed it. With Ellen, she could never be sure when that starchy Jamieson propriety would re-emerge. This was probably one of those moments. She guided the van into her carport, careful not to disturb the two girls, who were racing scooters along the street that intersected with Christy's. As she cut the engine, she could hear their competitive squeals of delight. She had to grin, her mood lightening.

The children's obvious joy in their game couldn't lift the gloom that enveloped Roy, however. Olivia's willingness to abandon the daughter she'd borne, but not raised, had shaken some basic part of him. At one point during the drive back from West Van, he had confided to Christy that he feared Quinn might be caught in a net from which he wouldn't be able to break free.

Christy had reached over and taken Roy's hand. "It looks bleak now, but we'll sort this out."

"Yeah. Sure," he'd said, polite but disbelieving.

"We've done it before," she said. She gave his hand a comforting squeeze. "We'll do it again."

That had cheered Roy to the point that he began to talk about his pride in Quinn's successful career, and how much it had meant to him when his son had decided to stay in Canada after Vivian Armstrong, Quinn's mom and Roy's beloved wife, died.

Christy let him talk. The visit to Olivia had depressed her, as well, and she didn't have a lot of positivity to pass along to Roy at this moment. She had to push down a panicked thought that Roy was right—they would never get to the bottom of who killed Frederick Jarvis, leaving Quinn and Tamara as the only suspects. Long, contentious trials, and the possibility that both Quinn and Tamara would be held without bail, loomed in this dark potential future. Christy had to resist the urge to shiver as she visualized it. She couldn't let Roy see her distress. He was upset enough on his own.

With her daughter's joyous cries ringing in her ears as she exited the van, she felt a renewed determination to continue her investigation and was hopeful that she'd find something to exonerate Quinn and Tamara.

Ellen pricked that optimistic bubble almost immediately. "Fortier and his gang of thugs came to visit while you were out."

"Fortier?" Roy's voice rose sharply as he climbed out of the van.

Fortier's appearance explained Ellen's dress-to-impress clothes. "What did he want?" she asked.

Ellen's eyes were worried. "Roy. And he had a search warrant."

"Did they break the door down?" Roy sounded almost hopeful as he stepped out of Christy's driveway and headed for his home. Ellen and Christy followed.

"No," Ellen said to his back. "I called Trevor and asked him what I should do. He said to stall them as long as I could, but ultimately to let them in. So I did."

"Pity," Roy said as he stopped at the end of his front walk. "I would have enjoyed suing them."

Ellen came up beside him. Christy stood to one side. The cat perched on the flower box. They all surveyed his front façade.

"Looks undamaged," he said. "I suppose they left a mess inside."

"Some," Ellen said. "Less than they might have."

"What does that mean?" Roy was still staring at the closed front door.

"Inspector Fortier seemed to think that it was permissible to dump the contents of drawers for no purpose other than to annoy you. I pointed out to him that vandalism had little to recommend it, certainly not for a civilized person. We had quite an interesting conversation about that. I fear he wasn't paying much heed to what I was saying until I began shadowing his men, cleaning up after they'd dumped. They became quite agitated. So did the inspector."

"I'll bet," Roy said. His eyes had brightened and Christy thought she saw mischief in his gaze.

Ellen allowed herself a small, thin smile. "He threatened to arrest me for obstructing justice, until I pointed out that I wasn't obstructing anything, merely restoring order from the chaos induced by his men. We agreed I would remain away from the areas being searched and his men would show your possessions more respect."

"Bravo," Roy muttered.

Christy could imagine Ellen squaring off against the highhanded Fortier, pitting her most imperious manner against his bluster. She suspected the conversation had been more polite on her side than his, and that voices—more than likely just Fortier's voice—had been raised.

Ellen drew a deep breath, the way someone did when they were confessing an error in judgment. "They took the computers, Roy. Both Quinn's and yours. I tried to make them stop, but they would not. Trevor arrived before they left and he made them sign a document stating that they had taken them."

Roy smiled grimly. "No matter. The hardware can be replaced."

"But what about your files? Your books? Your current project?" Ellen's dismay sounded in her voice and showed in her expression.

Roy's smile turned into a rather feral grin. "Quinn's a smart boy. He made sure we each backed up everything onto external drives. Those drives are now deposited in a secure place."

The front door opened and Trevor appeared. He scanned them for a moment before he said, "Fortier wants to question you downtown."

Roy nodded. "I expected that."

Trevor ran lightly down the stairs so he wouldn't have to raise his voice for the next of his comments. "I told him you wouldn't come in unless you had a legal representative present."

Roy nodded again. Ellen said, "Are you going to the station now?"

Trevor shook his head. "We're waiting for Mallory Tait. She's a hotshot criminal lawyer from my firm. She's going to represent you, Roy, and Quinn. Tamara too, if Olivia Waters isn't going to provide her with legal counsel."

"Considering the interview we just had with Olivia, I doubt that's going to happen," Christy said. "She's completely accepted that Tamara is the mastermind behind an international terrorist plot to kill Fred Jarvis."

"Then Mallory will represent Tamara as well," Trevor said, nodding. "I briefed her on the case when I arranged for her to hold the external drives in trust. She's already researching the details and she's excited by the opportunity."

Roy leveled a hard look at Trevor. "She understands that extricating Quinn is the primary goal?"

Trevor met his gaze squarely. "Her primary goal is to ensure that no one gets railroaded. Here's what is going to happen. When Mallory gets here, we will both escort you down to the station. Mallory will be with you when Fortier questions you." He pointed his forefinger at Roy, wagging it for emphasis. "And you will listen to her when she gives you instructions. If she says not to answer, don't."

"I didn't go through all this crap to make it easy for Fortier to scratch me off his list," Roy said heatedly.

"Listen up, Armstrong. Mallory Tait is a lot smarter than you and she understands the nuances of what is going on here. If she says shut up, you shut up!"

Roy's eyes narrowed and his expression hardened. He opened his mouth to argue. Christy said calmly, "Does Mallory know Patterson asked for my help?"

"Yes," Trevor said. Roy looked impatient at the interruption, but he allowed himself to be diverted, for the moment, at least.

"She won't divulge it to Fortier, will she? I think Patterson is right and Fred Jarvis' personal life is the key to the murder, not his professional one. Fortier is adamant, though. He won't let the taskforce be diverted away from his terrorist theory."

Trevor laughed. "Mallory is a firm believer that the less the prosecution knows the better."

"Good." Christy turned to Ellen. "When Roy and I talked to Olivia she mentioned that Marian Fleming was one of Fred's mistresses. We need to interview her. Do you know her?"

"We've met," Ellen said.

"Marian Fleming?" Trevor said. His brows rose. "The wife of Archie Fleming, Jarvis' main competition for the party leadership?"

Christy nodded. "Now you know why I think his murder had personal roots, not political ones." She turned back to Ellen. "Do you think you could arrange an interview with her?"

"I can try." Ellen sounded doubtful, though. "Do you really think Marian Fleming could murder someone?"

Christy noticed a car coming slowly down the hill. While her eyes tracked the progress of the vehicle, she said, "Probably not, but she could hire someone to do it. Patterson told me that Fred Jarvis was killed by a clean shot to the head, the kind of thing a professional sharpshooter would do. That's why Fortier is looking for terrorists or a politically motivated killer. The murder method doesn't have the hallmark of an act of passion."

The car stopped a few feet away from where they were standing clustered around Roy's front walk. The driver side door opened and they all paused a moment to watch as a woman emerged. She was young, blonde, had a killer figure covered by a beautifully tailored skirt suit, and wore sky-high heels that emphasized her long legs.

Inside her head, Christy distinctly heard a wolf whistle. She narrowed her eyes and glared at the cat. Stormy returned her gaze with wide green eyes. He meowed in what Christy took to be an apology, then jumped off the box to twine around her ankles. "Thank you, Stormy," she said, patting him. "I can't say I feel so positively toward your roommate at this moment."

Marriage didn't take away my license to look! The voice was indignant and not a little defiant.

Roy raised his eyebrows at this exchange, and Ellen looked disapproving. Trevor lifted his hand to wave the woman over.

In a voice loud enough for the woman to hear, Roy said, "The people around Fred Jarvis are wealthy, connected, and smart. If one of them wanted to kill Jarvis, they would do everything in their power to make sure they weren't implicated in the murder." He cocked an eyebrow at Trevor. "Can we get your Mallory Tait to sell that to Mr. Pompous Ass Inspector Fortier?"

The woman reached them and held out her hand. "You must be Roy Armstrong." Roy nodded. "I'm Mallory Tait," she said, and they shook. "I will certainly be proposing that the taskforce should broaden its search parameters, since none of my clients are guilty. Whether Inspector Fortier will heed my suggestion, I cannot say."

Trevor introduced Christy and Ellen and they shared a few conversational pleasantries before Mallory said, "We had best be on our way, gentlemen. Fortier was adamant he speak to Mr. Armstrong today. He's a classic hunter and he's under pressure to find the killer. I want to keep him off balance, not dug into a hole he won't bother leaving."

Trevor nodded. "Agreed." Together he and Mallory herded Roy into Mallory's car.

Ellen and Christy watched them drive away. Noelle took advantage of the moment to shout, "Mom! Mary and I are racing. Mary won six times more than me! Isn't she awesome?" Mary gave Christy a bashful smile. "Come on, Mary. Let's go again. Watch us, Mom." They sped off.

Christy laughed and said, "Okay," to their retreating backs. She doubted either girl had heard her.

"While you watch the hooligans, I'll go inside and see if I can make arrangements to meet with Marian," Ellen said.

Christy nodded as she glanced over at Ellen. "The sooner the better."

CHAPTER 19

Marian Fleming agreed to meet with Christy and Ellen the next morning. She suggested the Pacific Centre shopping mall downtown, shortly after the mall opened at ten. That gave Christy enough time to get Noelle to school and her and Ellen down to the mall. They found Marian at the entrance to Holt Renfrew, a high-end store where both Ellen and Christy shopped.

"Good morning, ladies," Marian said. She was wearing black slacks and a dark gray silk blouse that flowed elegantly around her well-endowed frame. On her feet were well-worn low heels.

Shopping clothes, Christy thought. Easy on, easy off garments; shoes that were comfortable for long hours of walking on hard floors.

"I'm glad you called, Ellen," Marian said. She smiled, but her gaze was sad. The concealer she'd used only partially covered the dark shadows that were evidence of sleepless nights. "I need a shopping fix and I don't like browsing alone." She led the way into the store and headed for the ladies' apparel section.

"Well," Ellen murmured to Christy as they followed Marian into the store. "This is an interesting development."

"Do you think she's trying to ignore a guilty conscience?" Christy whispered.

Ellen eyed Marian's back as she moved forward with a determined stride. "Maybe." She chuckled. "I guess we're about to find out."

Marian bypassed women's dresses, slacks, tops, and coats, heading straight for the lingerie section. At the edge, she paused and sighed as she looked around at the goods offered. "I miss Fred," she said. "I love pretty underthings and so did Fred. I used to think about him when I shopped. How would he respond to this bra or those panties? Would he like me to wear a thong under that dress or nothing at all?" She reached up to brush a tear away from the corner of her eye. "Archie doesn't care about my underwear. He's a practical man and likes to dive in without a lot of embellishment."

Christy glanced at Ellen to see if she was as horrified by this conversation as Christy was. She didn't mind girl talk, but not with a complete stranger and a stranger who was of her mother's generation to boot. Ellen didn't look horrified, but her expression said she was amazed at Marian's openness, and not a little intrigued. Christy decided she'd let Ellen do most of the talking. She'd probably be able to invite more confidences from Marian than Christy would.

"I would never have pegged Fred Jarvis as being a sensual man," Ellen said. Her tone of voice mirrored her intrigued facial expression.

Marian laughed as she plunged into the section. "Lord, yes. The man adored women, everything about women. He loved to look and touch and incite. *Your pleasure is my pleasure* was his motto." Her amused smile slipped into one that was nostalgic and not a little melancholy.

She picked up a bra that was mostly thin transparent silk, designed to do nothing but entice as far as Christy could tell. Sighing, Marian replaced it on the rack. Christy took a moment to touch the smooth fabric. A few months ago, she might have bought a bra like this for her own use. She pushed the thought away.

"Even after Fred and I broke up, we remained casual lovers," Marian was saying as she poked through a rack of nothing-there undies. "So I had a reason to indulge my habit. Now? What's the point?" She shrugged, obviously thinking about her no-nonsense husband.

"Didn't Archie mind that you and Fred were lovers? That you continued to be lovers until ... " Ellen waved her hand as she let her sentence drift away.

Marian raised her brows, surprised. "No, of course not. Archie and Fred were friends. Archie is as broken up over Fred's death as I am." She made a hiccup of sound, somewhere between a laugh and a sob. "That was Fred's way. If he wanted to spend time with a married woman he made sure her husband accepted the relationship. He and Archie were already friends and colleagues when Fred seduced me. He took care to ensure Archie was part of the arrangement."

In the act of putting the pretty scrap of a bra back on the rack, Christy froze. "Was Fred into ménage situations?" Her voice came out as a squeak. She knew she sounded naïve and so provincial, but she didn't care. Her brain couldn't process the concept of a man who might have one day been the leader of her country being into group sex—and who knew what else.

Marian laughed. "Of course not." A dreamy look settled into her eyes. "How can I explain? Fred was ... in the moment when he was with a woman, but he never forgot the bigger picture. That the woman had a husband and that her husband had value too. Everybody in Fred's life served a purpose." She giggled. "I like to experiment and wear pretty things, so I provided Fred with adventure, as well as sexual gratification. Archie became his political ally." She sobered, and the amusement seeped away, once again leaving melancholy behind. "Everyone came away with something positive. It worked beautifully for all of us."

Okay, Christy thought. Time to move on from Fred Jarvis's sex life to something more concrete. "The news of Fred's death must have been a terrible blow. How did you hear about it?"

Marian cast a last lingering look at a revealing negligee, then headed toward the shoe section. "Archie and I were campaigning in Calgary. His security detail was informed immediately after Fred's body was found, to ensure Archie was safe and had not been targeted too. He told me right away. We cried together. He had his staff cancel all our events, even though one of them was a thousand dollar a plate fundraiser." She sighed again. "People weren't happy about that."

Marian Fleming did a lot of sighing, Christy thought, but the mental image of Marian and Archie sobbing out their grief for Marian's dead lover and Archie's prime competition for the leadership, was more than she could handle. "Do you think Tamara Ahern is guilty of the murder?"

They had reached the shoe section and Marian was in the act of picking up a dainty sandal with a spike heel. She looked at Christy with surprise in her expression. "Who else could it be? I'm sure if the poor girl hadn't been traumatized, she would never have done it." Marian put the sandal back on the display. "Everyone who knew Fred loved him. The person who killed him had to be an outsider. There's no other possibility."

Christy thought there were plenty of other possibilities, but she was here to mine Marian Fleming for information, not prove her own point.

The shopping expedition continued with a more detailed shoe inspection, followed by a browse through the women's dresses section. They broke for lunch around noon, eating in the store's chic little café. Throughout the meal, Marian talked about Fred, her relationship with Fred, Archie's relationship with Fred, and how his death would impact both their lives.

"He was that kind of man," Marian said wistfully. "He was a force to be reckoned with. Once he was in your life you couldn't bear for him to be out of it." She was deep into pre-lunch margaritas by that point and was even more open than she'd been in the clothing sections.

Christy, who wasn't drinking, found her rather sad. Ellen was nodding agreement and seemed to have bought into the Fred Jarvis mythos. She tackled Ellen on that as they were driving home an hour later, just in time to pick up Noelle from school. "Since Marian was in Calgary with Archie, she couldn't have done the murder herself, but do you believe all that stuff about what a wonder Jarvis was, and how much both she and her husband loved him?"

Ellen stared out the windscreen and didn't respond for a time. "I've met Fred Jarvis at events over the years. Brief encounters that were little more than a few moments of polite chitchat and nothing like the intense relationships he had with Olivia and Marian. Still, Marian is right. He had a way of focusing on you and only you when he was talking to a person. His smile invited confidences and he was a handsome man, with deep brown eyes that could be as warm as melted chocolate and just as enticing."

They stopped at a light and Christy spared a moment to look over at Ellen. "You found him attractive."

"I did," she said promptly. "But I as I said, I met him briefly from time-to-time. I remembered him, but he never remembered me. That was the difference between Fred Jarvis, the intimate friend, and Frederick Jarvis, the politician."

The light changed and traffic began to move again. Christy kept her eyes on the road, even though she frowned. "Personal and impersonal charm. Someone like Marian Fleming, who was bathed in his potent personal charm, might not be able to believe that another person didn't find Fred wonderful."

"Exactly," said Ellen.

"A person who was caressed with that delightful charm, but forgotten the minute he or she was out of range, might feel excluded, and not understand why. Not understanding can cause resentment and resentment brings with it anger and bitterness."

"And perhaps violence," Ellen added quietly.

"Is that who we're looking for, Ellen? Someone who believes he or she should be inside the golden circle, but who was not?"

"Possibly, but not exclusively. It might be a complete outsider. Someone who was immune to his personal style, who was perhaps able to look past it to see the man beneath."

Christy sighed. "You're talking about Tamara."

"She's one. I hate to say it, but ... " Christy could feel Ellen's eyes on her, searching her face, watching her expression. "Quinn is another."

Denial came quick and easily. "Quinn didn't kill Fred Jarvis."

"No, I don't think he did." Ellen hesitated, then she said, "If Quinn had wanted to harm Jarvis he would have used his reputation and his skill with words to destroy the man's chance to win the leadership. I think all Quinn was interested in was minimizing the damage Jarvis could do to Tamara."

"You could be right," Christy said. They turned into the development. "I wonder how Quinn and Tamara are doing?"

"And Roy. I didn't see him come home last night."

As soon as they reached the top of their street it was obvious that something was happening at the Armstrong house. People were emerging from either side of a new model Ford that was parked in front of the driveway. Christy recognized Mallory Tait's beautifully styled blond hair and svelte figure on the driver's side. More importantly, she saw that one of the men exiting the passenger side of the car had Quinn's dark hair and broad shoulders.

Relief bubbled up inside her. "Looks like Quinn has been released. Let's find out what's been happening while we were cruising the mall with Fred Jarvis's mistress."

CHAPTER 20

B y the time Christy and Ellen were parked and out of the car, there was an argument going on at the Armstrong's driveway.

"It will be an interview," Quinn was saying.

"It won't. You're not an impartial observer. You're involved." That was Mallory Tait, the hotshot lawyer from Trevor's firm. She sounded annoyed.

Christy raised her brows and shared a glance with Ellen. The cat appeared out of nowhere and rubbed against her ankles. She reached down and picked him up. He purred as she scratched behind his ears.

Quinn's upset. He wants to interrogate Archie Fleming. He says Fleming is the key.

"Does he, now?" Ellen murmured. "I wonder why that is?"

He's bought into the idea that the killing was politically motivated. Who else could it be, but The Competition?

"Fleming could also be implicated if it was personal," Christy said. She was thinking about Marian's day-long paean to Fred Jarvis. Surely such devotion to a lover would be hard for a husband to bear. What Marian believed and what the real emotions were might be very different.

"Fortier has Tamara all but hung, drawn, and quartered," Quinn said. His expression was grim. "He's stopped looking for the killer. He figures he has her. He's wrong. I know it. So if he won't keep searching, someone else has to."

"And that would be you?" Mallory asked, a sneer liberally mixed into the annoyance in her voice.

"No. That would be us," Christy said as she reached the little group.

Mallory frowned at the interruption, but ignored it, keeping her focus on Quinn. When she spoke, it was clear she was determined to stop him from meeting with Archie Fleming. "How do you expect to get a private meeting with him? Not only are you still a person of interest in the case, but he's a politician on the campaign trail. He may have taken time off after Fred Jarvis's death, but his days will be filled with events and meetings."

Quinn's gaze didn't waver. "I'm a journalist. Politicians love us. If he doesn't respond right away, I'll try again. If he won't see me I'll camp on his doorstep. Whatever happens, I'll get in to see him somehow."

"Listen to me, Quinn! That's harassment. It's not good strategy—"

Christy lowered the cat to the ground. He twined around Mallory's ankles, distracting her. Christy ignored Mallory and looked at Quinn. "I may be able to help with that. Ellen and I have come from shopping with Marian Fleming. I'll call her and see if I can arrange through her for you to meet with Archie."

Mallory frowned as she gave Christy a thorough onceover. Her expression said she found it difficult to equate schmoozing with the wife of a national politician and a modest Burnaby townhouse complex. Evidently she hadn't received the memo that not only did a world-renowned author and his journalist son live in the townhouse complex, but so did the two senior members of the powerful Jamieson family. Mallory's frown deepened as she met Ellen's imperious stare, but she was made of tough stuff. She wasn't about to back down from her primary goal. "It doesn't matter how you get the interview. It's still a bad idea. Fleming will be hostile. He won't speak freely to you, which means you won't get the information you think he's hiding."

Ellen laughed, which made Mallory turn her glare on her. "You clearly don't know Fred Jarvis or the bizarre relationships he formed."

Mallory's gaze sharpened. "What do you mean?"

"Fred had a way of creating extended family through his lovers," Christy said. "I think Marian has picked up the habit. I'm her friend now, so my friends are her friends."

"And her friends are Archie's friends," Ellen added.

Quinn's gaze burned into Christy's. "Go for it," he said. "If you can get Archie to agree to meet with me just tell me when and where and I'll be there."

WHEN AND WHERE turned out to be the Fleming's house that evening. "After dinner drinks," Christy had said when she called to let him know. "Wear a suit."

So here he was, standing beside Christy outside the Fleming's British Properties home in West Vancouver, wearing a suit and being frisked by one of Archie Fleming's security detail. Finally, they were waved through the security perimeter and allowed to proceed to the front door. Marian Fleming opened it herself.

"Darling!" she said to Christy as if they were the best friends in all the world. The two women engaged in the air kisses ritual, barely touching cheeks, smiling all the while. He'd always known Christy was smart and capable, but he was impressed—and not a little saddened—by how quickly she'd adapted to being the senior Jamieson and the family representative.

The air kisses ritual over, Marian turned to scrutinize him. "And this must be your Quinn," she said as she looked him up and down. He fancied he saw approval in her smile as she reached for his hand. She clasped it strongly, giving it a little squeeze to go with the warm smile. It was the kind of grasp you gave a friend you liked, perhaps even cared for, but hadn't seen in a long time.

"It is," Christy said as she performed proper introductions. She didn't indicate what she'd said to Marian to convince her Quinn was okay. He could wonder, even guess, but he didn't really want to know the exact details. It would confuse an already confused situation and bring up emotions he wasn't prepared to deal with now while he was with Christy.

Marian ushered them into a spacious central hall. The floor was tiled with natural slate, the walls wood paneled and gleaming with a rich patina of care and age. Above the paneling, the walls were painted a mellow ivory and hung with fine examples of West Coast native art. A console table made of teak, with the spare clean lines of mid-century modern design, was set against one wall. Chairs in the same style were arranged on either side of the table, and on one corner was a large painted bowl in West Coast First Nations style, apparently used to hold keys. At the other end, was a silver tray with the hallmarks of the Georgian era. On it were several envelopes, old-fashioned snail mail, either on the way in or out. A chandelier hung from the high ceiling, casting a mellow glow over the entire space.

"What a lovely house," Christy said, smiling.

Marian beamed. "We bought it fifteen years ago when Archie first won the riding." She shuddered theatrically. "I thought the price was horrendous then, but now? We had it evaluated recently and I was shocked at how much it had appreciated. Of course, we had to do extensive redecoration. The old couple who originally owned it were lovely people, but the interior was so outdated."

Christy made a pleasant reply, encouraging Marian to expound on the history of the house and the changes she'd made as she led them through an archway and down a corridor to a snug room decorated with the same mix of traditional and modern. Archie Fleming was waiting inside and it soon became clear that the coming interview was expected to be private.

Once the introductions were made, Marian kissed her husband

on the cheek and said, "Enjoy your talk, you two. Christy and I are going to indulge in a glass of wine and a chat in the family room."

Archie watched his wife gently close the door. "I don't know what Mrs. Jamieson did, but Marian came back from their shopping trip more cheerful than I've seen her since Fred died. So thank you." He turned away, moving over to a built-in drinks cabinet. "What would you like?"

Normally, Quinn didn't drink on the job, but he wasn't interviewing Fleming with the intention of doing an article, so he said, "Scotch, neat, please."

Archie nodded and poured himself a whisky as well. He handed Quinn a glass. "You want to know about Fred."

"I don't think Tamara Ahern killed him." Best to put where he stood out in the open. If Fleming didn't like it, he could end the interview and tell Quinn to go.

Archie indicated a chair beside an unlit fireplace. Quinn sat. Fleming eased into the second of the matching pair, opposite. "Why?"

Quinn frowned. "Why what?"

"Why do you think Fred's daughter is innocent? Inspector Fortier believes she's—if not the killer, then at least the instigator of the crime. Letitia Jarvis agrees with him."

Quinn watched the Scotch swirl as he tilted his glass from side-to-side while he gathered his thoughts. This was supposed to be about him questioning Archie Fleming, not the other way around. Still ... He looked up and met the Fleming's gaze. "I think Fortier has one thing right. The person who killed Fred Jarvis was a professional. The cops showed me pictures of the victim while I was being interrogated. The shot was too precise, too clean, to have been done by someone not familiar with firearms. The next step is to wonder who hired a hitman to eliminate Jarvis. A professional hit implies planning, motivation, and money. Tamara doesn't tick any of those boxes."

Archie raised his brows. "Fortier thinks she does."

Quinn kept eye contact as he shook his head. "He's wrong. Planning? How could she organize a hit when she didn't know Fred Jarvis was her father until Olivia Waters introduced him to her two days before his murder? Motivation? Why kill him? Okay, their first meeting went badly and she didn't like him, but to murder him? He wasn't part of her life. It would be easy to walk away and not look back. Money? None there. The only real money in her life came from the trust fund Olivia Waters created for her and there's no evidence she has accessed it since before her kidnapping."

Archie watched Quinn as he spoke, sipping whisky and listening carefully. "Good points," he said in reply. "But the people who kidnapped Dr. Ahern could have found out about her relationship to Fred."

"How?" Quinn hadn't intended to bark out the word, but that was how it sounded.

It didn't faze Archie. He smiled faintly and said, "Dr. Ahern's parentage may not have been widely known, but was it a close kept secret? Letitia knew Olivia was pregnant. Hell, that's why Fred broke off with her all those years ago. Sure, he assumed Olivia had an abortion, but if you knew she'd been pregnant, it would be possible to trace the links and discover that she had carried the child to term."

"Not likely, given the circumstances."

Archie shrugged and sipped his whisky. "You're a journalist, Armstrong. You know there's always another story buried under the surface."

"Yes, I do. And I think that's the story here. If you buy into the idea of Tamara as the center of an international terrorist conspiracy, then it's easy to assume she was put in place to gain access to Jarvis, then lead him into a trap where he could be assassinated. But that's the surface. When you start asking why, you realize the picture is hazy, and if you keep asking questions the image starts to shimmer, then break up."

"What's the new picture you see emerging?" Archie's eyes were watchful as he waited for Quinn to reply.

"I see it as still being political, just not the kind of political that involves an international terrorist conspiracy."

Archie lowered his glass. He looked and sounded incredulous. "Are you accusing me of arranging Fred's death?"

Quinn raised his brows. "Did you?" He expected Archie to react with outrage, anger, perhaps insult in response to his question. What the man actually did surprised Quinn.

He laughed. "My God! I thought your Christy had explained the situation."

Quinn stiffened. Resisting the urge to say, *she's not my Christy, not anymore,* he said instead, "What situation?"

Still chuckling, Archie shook his head. "Heavens, Fred would have laughed if he'd been here."

"I'm afraid I don't understand."

"Fred and I were competitors, yes. We both knew one of us would win the leadership. We also knew that we were stronger together, as a team, than as individuals. So we had an agreement. Whichever one of us won, the other would become his most senior minister. If Fred won, I was going to take Finance. If I won, Fred wanted Foreign Affairs."

He paused to stand up and move over to the drinks cabinet. He poured whisky into his own glass, then held up the bottle, offering Quinn a top up. Quinn shook his head and Archie sat down again. "Initially, we'd be in opposition, of course, but once the party won the general election, together we'd lead the country to a greater strength and prosperity than we've had in decades. It didn't matter to either of us who won. What mattered was the party and the country."

Quinn stared at him and wondered if Archie Fleming really believed the rhetoric he was spouting. "Sounds very high-minded." He knew his tone was cynical and perhaps even snarky. He made an effort to moderate his voice. "It's easy to say now, when Jarvis is gone. But what if he'd lived, if he won the leadership, not you? Here's a guy who took your wife and now he's grabbed the top job. How would you feel? Do you really believe you would have been satisfied as the second banana?"

"Ah," said Archie. "I detect an element of disapproval in that question. A Puritanical attitude to the roles of men and women in relationships." He wagged his finger at Quinn. "Let me tell you this, young man. Since Marian became involved with Fred, my personal life has blossomed and my career has taken off. I have nothing to complain about. And I trusted Fred. We were allies in a tough business. He had my back. Always."

"Still, if he won—"

Archie made a little sound of impatience. "He wasn't going to win. I was! We both knew it. Fred was a presence in the provincial wing, but I represent this riding in Ottawa and I am a senior member of the national party. Sure, there was a possibility Fred would win, but it was unlikely. We both knew it. We both accepted it." He tossed off the last of the whisky in his glass and gathered himself. "Look, I didn't kill Fred or arrange his murder. Nor did Marian. We both loved the man in our own way." Compassion sounded in his voice. "I know you are looking for a way to exonerate Dr. Ahern, but you won't find it here."

CHAPTER 21

Burnaby Mountain Park was quiet, the parking lot virtually deserted, as it had been the first time Christy met Detective Patterson here. That day the sun had been out and the mountains across Burrard Inlet rose high in a vivid blue sky. Today, clouds wreathed their tops, a heavy gray covering that brought the heavens down to earth. A misty drizzle was falling as Christy parked her van beside Patterson's car, but she hardly noticed as she stepped out.

Patterson came round her car. She was holding two paper cups in her hands. She offered one to Christy. "You drink your coffee black, right? I brought extra sugar and cream if I guessed wrong."

Raising a brow, Christy said, "When I'm not indulging in super sweet concoctions that are more dessert than coffee, I do. Thanks, Detective." She accepted the offered cup and took a sip.

"You said you had info for me when you phoned."

Christy looked at the detective over the rim of her cup. "I do and I don't."

Patterson didn't say anything. She drank her coffee and leaned against her car, a woman who had all the time in the world. Though of course she didn't. Christy took another sip of coffee then put the cup on the roof of Patterson's car. She reached into the pocket of her jeans and pulled out several pieces of paper. Patterson's brows rose.

The pages were the result of a brainstorming she and Ellen had done that morning. Ellen, in her self-nominated role as secretary and recorder of the Jamieson-Armstrong detection group, had made notes from the session. She used her expensive blue letterhead and her many fountain pens, each filled with a different color of ink. Her handwriting was a flowing copperplate that suited the writing implements and paper.

When Ellen wrote the document, the paper had been crisp and smooth. Now, after being wadded up in Christy's pocket, it was crumpled, but still elegant. Christy held it up in evidence. "Details and questions," she said. "Frederick Jarvis led a very interesting life."

"Interesting as in visiting new places and meeting new people is fun and exciting. Or interesting as in yikes, this is weird and scary."

Christy met her eyes. "Weird. I'm not sure about scary."

Patterson sighed. "I was afraid of that. Okay, what have you got?"

Christy crumpled the papers further and reached for her coffee. She took a sip as she gave herself time to organize her thoughts. She needed to present what she'd found coherently, or else Patterson would think she was making it all up. "Fred Jarvis had mistresses."

"We know that," Patterson said with a shrug. "Tamara Ahern is his daughter from Olivia Waters, his mistress."

"She is," Christy said. "I guess it wouldn't surprise you if I told you that Marian Fleming was also his mistress."

That statement was greeted with silence as Patterson stared at her through narrowed eyes. "Marian Fleming, as in Archie Fleming's wife."

Christy nodded. "The same."

Patterson said curtly, "I don't believe that."

"Marian admits it freely. Ellen and I had a very interesting shopping excursion with her where we cruised the lingerie department at Holts and she told us exactly what Fred liked to see her wearing."

About to take a sip, Patterson slowly lowered her cup. "Seriously?"

Christy nodded. "It gets better, Detective. Marian said that her husband not only knew about the relationship, but was okay with it. She says Archie and Fred were best friends."

"Oh, hell," Patterson said.

Christy imagined the detective was envisioning the kind of political fallout that would occur if it came out that two of Canada's most popular politicians were entangled in some kind of sexual triangle. "Marian gave us no indication that Archie was involved in Fred's sexual activities with her. She made it clear the men were friends, allies, and competitors who respected each other."

"Even so," Patterson said. She'd recovered enough to gulp down more coffee.

"Yeah," Christy said. She paused to drink her own coffee. "I find it hard to believe too. I mean, Fred was sleeping with Archie's wife. Most men would be furious and starting divorce proceedings."

The coffee had apparently revived Patterson cynical side. "Marian Fleming comes from old money. Maybe Archie couldn't afford to divorce her."

"I don't think that's it," Christy said. This was the tricky part. She had to provide Patterson with the information Archie had given Quinn last night, but she didn't want to admit that Quinn was the one who talked to Archie Fleming. There was no telling how the detective would react, what she might feel she was required to do. Quinn may have been released without being charged, but he was still a person of interest and would be until the real killer was found.

She sipped her coffee while she marshaled her thoughts. "During our shopping trip, Marian talked a great deal about her relationship with Fred. I have to admit, I was skeptical about Archie's position. She invited us to drinks last night." She toasted Patterson with the mostly empty coffee cup. "Archie opened up and told all."

Patterson's brows went up and she tilted her head in an enquiring way. "I'm listening."

Christy grinned. She couldn't help it. "Archie's sex life is much better since Marian started sleeping with Fred."

"Oh, dear God!"

Christy laughed. "Yeah, that about says it. The important thing is that Archie and Fred had a pact. No matter which one of them won the leadership race, the other would benefit with a senior cabinet post. Archie truly believes that he will win and would have even if Fred were alive. He says Fred knew it too."

Patterson contemplated nothing in particular for a minute, before she refocused on Christy. "So Fleming and Jarvis are allies, running together and basically ensuring that no other candidate can come up from behind and snatch the election away from them."

Christy nodded. "Sounds that way."

With a sigh, Patterson said, "There's a whole bunch wrong with that, but it doesn't provide a motive for murder. In fact, it argues against Archie or Marian being involved."

"Possibly, but Ellen noted that Archie is a politician, a good one. He knows how to talk around an issue so it sounds like he's coming down strong on one side, when he is actually inclined differently. It's a good point. I think it makes Archie worth talking to. We only know about the pact from Archie. What if he was lying about that and about his sex life? Jarvis wanted to use Tamara to help his campaign. What if Archie thought her participation would push Fred ahead of him in the polls? He kills Jarvis and makes it look like Tamara is the murderer. All those people who were thinking of voting for Fred then turn his way. Now he's the sole front runner for the party leadership and the man who stole his wife is no longer around to taunt him."

"Archie Fleming was in Calgary at the time of the murder. He has an unbreakable alibi."

"So he said. But you said the murder appeared to be carried out by a professional. Archie has money and influence. He could have hired a hitman."

Patterson stared at Christy for a moment, then she said, "Easier said than done. Anything else?"

"Letitia Jarvis was aware of her husband's string of mistresses and didn't mind. Or she says she didn't mind. Her big issue was kids. According to Olivia Waters, Letitia was happy to let Fred stray wherever he wanted as long as no children resulted. In fact, that's why

Jarvis dumped Marian. She got pregnant. It was Archie's child, but that was the end of her relationship with Fred."

Patterson drank more coffee as she listened to this. "So Letitia had it in for Tamara, her husband's love child?"

Christy nodded. "She's quite certain Tamara killed Fred."

"How do the kids feel about their half-sibling?"

Christy sipped her coffee before she replied. "I don't know. I haven't had a chance to talk to them yet. Ellen thinks there may be more mistresses lurking in the wings. She's heard rumors for years, but had no proof." She swirled her coffee cup, watching the liquid crawl up the sides of the paper cup. Then she looked straight at Patterson. "She may be right. When we were waiting to be admitted into the church for Fred's funeral, I spoke to a woman who was ahead of us. She mentioned that Fred liked cats. She has a Persian and he told her stroking it was a stress reliever for him."

Patterson grinned. "That was your cat, wasn't it? The one who crashed the funeral?"

Christy drew a deep breath. "Yeah. He hitched a ride with Roy Armstrong."

Patterson laughed, then got back to business. "So Jarvis liked to pat cats. Doesn't mean the woman was his mistress."

"No, it doesn't. It was an impression I got from the way she teared up and the emotion in her voice when she spoke of Fred."

Patterson pursed her lips, then clicked her tongue. "Okay, so what we have is a man with a screwed up personal life. He behaves like a medieval seigneur who figures every woman is fair game and their men own him their allegiance—"

She broke off as Christy shook her head vehemently. "It wasn't like that. Not at all." She paused, lifted her hands as she tried to find the words to explain. "Fred Jarvis seduced people," she said. Her brow wrinkled as she chose her words, slowly piecing together a picture of a life that was highly individual and perfectly reasonable for those involved in it. "If Fred wanted someone, he made her—or him—want to be with him. Marian Fleming loves her husband, Archie. She also loved Fred Jarvis. It was a different kind of love, but

... " She shook her head. "How do I explain? With women, it was sensual. Fred gave them pleasure, made them feel desirable, needed, powerful. For men, he was their best bud. The guy who had their back, the man they could depend on. And when he broke off the physical relationship a woman, he did it carefully, so no one was hurt. Then the woman became his friend, like her man." Christy paused, drinking more coffee, looking inward. "It was not a style I could have handled. Nor Frank, I think. More certainly, not Quinn. Maybe it was a generational thing? A variation on the free love days of the baby boomers."

Patterson snorted. "Or maybe it was just weird and all these people are pretending they're okay with it, but they weren't."

Christy nodded. "Could be."

Patterson sipped coffee and ruminated. Christy finished off hers and waited. "Okay," Patterson said finally. "Here's what we do. The taskforce has taken statements from everybody involved in Jarvis' life. I'll review them and check the alibis. Could be some are not as airtight as they look on the surface. I'll also check bank records to see if any of the people in his personal circle recently withdrew a large sum of money. You talk to his kids and also see if you can dig up any more mistresses."

Christy nodded agreement as Patterson hesitated.

"I think you're on to something here, but I have to tell you, we're pushing water up hill. Fortier believes this is a political murder brought about by an international conspiracy. He likes Tamara Ahern for it and she doesn't have anyone who can corroborate her story that she was walking in Stanley Park when the killing took place." Patterson shrugged. "In fact, you're right. The actual killing could have been done by a hired pro, but if so, Tamara could have been the one who did the hiring. Fortier doesn't care if she is the planner or the doer. To him, she's still guilty."

"Does he still think Quinn is involved? That he's the one who pulled the trigger? Because, if he does, he's wrong!"

"You probably know that he cut Armstrong loose. I don't think he's likely to charge him."

Christy breathed a sigh of relief. "Thank God."

Patterson shot her a sympathetic look that made Christy blush. "Okay, Mrs. Jamieson. Keep in touch. But we have to move quickly. Fortier wants an arrest—and so do our bosses."

"I'll do what I can." She held out her hand. "There's a recycling station over by the restaurant. I'll get rid of our cups."

"Thanks." Patterson handed her the cup, then slid into her car.

Christy watched her drive away before she trudged slowly over to the disposal area. Patterson seemed to have bought her implication that she and Ellen had talked to Archie Fleming. She'd also accepted that it was Christy and Ellen who had come up with the idea that Archie might be lying, when in fact, it was Quinn who had brought it up as they drove home from West Van last evening.

Talking to Quinn about the case, discussing suspects, pulling apart their statements, all of it had been bittersweet, dredging up memories from previous cases when they were working together on their relationship, not just to solve a murder. He had a sharp, incisive mind that was a good counter to her more instinctive way of reading people and situations. They made a good team.

She hugged that thought close as she watched the cups disappear into the depths of the recycling box. Her future was complicated as she took up her new position as The Jamieson, even as she dealt with old emotions and figured out new ones. She suspected Quinn was in a similar position. Tamara's home base was Toronto. That would mean a cross-country move for Quinn, if they were to get together. Then there was her international aid work, another set of emotional challenges.

A lot of decisions coming up, for both of them. Decisions that could only be made after they cleared Tamara and found Fred Jarvis' killer.

She turned away from the recycling bin and walked quickly back to her van.

CHAPTER 22

Christy parked her van in the visitor parking of the West Vancouver townhouse complex. The parking lot was at the base of the development, which crawled up Cypress Mountain. Below them the always busy TransCanada Highway was screened by an environmental fence and a row of tall cedars. It muffled the traffic noise, but didn't quite eliminate it.

Christy peered up at the stacked townhouses above them. Each residence looked out toward the city of Vancouver, and their fronts were a wall of glass that glinted in the midday sunlight, making the most of the location. "The view from those windows must be spectacular."

"There is more to a residence than the view," Ellen said. She sounded like she'd already made up her mind not to like the townhouse that was for sale. Miss Krippen, their long-suffering realtor, had her work cut out for her.

"Okay," Christy said. "I see Miss Krippen's car on the other side of the parking lot. Let's get this done."

Ellen sniffed.

It had been Ellen who suggested that Miss Krippen expand her search for an appropriate new residence for Ellen. She had been looking in the downtown and West End area, but Ellen had been intrigued by Christy's description of Olivia Waters Dundarave apartment in West Vancouver, and she decided she might enjoy living on the North Shore. Miss Krippen had accepted the challenge with enthusiasm and sent over a dozen listings for Ellen to consider. This Cypress Mountain complex was the first she and Christy had been to see.

Seeing them alight from the van, Krippen bustled over, smiling cheerfully, as she always did—until Ellen rejected yet another of her options. Christy didn't know how she remained so positive. In Krippen's shoes, she would have been wreathed in constant gloom.

"Good morning, ladies," Miss Krippen said when she was near enough not to shout. "Isn't this a lovely development?" She didn't wait for an answer. "Because I know your neighbors are important to you, Miss Jamieson, I've arranged for you and Mrs. Jamieson to meet with the chairperson of the Strata Council after we've done a tour of the unit. I have the details about the management of the complex, but she will be able to tell you about the community itself."

She looked so hopeful as she outlined her strategy that Christy had to smile back as she nodded. Ellen raised her eyebrows. Miss Krippen gulped and headed out to give them the tour.

At the end Ellen had to admit that the unit was spacious and well laid-out, with a breathtakingly spectacular view. Heartened by this evidence of thawing, Miss Krippen's optimism reached new heights. "Mrs. Conroy is meeting us in the community building. They have an indoor aquatic center with a swimming pool, sauna, and hot tub. As well, there is a common room with a lovely little kitchen. They use it for their strata meetings and neighborhood parties. Owners can also book the space for their own events."

The common room was decorated to look like the great room in an upscale mansion. Squishy sofas and chairs were positioned to make the most of the stupendous view of the city and seascapes. A round table covered with a starched, crisply ironed white linen tablecloth had been set up in a cozy corner. On it were the trappings of coffee service for four. There was a woman sitting at the table, presumably Mrs. Conroy. As they neared, she stood, smiling in welcome.

She was a woman in her mid to late forties and Christy knew her instantly. She'd sat in the family row at Fred Jarvis' funeral.

After the introductions had been made, they talked about the management of the strata while they all shared a cup of coffee and a pastry, then Miss Krippen quietly excused herself to allow Ellen and Christy to talk privately with Sharon Conroy.

Christy said, "I'm sorry for your loss, Sharon." When the woman looked blank, she added, "You were at Fred Jarvis' funeral, sitting with Letitia."

Sharon Conroy blinked then said cautiously, "Were you one of Fred's ... friends?"

Christy sucked in her breath. It hadn't occurred to her that anyone might consider her in the role of one of Jarvis's mistresses.

Ellen set her teacup down into the saucer with a clink of bone china. "Of course not. She's a Jamieson," Ellen said, as if that explained everything. "We were both there, as representatives of the Trust."

Sharon looked down at her cup, then reached for the coffee urn to pour a refill. "Where were you seated?" she asked in a neutral voice.

"In the balcony," Christy said. She exchanged a glance with Ellen, who didn't appear to be impressed by the route the conversation had taken.

Sharon was nodding as she poured. "Good," she said. "Fred's women were assigned places close to the family seating." She set down the urn and seemed to come to a decision. "Since we may become neighbors, you'll find out anyway. Letitia Jarvis is my sister. Fred Jarvis was my brother-in-law."

"This is probably not a good time for you, then," Christy said, deciding to go the sympathetic route.

Sharon flicked her wrist dismissively. "I'm fine. And so is Letitia, really. My brother-in-law may have been a brilliant politician, but he was a lousy husband. And father, for that matter. I put up with him for Letitia's sake, but I never liked him."

Christy glanced at Ellen. Sharon Conroy's attitude was what she had expected from the women in Fred Jarvis' life—dismissive, disdainful, perhaps even angry. "It must have been hard on Letitia to have to share him with another woman."

"Another? As in one?" Sharon laughed without humor. "The man was a serial philanderer, Christy. Over the period of their marriage, Fred had a dozen or more other women. I lost count over the years. I did notice that they kept getting younger and younger, though."

Christy thought about the woman at the church, the one who owned the cat Fred liked to stroke. She had been in her thirties, younger than Olivia, who was in her fifties, and Marian, who she thought was in her late forties. She had guessed the woman had been one of Fred's mistresses. Now she was sure.

Ellen said, "I gather you don't approve of Mr. Jarvis' lifestyle. How curious, since Letitia doesn't seem to mind."

"She doesn't, and she does," Sharon said. "Fred made sure she knew she was first. His legal wife, the mother of his children, the woman who would always be there. But, as you say, she had to share. That took its toll."

"I'm not surprised," Ellen said.

Christy hid a smile. Ellen was making no attempt to hide her disapproval.

"Your viewpoint on Fred's lifestyle is different from everyone else we've spoken to," Christy said.

"It's refreshing," Ellen said.

Sharon sipped her coffee. She put her cup down, toyed with it for a moment, then said in a low voice, "That's because I knew Fred was selfish and self-absorbed. He made people think they were important to him, but really, they weren't. All he wanted was his own pleasure and he didn't care who he hurt in the process." She stopped just before her statement turned into a rant.

"Did something happen?" Christy asked.

Sharon fiddled with her teacup some more, then she shrugged. "The man is dead. He'll never be Prime Minister now, so I suppose I don't have to keep the secret any longer." She lifted her head and looked Christy right in the eyes. "Fred propositioned me. Me! His sister-in-law."

"When?" Christy asked. If it was a recent occurrence it might be a valid motive for murder.

"It was after he'd dumped Olivia Waters for getting pregnant." She sounded belligerent. "He told me he'd decided to keep his ladies in the family." She snorted. "Imagine that, making a pass at his own wife's sister. Horrible man." She shook her head. "Later on, I realized he'd taken that idea of making his women family and run with it. That's why he had that weird relationship thing with the husbands. So not only did Letitia have to accept that he went to other women, but she had to socialize with them."

"That must have been hard on her," Christy said.

"Of course it was! He was such a bastard. I hated him for that, for what he did to Letitia. Belittling her, making her part of such a distasteful arrangement. Making me part of it."

Ellen frowned. "I assumed from what you said that you rejected him."

"I did, but Letitia is my sister and I wasn't about to let her go because she'd married a jerk. To stay within Frederick Jarvis's magic circle, I had to accept his ways too. I had to socialize with his women —and their men. I had to make nice and pretend that I thought everything he did was okay." She stopped, drew a deep breath. "I hated it. I hated him. I just didn't realize how much until he was dead and I didn't have to pretend anymore."

CHAPTER 23

Q uinn jabbed the End Call button on his phone with more force than was required. In fact, he didn't need to touch the button at all, since Mallory Tait had already disconnected. Her voice echoed in his mind. *You need to be prepared. I expect it to happen any time. Short of finding the real killer, there's no way to stop it.*

It was Tamara's arrest. He closed his eyes, imagining her in a cell down at the remand center. A Canadian cell this time, but still a small space surrounded by four solid walls and a locked door. It would bring back memories of her captivity in Africa. Being locked up would cause her mental pain at the very least. At worst? He feared it would break her forever.

The Tamara he remembered had been bold, passionate, confident. The woman who had returned was introspective, cautious. She'd confided to him that she still wanted to help people caught in war zones or existing on the margins of societies in crisis, but she couldn't do it on the ground anymore. She'd been thinking about creating a foundation that had the goal of exposing underlying causes of armed conflicts as well as the atrocities that resulted. They'd brainstormed ways and means, the kind of reporting that would need to be done, how to structure such an organization, the kind of money required to fund it.

Her meeting with Fred Jarvis and her initial rejection of him was based on his complete disinterest in her as a person and his child. She'd been angered by his enthusiastic assumption that she'd be an asset to his campaign, nothing more. The irony was that after reflection, she'd come to the conclusion that joining with him to win the leadership of his party would provide her with an incredible wealth of opportunities to help her in the creation of her foundation. If he won, his position—and hers as his daughter—would provide a solid base for the foundation to grow. She'd planned to tell him of her change of mind the day he was killed. She never had the chance.

Archie Fleming assumed he was the obvious choice to win the leadership, and Quinn thought that might have been true before Tamara arrived in Vancouver. How would the sudden revelation of a daughter, one who believed in just causes, who had endured suffering in the pursuit of those causes, have affected the political balance between the two men?

Archie told him that Fred wanted the Foreign Affairs portfolio if he lost the leadership bid. That meant he already had an interest in international relations. He would have known how to use Tamara and her experiences to his advantage. In Quinn's estimation, Fred's support would have grown, while Archie's remained static or diminished.

A powerful motive for a politician in pursuit of power.

Quinn firmly believed that Fred Jarvis' murder was rooted in his political life. Fortier thought it had international implications, so he was focused on Tamara, but Quinn believed he had discovered a solid political motive for Archie Fleming. What he needed to do now was dig deeper, find a connection, the proof he needed, before Fortier charged Tamara, locked her in a cell, and convinced a judge to refuse her bail. He settled down to work.

His research brought to light the fact that Archie Fleming's chief strategist was Colin Jarvis, Fred Jarvis' only son. Now that, Quinn thought, sitting back in his desk chair and staring at nothing in particular, was very interesting indeed. Why would Colin Jarvis support his father's main opponent? According to his sources, Colin Jarvis was both shrewd and farseeing, with the kind of mind able to leap past the obvious and see the pitfalls ahead. Some said Colin was the main reason Archie had achieved such success in the party, why he was the frontrunner in the leadership race. None of Quinn's sources could pinpoint why Colin Jarvis stayed with Archie Fleming when his father put in his own bid for leadership. There was no overt break between father and son, no particular reason why Colin would remain loyal to Archie instead.

Clearly, he needed to talk to the man himself. Quinn set his mind to figuring out how to get an interview and what questions to ask when he did.

He arranged a meeting with Colin Jarvis through an unsuspecting secretary who thought he wanted to profile Archie Fleming for one of the major Eastern dailies. Since Colin made the decisions on who had access to Archie, she blithely told Quinn he'd have to pitch his idea to Colin before she could schedule a meeting with Archie.

Perfect. Even better, she said Colin had an opening in his schedule this afternoon at five. Could Quinn make it? Oh, yeah, he could.

Archie Fleming's national campaign headquarters were located in a sleek glass and steel tower on West Georgia. Like all such buildings, the inside was a shell that the tenant could make of what he or she would. Archie's style of decoration was lots of desks loaded with computer equipment and telephones, arranged bull pen style, a few partitions for calls that demanded a bit of quiet, a conference room for meetings, and one office. His.

And Colin's, Quinn discovered. That suggested a level of trust and intimacy that fit well with the weird pseudo-family relationship that seemed to exist between Archie and Fred.

"I have a half an hour," Colin said as he ushered Quinn into the office.

Unlike many of his staffers, he was smartly dressed in an expensive suit, a dark charcoal wool and silk blend, if Quinn guessed right, a pearl gray shirt, and a conservative blue tie, establishment clothes that implied the right to govern.

He indicated a visitor chair as he sat down behind the desk visible from the bull pen and Quinn realized that there was a second desk tucked away at the back of the room, away from the doorway and the prying eyes of the mass of staffers and volunteers who populated the main area. Colin Jarvis was not only Archie's strategist, he was also his guard dog. "My admin assistant didn't know you are tied to the woman who killed my father, but I do. If this is a legit interview tell me what paper you're targeting and what angle do you intend to take."

No sense in trying to build a rapport. Time, Quinn thought, to just dive in. "How about this? Archie Fleming ordered the hit that killed your father."

Colin froze. Quinn watched shock fade and anger bloom. "What the hell kind of statement is that?" He jerked to his feet. "I think you'd better leave."

Quinn stayed put. "Did you know that your father and Archie Fleming had an agreement in place that whichever of them won, the other would have a senior cabinet position in any future government?"

"Of course," Colin said, still standing, his voice scornful. "Agreements like that happen all the time in politics. If you're as good as you're supposed to be, Armstrong, you'd know this."

Quinn nodded. "I do. It's just odd in this case, since one guy was sleeping with the other guy's wife and they both seemed to see it as one big happy family."

He could see at once that Colin knew exactly which guy was doing the sleeping with the other guy's wife. His face whitened and he sat down abruptly. "That's bullshit. You have no proof."

"I talked to Archie last night."

"Archie wasn't meeting the press last night," Colin said.

"It was a private conversation, over drinks with Archie and Marian," Quinn said, watching Colin intently. He could see signs of fear, perhaps even panic that Colin was struggling to control. He was sitting very still, but there was a tremor in his hands, which were lying flat on the desktop. His skin, if possible, was paler than before. Quinn would swear that he didn't know about his father and Marian Fleming, but he did know something. What?

Colin moistened dry lips. "You're wrong."

"I'm not." Quinn watched emotions of betrayal and anger flit across Colin's face and pressed gently. "You didn't know about the relationship?"

"Of course not!" Agitated how, he sprang up and started to pace. "Do you think I would have supported a man who pimped his wife out to tame the competition?"

"Harsh, and not quite accurate," Quinn said. "From my understanding, the relationship was Marian's choice."

Colin snorted and waved a disparaging hand. "He let her think it was her choice."

He was obviously Fred Jarvis. Quinn thought it very interesting that Colin had not yet expressed any warm feelings for his late father. He didn't comment, though, just let Colin continue on, hopeful the man would reveal something valuable.

"That's how he worked," Colin said. He kept pacing, his eyes anywhere but on Quinn's. "He targeted women he thought could be useful, then he seduced them until they abandoned their morals and forgot about any ethics they'd ever had. Along the way he made them, and everyone around them, think the relationship with him was the best thing that had ever happened to them." His voice died off as his agitated pacing brought him to the open doorway and the bull pen full of staffers. He closed the door gently, his expression stricken.

Quinn shifted in his seat to keep Colin in view. "Your description is precise and it fits with what Archie told me last night, although he described it in a more positive way. You claim you didn't know about Marian and your father. Where did you get your knowledge of his methods, then?"

Colin turned away from the door. He walked slowly back to the desk. The expression on his face was bleak, the kind of look Quinn had seen more often than he cared to remember, when a person learned a loved one had died. The look of loss, of realization that nothing would ever be the same again.

Reaching the desk, Colin pulled open a top drawer and began unloading the contents. "I was in grade ten when I discovered my father was sleeping with the principal of my very expensive private school." He pulled a Mont Blanc pen from amid the regular bits and pieces found in every desk drawer and pushed it to one side. A tiepin with the party logo and Archie's name followed. "Turned out that he'd started the liaison shortly after my name was submitted for admission to the school." He looked up from his agitated, almost obsessive, sorting. "It was an exclusive institution and not even Jarvis money and my mother's Eastern Establishment family could ensure I would get in." He went back to rifling through his desk. "She was a prize, that one was. Her husband was a senior administrator at the university I chose to attend." He stilled. "I chose to attend," he muttered derisively. With a sudden violent move, he picked up the expensive pen and the gold tiepin and flung them at the desk in the back of the room.

"How did you find out?" Quinn asked as the clatter of the falling pen died off.

Colin fell into the desk chair with a plop. Leaning forward, his elbows on the desktop, he rubbed his temples, soothing himself, letting the poison flow. "My father was one of the parents who always showed up at the school. My friends noticed it. The kids I didn't hang with, noticed." He lifted his head and met Quinn's gaze. "One afternoon, halfway through the term, a group of us were working on a class project after school hours. When I was leaving, I saw my father's car in the school parking lot—so did all the others. They wanted to know why my dad was there and they pretty much dared me to go inside and find him." He shrugged. "So I did. I caught them at it. The principal and my dad. She didn't see me, but he did."

He stopped talking, his eyes staring blankly into the past, Quinn thought, as he saw again that pivotal act of betrayal. "What happened?"

"Nothing. We talked it out. Like men, my father said, as he explained that people like my principal could be useful." His lip curled. "I remember feeling proud that he was talking so openly to me, sharing his viewpoint, his way of being. He promised me he'd split with her." The curled lip turned into an outright sneer. "All he did was move the site of their meetings somewhere else. When I graduated, I was steered to the appropriate university, where I received early admission and a scholarship. That was when he dumped her. Even then, she and her idiot of a husband remained part of his so-called extended family. She was one of the ones at the funeral. Bastard."

He swept the pens, pencils, and highlighters on the desk back into the top drawer, opened another, and hauled out a pair of dress shoes, a white dress shirt, folded and bagged from the drycleaners, two silk ties—both solid variants on the party's signature blue. Slamming the drawer shut he glared at Quinn. "Think I'm a chump?"

"I think both men realized you would never agree to work for Archie if you knew about your father and Marian. You were manipulated by a man who was a champion manipulator." Colin went back to methodically emptying his desk. Quinn watched him for a minute, then he said, "The question is, did you just find out about Fred and Marian because I told you? Or did you learn about it yourself?"

Colin slowly straightened, "What are you suggesting?"

Quinn didn't flinch. "That you found out your father was banging your boss's wife and he'd set you up. You couldn't stand that. Bad enough when you were a teenager. But now? When you should have known better, here you were again, so you killed him in a fit of rage. Just like you threw that fine pen across the room because you were angry at the man who gave it to you."

"You need to leave. I'm not going to ask again," Colin said. His eyes were narrowed, his expression hard.

Quinn shrugged and stood. He hadn't expected a confession. In fact, he'd gained a lot more than he'd anticipated from his meeting with Colin Jarvis.

As he headed for the exterior door to the suite, he saw Colin pull out a leather backpack from beneath the desk. He started to stuff his personal items into it as Quinn was strolling out of Archie Fleming's campaign office.

Looked like Archie just lost his chief strategist.

CHAPTER 24

"He didn't know about his father and Marian Fleming," Quinn shifted restlessly in his lawn chair. "I think he really believed in Archie Fleming. Discovering his father and Fleming were more than just political allies infuriated him. It also brought up memories from his past, but this betrayal was fresh. He didn't see it coming." Quinn shook his head. "Colin Jarvis isn't the killer."

He sounded disheartened, Sledge thought, which wasn't surprising, since Tamara was still in police custody. This was apparently gnawing Quinn harder than it was Tamara, though. Mallory Tait had seen and talked to her, and said she was holding up well. Tamara was calm, polite, and firm in her denials. Clearly, she was coping. In Sledge's opinion, Quinn wasn't. He could understand why. He and Quinn shared a core belief—if a man cared for a woman and that woman was in trouble, then the man needed to help her out. If he couldn't ... Well, he was entitled to freak out and do things that were, perhaps, not in his usual style. Like confronting Colin Jarvis and accusing Archie Fleming of murdering Colin's father.

Sledge reached for the box of pastries Christy had brought to this morning's brainstorming session and picked out a Danish. He held up the box to see if anyone else wanted to refuel, but Roy and Ellen shook their heads. Christy was watching Quinn with a single-minded focus and worry in her eyes. She didn't even notice Sledge's gesture.

Since the morning was clear and warm they were sitting in the Armstrong's backyard. He was representing his father, who was still down at the cop shop trying to breakout Tamara, with the help of Mallory Tait. The cat was sitting at the edge of the greenbelt behind the garden, watching the trees, his eyes glued to the canopy above, his ears flicking at each new sound. High in the branches a squirrel twittered. The cat's tail twitched and he crouched, ready to spring. Frank wasn't adding a lot to the discussion at the moment.

"When Christy and I shopped with Marian Fleming, she was very open about the relationship," Ellen said. She had her leather portfolio in front of her and her collection of pens arrayed beside it. She'd already started a ledger of suspects and the clues they offered.

Sledge munched the Danish and resisted the urge to shake his head. He thought the music industry had some strange behaviors. The political world made his seem wholesome by comparison.

Christy frowned. "Letitia Jarvis was more circumspect, but she made reference to his extended family, which meant his mistresses."

Ellen tapped her chin with one of her fountain pens. "I came away with the impression she guarded her children carefully." She turned to Christy. "Do you think she knew Colin was aware that his father had a mistress?"

"Good question," Roy said. Like his son, his mood was subdued. He was holding a coffee cup and watching the steam rise lazily above the rim.

Quinn stirred and shrugged. "Does it matter?"

"It might," Roy said. "If she was determined to keep her kids ignorant of their father's extracurricular activities."

"Colin Jarvis was in grade ten a long time ago, Dad. If Letitia was angry at her husband over this, she'd have dealt with it years ago."

Roy leaned forward and put the coffee mug onto the table with a thump. "Maybe. Maybe not. That family was full of secrets. What if Colin Jarvis was as good at keeping quiet as his father was? What if

Letitia only found out what her son knew when Tamara showed up and blew the family secrets out into the open?"

"She discovers that her now adult son's teen years were less innocent than she thought. So what? No one is going to kill their spouse because he made a parenting mistake long ago." Quinn and Roy glared at each other. Roy picked up his mug again and sat back in his chair.

Roy's right. The key to this thing is in the mistresses—

Frank's thought ceased abruptly as the cat lunged at the black squirrel who was unwary enough to descend from his place in the treetops. There was a burst of speed from both animals as the squirrel raced for the nearest tree trunk with Stormy hot on his heels. There were zigs and zags, then suddenly the squirrel was bounding up a tree trunk. The cat lunged and almost caught the squirrel's bushy black tail, but missed by inches. The squirrel scrambled up to the nearest branch, tail quivering, raced to its end, then leapt onto a branch of another tree and disappeared into the canopy of fresh green leaves.

Once again, Stormy was defeated. He stalked to the edge of the Armstrongs' yard, glared at everyone as if it was their fault the squirrel had escaped, then turned away. Sledge heard Frank protest that he needed to be part of the deliberations, but the cat was having none of it. He trotted into the trees and disappeared from sight.

The only one at the table unable to hear Frank's comments, Quinn continued on his theme. "If Jarvis had died because he was poisoned or pushed down the stairs, or had his head bashed in, we could probably make a case that one of his family—nuclear or extended—killed him, but he died from a clean shot to the head. That takes skill with firearms, which none of the family apparently had."

Roy glowered at him over the edge of his coffee cup. "So, one of them hired a professional assassin."

"Easier said than done, Dad!"

"Open your mind, boy," Roy snapped. "Entitled people with too much money figure they can buy anything. Including hitmen."

"Fortier is right. This was a political kill. What he has wrong is the kind of politics involved and the person behind it. I spent the whole time I was in custody—hours, if not days!—trying to convince him of that. Would he listen? No," Quinn said bitterly.

The atmosphere around the table had turned from gloom to dismay as father and son battled. Christy was wide-eyed and exchanging frowning glances with Ellen. They were both scanning the faces around them as if to find some way to defuse a situation was escalating with spectacular speed.

Sledge was of the opinion that an altercation was necessary. Quinn needed purge the poison left from his interrogation by Fortier. He was a passionate guy, a person who believed in rights and freedoms and innocent until proven guilty. Being interrogated by a man who thought he could be a terrorist had probably shaken him to his core. He needed to regain his equilibrium and start believing in the system again before he'd be able to use that incisive brain of his to sort through this sorry mess. If a donnybrook between him and his father was what was needed to make that happen, Sledge was up for it.

Except that Christy was clearly disturbed by the argument. And Sledge didn't like the idea of Christy upset. He put his mug on the table with a *thunk* and reached for the coffee beaker that was sitting beside the pastry box. Quinn's glanced flicked his way as he lifted the urn and sloshed coffee into the mug with a flourish that would have done a professional server proud. "Fortier's under the gun."

"So what?" Quinn said. He sounded impatient. Dismissive.

"Our job all along has been to throw roadblocks in his way. Anyone want more coffee?" He held up the beaker.

Christy nodded and held out her cup as Quinn said, "What are you talking about?"

Quinn's attention was now directly on him. Christy's eyes said thank you for things other than a mug full of coffee. Sledge smiled lazily in a way that he was sure would annoy Quinn. "Maybe it is farfetched that one of the Jarvis family would hire a hitman to knock off old Fred. The thing is, if we make a case for that, Fortier will be

184

forced to look into it." He wasn't a lawyer's son for nothing. He might not know the law the way some did, but he understood the art of using what you had in hand to the utmost effectiveness.

Quinn frowned and sat a little straighter. That was good. He was starting to think.

"In the meantime," Quinn said, "Tamara is held in a cage for that much longer."

Well, maybe not. "Better a couple more days of Fortier badgering her than a lifetime in prison."

Quinn shoved his chair out, anger blazing from his eyes.

Not quite the result Sledge had planned, but at least Quinn wasn't at war with his father. That would ease some of Christy's dismay at the way the morning meeting was going. He watched Quinn warily, ready to dodge a verbal spear, or even an actual punch.

Quinn started to speak, but his words were drowned out by the opening notes of SledgeHammer's first international hit. The song meant Trevor was texting. Sledge pulled out his phone and read.

He was hit by an overwhelming sense of grief, not for himself but for his friend. He looked up from the screen to find they were all staring at him.

"What is it?" Christy asked. Her voice was low, distressed, almost frightened.

"Bad news, I think," Ellen said, observing his expression.

"I'm sorry," Roy said. He must have seen the same emotion that Ellen had.

Sledge looked helplessly at Quinn. He didn't want to say what he knew he must. "Fortier has charged Tamara with being the agent of a terrorist organization and with planning and executing the murder of a government official."

Look who I found lurking by the front door?

Christy twisted in her chair. Stormy the Cat, tail held high, pranced into view. Behind him sauntered Detective Billie Patterson.

Christy leapt to her feet, the bottoms of her chair legs scraping against the concrete patio tiles as she roughly shoved back her chair.

As if it wasn't bad enough they'd just found out Tamara had been charged. They didn't need Patterson here too. "What have you done?" she cried. She heard the anguish in her voice and struggled to control it, but it was no use.

The cat likes her. He thinks she's good people. She pats him.

"I pat him too, but he doesn't expect me to follow him around!"

"Christy." That was Quinn. He too was standing, and he was watching her with a grave expression. His eyes flicked a look at Patterson. Heat flooded her cheeks and she knew she was blushing a bright red.

"Good morning," Patterson said. Her eyebrows were raised, but her expression was neutral.

She was good at that, Christy thought, taking in whatever was happening around her, absorbing information, but not showing her own thoughts.

"What are you doing here?" Roy hadn't stood as Quinn had. Instead he was lounging in his seat, his position one of studied insolence, provocative body language designed to annoy.

Patterson didn't bite. "I came to give you the news of Dr. Ahern's arrest personally. I gather Mr. McCullagh beat me to it."

"We've been filled in," Quinn said. His voice was quiet and steady, without the hint of a threat, but there were storms in his eyes. "Consider the job done. There's no need to linger."

"Seconded," said Roy.

"I must add my voice to theirs," Ellen said.

Since she's here, why not grill her? The cat hopped up onto the table and sat down beside the pastries. He fixed wide green eyes on Patterson.

"I doubt she has anything useful to tell us," Ellen said. She didn't look at the cat.

At least Ellen's comment fit with the tone of what the others were saying, unlike Christy's outburst. Ellen had a particularly disdainful expression on her face, which made it seem as if she was deliberately talking about Patterson as if she wasn't standing on the path in plain view.

"I don't know about that," Christy said. She stared at Patterson but spoke to the others. "She asked me to act as her unpaid informant, to help her find out about Fred Jarvis' personal life. I've done that. And what I've found out? What can I say? I'm amazed the man wasn't murdered years ago."

"There have been rumors for years." Ellen sniffed. "However, Fred Jarvis had friends and we know those friends protected him."

Christy raised her brows and looked at Quinn. "Didn't Archie Fleming address this question, Quinn?"

His moody glance met hers. "His specific comment was that they had each other's backs."

Christy looked back at Patterson. "That was Fred Jarvis' signature style. He made connections with people who mattered, then he found a way to bind them to him, either directly or as part of a network of sexual and emotional relationships. It worked perfectly when everybody was on board, but what if someone decided they'd had enough? Fred wasn't the kind of man who let people escape once he'd bagged them. You were part of the club for life. The only way out was to eliminate Fred himself."

Patterson frowned. "Are you suggesting a conspiracy?"

"Why not?" Roy said. "And who knows who was part of it."

Patterson's frown deepened.

Roy took note. His expression turned gleeful. "That's the best part of conspiracies and secret societies. No one knows exactly who's involved. Just think, it could be a member of your taskforce. Have you met Inspector Fortier's wife? Maybe she was one of Jarvis' lovers."

"A step too far, Mr. Armstrong."

"Going to arrest me, Detective?"

Patterson said nothing, just sent him a level look that said she knew he was baiting her. She looked at Quinn, then back at Roy. "I'm officially here to speak to both of you. Is there somewhere we can talk privately?"

"You can say what you have to here," Quinn said. He moved to stand beside his father's chair.

If she's going to arrest Quinn and Roy, why didn't she bring the goon squad?

Ellen stood up and moved beside Roy. Patterson's brows rose.

Sledge stood too, then sauntered around the table, where he ranged beside Quinn, his hands in the pockets of his jeans. There was a lazy smile on his face, but his eyes were watchful.

The cat leapt from the table into Roy's lap. He landed hard and Roy's breath exhaled in a huff. "What have you been feeding this cat, Christy? Feels like you need to put him on a diet."

Thanks a lot! Undeterred, Stormy circled Roy's lap, then settled facing Patterson.

Christy stayed where she was, the intermediary between opposing forces.

Patterson observed this closing of ranks without comment. She said, "Archie Fleming contacted the taskforce this morning and accused Quinn Armstrong of harassment."

Quinn raised his brows. "Isn't that interesting. Are we talking about the same Archie Fleming with whom I shared drinks and frank conversation about his wife's sexual relationship with Fred Jarvis just a couple of nights ago?"

Patterson shot Christy a penetrating look. Since Christy had not mentioned that Quinn had been at the Flemings with her, she figured the detective had a right to be annoyed.

She refocused on Quinn without comment. "Apparently, your conversation with Colin Jarvis caused him to resign his position on Archie Fleming's leadership campaign, Mr. Armstrong. Mr. Fleming feels this was deliberate harassment on your part. He claims you went to his offices to purposefully alienate Colin Jarvis."

Quinn shrugged. "I went to talk to Colin about the possibility of an official interview with Archie Fleming. During our conversation we spoke about Fred Jarvis. I assumed Colin knew the kind of man his father was. I was surprised he wasn't aware of Marian and Archie's bizarre relationship with Fred."

"The last time we spoke, Detective, you were going to check out bank accounts and alibis," Christy said, redirecting. "Letitia Jarvis, her children, Marian and Archie Fleming. If they didn't have the capacity to kill Fred Jarvis themselves, they are all wealthy enough to hire someone."

Patterson flicked her a glance that said she knew what Christy was up to. "All the people in Jarvis' inner circle have alibis for the time of the murder. There are no large, unsubstantiated withdrawals from the bank accounts of any of them. There is no evidence that anyone hired a professional assassin." She hesitated, then said, "I'm sorry, Mrs. Jamieson, Mr. Armstrong. The taskforce has found the killer. The case is closed."

Sledge, the lawyer's son, said, "Only from the prosecution's point of view." He shot her one of his trademark grins. "The defense is still gathering evidence."

Annoyance crossed Patterson's features. "The proof is irrefutable. Mr. Jarvis received a text from Dr. Ahern asking him to meet with her privately in Stanley Park. To get there he would have to use his vehicle. She lured him into the underground parking, where her sniper was able to execute him."

Quinn took a quick step forward. "She wanted to start over, to see if there was a way they could work together. Yes, she knew he'd have to drive there, but she assumed he'd have his security people in his vehicle with him. She was not setting him up for assassination!"

"So she says." Patterson sounded resigned, almost weary, as if she was no happier with the outcome of the investigation than the others were. "She organized it. She wasn't the one who pulled the trigger."

"Why would she do this?" Christy demanded. "She has no motive."

"We believe she was turned during her captivity."

"You have no proof of that," Roy said.

Patterson turned her attention to him. "But we do, Mr. Armstrong. Dr. Ahern is known to have behaved differently after her release and return to Toronto—"

"Not surprising," Ellen said briskly.

Patterson flicked her a glance, but didn't acknowledge the interruption. "Prior to being kidnapped, she never showed any interest in finding her birth parents. Yet upon her return she deliberately sought them out."

"She spent months afraid for her life. She wanted to know why she was on this planet and who made her. She came to Vancouver to ask for help finding them. It was sheer coincidence that Olivia Waters was her birth mother," Quinn snapped.

"Was it? When Dr. Ahern returned to Toronto she spent a great deal of time helping people who are in the country illegally, people who claim refugee status, but have no proof to back it up."

Quinn's hands clenched and his eyes narrowed. "She was trying to help. That's who Tamara is. That's how she's spent her life. That's how she got herself kidnapped in the first place!"

"Dr. Ahern's adoptive father is a minister who works closely with the underprivileged. Why didn't she work side-by-side with him?" When Quinn didn't reply, Patterson continued on. "Many of the people she worked with were part of the same African community as the men who kidnapped her."

"The same country and ethnicity, perhaps," Quinn snapped. "They were not terrorists, though."

"Some of the people she helped were suspected of supporting terrorist groups."

"She was helping their wives and daughters."

Patterson raised her brows. "You don't think women can be terrorists?"

"Tamara saves people. She doesn't kill them."

"The woman you knew before, saved people. The woman who came back doesn't." There was compassion on Patterson's face, but no softness in her voice. "I'm sorry, Mr. Armstrong. The taskforce is still looking for Ms. Ahern's accomplice, the actual shooter, but we know she is the mastermind behind the murder. The case is closed." She turned to Christy. "Thank you for your efforts, Mrs. Jamieson, but there is no need for further investigation."

Christy was feeling sick inside. Quinn looked devastated and even

Roy's insolent position had shifted to one that was closer to a protective hunch. She lifted her chin and shot Patterson one of her Jamieson princess looks. "I'm afraid you are wrong, Detective. You haven't convinced me—or anyone else here—of Tamara's guilt."

Patterson's expression hardened. "Mrs. Jamieson. Mr. Armstrong. All of you, stand down. At this time, Inspector Fortier is not prepared to act on Archie Fleming's harassment concerns, but all of you have tried his patience throughout this investigation. He won't be so lenient if you continue to poke your noses where you shouldn't."

The cat jumped off Roy's lap and strutted over to Patterson, where he twined through her legs. *Time to go, Detective.*

Roy's chair legs grated roughly on the concrete as he pushed it back and rose to his feet, an imposing elder statesman flanked by his more youthful supporters. "You can tell the inspector we will not allow our rights to be trampled," he said, his voice booming out in true orator style. He shook his fist in the air. "Take heed. We will not be silenced. The infamous Fortier will rue the day he unjustly arrested an innocent!"

"Mr. Armstrong ... "

Before Patterson could say anything further, Stormy rose up on his hind legs and put his front paws on her thigh. Then he nudged her with his nose.

"You need to leave," Roy said, voice still projecting angry passion. He pointed to the cat. "Stormy will see you out."

CHAPTER 25

"At least Roy didn't suggest that Frank escort Patterson out." Ellen laughed as she gathered lunch dishes and passed them to Christy over the peninsula counter, so Christy could stack the dishwasher.

The meeting had drifted to an inconclusive close not long after Stormy had pranced ahead of Patterson and led the detective back to the street where her car was parked. When the cat returned, Frank announced he'd waited until Patterson drove away. He then thanked Roy for giving Stormy a mission. He said the cat was now feeling quite pleased with himself.

Tamara's arrest had put a pall over the assembled group, with Quinn seething with barely restrained anger, and Roy brooding over what he perceived as a betrayal by a Canadian government that ignored its citizen's human rights. Sledge was the first to find a reason to depart. Christy and Ellen left soon after.

As she accepted the dishes Ellen passed her, Christy grimaced. "I certainly goofed when Frank showed up with Patterson in tow. I'm pretty sure she picked up on the phrase I used. I was surprised she didn't call me on it."

"Patterson may be fairly good at solving murders, but she doesn't have the kind of mind that is flexible enough to accept that a person can take refuge in the body of a cat." Ellen sounded disapproving. Since her own acceptance that Frank's current residence was in Stormy the Cat was fairly recent, she had a tendency to believe with the passion of the newly converted.

"She's sharp," Christy said, dropping a plate into the bottom rack. "She noticed and she filed it away as one more oddity in the Jamieson world. I need to watch my tongue." She added the second plate, their salad bowls, then pulled out the upper rack to stack their glasses. "I was rattled by the argument between Quinn and Roy. I wasn't paying attention."

"They are two adult males, both with strong personalities, living together. It's made worse by their relationship as father and son. I'm surprised they argue as little as they do," Ellen said. She handed Christy the cutlery, then took a critical look around the breakfast nook and kitchen. "I think we're done here."

Christy nodded agreement. "I have to get Stormy into the tote and we can be off." Off was to the school where a dress rehearsal for the annual end of year concert was being held. The principal strongly believed that children were more focused and gave their best if an audience was included at every performance, rehearsal or official concert, so parents had been invited to attend the afternoon presentation. Christy thought the evening performances would be too crowded for Stormy's comfort level, so she and Ellen were taking him to the dress rehearsal so Frank could enjoy seeing his daughter in action.

Stormy entered the tote with his usual fussy care, one prim step at a time. He settled at the bottom calmly enough and Christy and Ellen set off.

Though it was mid-week and midday, there was a substantial audience in the school's gym where the concert was being held. A stage had been set up near the main access. Wooden benches for the audience to sit on were laid out in rows throughout the rest of the large room. Christy and Ellen found seats at one end of a bench near the wall and not far from the front. Christy settled the tote in her lap and pulled it open to let Stormy see. His head popped out, but he didn't try to jump out of the bag or off her lap.

She looked around at the rapidly filling gym. The audience, she noted, was made up of a large percentage of grandparent-aged adults, plus a smattering of moms with toddlers, not yet school age, and babies.

The student body was also attending. They were sitting cross-legged on the floor in front of the benches. According to Rebecca Petrofsky, the evening concerts would be so packed that the kids would have to stay in their classrooms before and after their time on stage. During the dress rehearsal, however, they were allowed to watch. As each class had two songs the result was a constant procession of students from the audience to the stage.

Frank was totally charmed by the concert and particularly Noelle's class, which sang "Take Me Out To the Ball Game" and did a skit mimicking an audience watching a baseball game. They followed up with a modified version of John Fogarty's "Centerfield," which was both sweet and funny. Ellen and Christy clapped wildly at the end of their set. Stormy purred.

When the concert was over, Christy picked up Noelle and Mary Petrofsky, who was spending the afternoon with them, and they all walked home together. The concert had done a great deal to improve Christy's mood. How could it not? The enthusiasm of the kids, their energy, and the whole feeling of excitement had been exactly what she needed. She only wished Roy and Quinn had been able to attend today. They had both promised to take in the final performance on Friday night, however, and Noelle was looking forward to that.

The girls cavorted around Christy and Ellen, still so full of performance energy that their excitement lasted all the way home. When they reached the house, Christy said, "I haven't checked the mail in a couple of days. Anyone want to come up to the boxes with me?"

Both girls shouted agreement. Ellen took Stormy in the tote, and headed into the house. Christy set off up the hill with the girls skipping and dancing around her. When she unlocked her mail slot, she found six envelopes, a couple of flyers and another half-dozen pieces of unsolicited junk mail. She dumped the junk mail in the handy recycling bin kept beside the mail station for just that purpose, scanned the flyers and dropped both in as well, then took the envelopes home with her.

Noelle and Mary decided that this bright, sunny afternoon was the perfect day for a good game of hopscotch, especially since Christy had recently invested in a new box of pavement chalk that featured neon colors. Noelle grabbed the box from the shelf in the carport where Christy had stashed it and the girls got busy drawing the board, using multiple colors to make things interesting. Christy sat down on her front steps and sorted through her mail.

As usual, it was mostly bills. She opened each to make sure there were no surprises, then set it aside to be paid when she went inside. The final envelope had the distinctive logo of Noelle's former school, Vancouver Royal Academy.

Christy stared at it, puzzled. Noelle's departure from the school at the end of last year had been final. Hilda Toutov, the principal, had been polite, but dismissive. Even if Christy had the funds to pay the expensive fees, there was no room at VRA for the impoverished child of an embezzler. Leaving the institution she had attended from pre-school on had been a painful experience for Noelle, but she'd bounced back and found friends, and particularly her dearest buddy, Mary Petrofsky, here at this unpretentious school on Burnaby Mountain. Christy could think of no reason why VRA was writing to her now. She shrugged and tossed the envelope, unopened, on top of the bills.

She was watching and laughing along with the girls as they hopped from box to box on the hopscotch board, giggling whenever one of them made a mistake, when the door opened a few minutes later.

Ellen came out and sat down beside her. "We had the strangest message on the voicemail."

Christy sobered. Strange messages on voicemail did not usually bode well. "What's up?"

"Principal Toutov from VRA called. She wants you to phone her to set up a meeting."

Christy frowned. "Did she say why?"

Ellen shook her head. They exchanged thoughtful and not particularly happy looks.

Christy twisted away, reaching behind her for the stack of mail. She picked up the VRA envelope. "She sent me a letter, too."

Ellen raised her brows. "You didn't open it?"

Christy looked at the envelope, then at Ellen, before looking back at the envelope. "No. I thought it was probably a fundraising request." VRA had been an establishment institution in Vancouver for decades. Ellen was a graduate, as had been Frank's mother. Christy had no ties to the school, but the Jamiesons did and Noelle was a Jamieson.

"Well?" Ellen indicated the envelope with a nod. "Are you going to open it?"

"I suppose." Christy picked at the edge of the flap to make a hole, then used her thumb to rip away the rest. The letter inside was on heavy cream paper, like the envelope itself, and as Christy read the contents aloud her voice faltered from sheer astonishment.

The principal thought that she and Christy should meet to establish a program to ensure that Noelle's reintegration to the school and her year group occurred in the smoothest way possible.

Ellen looked at Noelle and Mary, still deeply focused on the hopscotch game. "I didn't know you were re-enrolling Noelle at VRA. I thought you believed she was happier at her school here."

"I do. She is." Christy began to laugh. "I don't believe this! What on earth is going on?"

Ellen remained somber. "Principal Toutov must have heard about the return of the Trust."

Christy looked at her sharply. "You think?"

Ellen nodded.

"Well! Of all the ridiculous ideas, this one tops it." She tossed the letter to one side. "There's no way I'm going to pull Noelle out of a warm, supportive school where her friends are close by so she can commute for an hour to and from VRA every day."

They watched the girls in silence for a couple of minutes, then Ellen said, "You should call and make that appointment."

Christy's breath caught. She wondered if Ellen resented her reluctance to have Noelle return to VRA. After all, the school was her alma mater. "Ellen ... "

Ellen must have guessed what Christy didn't want to put into words, for she straightened and shook her head. She shot Christy a long, raised-eyebrow look. "Candis Jarvis Blais, Fred's daughter, has a child at VRA. Am I correct?"

Understanding began to dawn. Christy nodded.

"Yes. We know that Fred had a liaison with the principal of his son's school. I think it is entirely possible that he did the same thing at his granddaughter's school."

Christy's eyes widened. "Principal Toutov?" She began to laugh. "The old dragon who considers bad manners a sin right up there with coveting thy neighbor's wife?"

Ellen was shaking her head before Christy had even finished. "Not necessarily the principal. One of the teachers, perhaps. Someone who had influence over the child's school experience."

Christy sobered. "The girl's classroom teacher."

"Or maybe her music teacher, if the child is talented. Or the librarian if she loves books and reading."

"Or the phys ed teacher," Christy said. She picked up the letter and scanned it once again. She looked at Ellen. "Can you watch the girls while I call? There's still time to catch Toutov before she leaves for the day."

CHAPTER 26

Hilda Toutov, the principal of VRA, was a formidable woman, all the more so because she had a warm, open manner that hid an implacable will. Her hair was short and impeccably styled. She wore a tailored dress that hadn't come off a rack, and dark leather pumps that were hand stitched and probably made in Florence or Milan. She was the CEO of an organization that catered to the very rich and she looked the part.

When Christy and Ellen were ushered into her office she held out her hand and smiled with apparent pleasure. "Mrs. Jamieson. Ms. Jamieson. Welcome. It is wonderful to see you again, Mrs. Jamieson. And Ms. Jamieson, it is always delightful to welcome back a returning alumna." They all shook hands.

Christy was wary of the principal's open bonhomie. Hilda Toutov was a prime example of the world Christy was cautiously stepping back into. The world of sharing air kisses with people you really didn't like and smiling agreeably just because someone had position and power.

Knowing she'd be meeting Ms. Toutov today, she'd taken a private moment with Noelle the previous evening and asked her how she felt about her current school and if she missed VRA. The answers had been a resounding "I love it" and an emphatic "no." When pressed, Noelle had said she didn't want to move—back to the mansion, back to VRA. She liked Burnaby, she loved Mary Petrofsky and her other new friends, and she was looking forward to the next school year because the grade four teachers were awesome.

Her conversation with Noelle gave Christy the emotional armor she needed to deal with Principal Toutov. Her clothing provided the mental freedom to go on the offensive.

When Noelle had been a student at VRA and Christy had chaired the parent council, she been Frank Jamieson's wife and Noelle Jamieson's mom. She'd worn casual styles, well made, of course, but still not the kind of clothes that said 'I'm in charge.' For this meeting, she picked an outfit from the ones she had been amassing for her new role as the representative of the Jamieson Trust. A stylish jacket in a cream-colored silk-wool blend, with a silk shell beneath, topped a straight skirt that ended a couple of inches above her knees. On her feet, she wore needle-heeled shoes that added inches to her height. The whole outfit was designed to generate a sense of quiet power. It certainly gave Christy's outlook an added boost.

After shaking hands, Ms. Toutov directed them to a grouping of club chairs set around a burnished walnut coffee table placed in near the windows, and away from her desk. "Mrs. Jamieson, I cannot tell you how pleased we will be to welcome Noelle back to this school. She is a delightful child. We missed her while she was away."

"How interesting," Ellen said, raising her brows.

Ms. Toutov didn't even have the grace to blush.

A smile quirked Christy's mouth at Ellen's comment, but she simply said, "I completely agree. My daughter is very special."

In her term as chair of the VRA parent council, Christy had never had cause to oppose Toutov on any major issue. There was no reason for the principal to now think that Christy Jamieson would be diffi-cult. She smiled and reached for a portfolio resting on the coffee table. "For her grade four year I've placed Noelle in a split three-four class—"

"You cannot be serious!" Ellen's eyebrows snapped together in a frown. She tilted her head imperiously. Her indignation was part of the plan she and Christy had worked out last night. Christy would be magisterial, Ellen passionate. As Ellen was an alumna, the principal would expect her support. Toutov would be unsettled if she didn't give it. Since their purpose in coming today was not to re-enroll Noelle, but to find out if Fred Jarvis had had a mistress amongst the faculty or administration, Christy figured that keeping Hilda Toutov on edge would not only be helpful, but necessary.

Christy raised her brows. "An interesting selection, Ms. Toutov. It is my understanding that VRA only uses split classes for children with learning problems. What is your reasoning for putting Noelle in such a class?" Inside she was seething, but there was nothing in her voice to indicate her feelings.

Toutov smiled in an encouraging way and said, "I am sure you are surprised and probably upset as well—"

"You are stating the obvious, Ms. Toutov. There is absolutely no reason to think Noelle couldn't cope in a regular grade four classroom." That was Ellen at her most imperious. Christy stifled a laugh.

"In a normal situation, I would agree, Ms. Jamieson. However, Noelle has spent the last year in a public school." The principal's expression was serious, even concerned, as she looked from Ellen to Christy.

"Are you saying that the level of education Noelle is currently receiving is sub-standard?" Christy asked in that same non-committal tone.

Toutov nodded. "Exactly. Noelle is a bright child. She will catch up, but she'll need help."

"I see," Christy said. "Have you assigned a teacher to the class as yet?"

"Yes." Toutov smiled. A little cautiously, Christy thought. She knew why when the principal named the proposed teacher. "Mrs. Boyle."

Mrs. Boyle was the teacher VRA used to whip the children who were lagging behind into shape. She had a reputation among the parents as being a no-nonsense teacher who got results. Christy happened to know that she was the terror of every child in the school.

"I see," she said, and thought she did, very clearly. Time to move away from the ostensible reason for the meeting and on to the real one. "When I was chair of the parents' council there were a number of projects on-going and the head teacher, Mrs. Fulton, was about to retire. Can you speak to those changes?"

Toutov looked relieved that Christy hadn't produced any parental theatrics over the class and teacher choice. She said enthusiastically, "Indeed I can! Our music room has been upgraded, which has allowed us to expand our music program. We have two new science labs. These are mainly for the upper year students, but children grow so quickly, it will be no time at all before Noelle will be using them herself." Here she smiled warmly, inviting Christy and Ellen to join her in celebrating the natural miracle of children growing and learning through the years. "Our new head teacher is Leslie Bankes. She came to us three years ago as a classroom teacher. She taught the late Fred Jarvis' delightful granddaughter, Frederika. Frederika was two years ahead of Noelle, so you might not have known Leslie when Noelle was here before."

"I didn't," Christy said. "Will we have the chance to meet her today?"

"Yes, of course," Ms. Toutov said. She smiled with satisfaction. She clearly thought she had Noelle's return wrapped up and in the bag. "I arranged for Leslie to give you a tour of the new facilities as soon as we finished going over the details of Noelle's placement. I'll buzz her now and she will be with us in a moment."

Leslie Bankes must have been hovering in Toutov's outer office, because she was opening the door almost before the principal's finger was off the buzzer button. "Ah, Leslie, excellent. This is Mrs. Christy Jamieson and her aunt, Ms. Ellen Jamieson. They are looking forward to getting to know you and to see our new improvements. Mrs. Jamieson, Ms. Jamieson, this is our head teacher, Miss Leslie Bankes."

The woman who entered the office appeared to be in her early thirties. She was of medium height, had short hair and wore a serviceable dark blue skirt with a plain, light blue polyester shell top, covered by a cream, summer-weight sweater. Christy heard Ellen draw in a quick breath as recognition hit her. She allowed herself a moment of satisfaction. It looked like finding Fred's mistress at VRA was going to be easier than they'd expected.

She smiled at Leslie Bankes and said, "I believe we met at Fred Jarvis' funeral, Ms. Bankes. It's nice to see you again."

Leslie nodded, her expression momentarily downcast. Then she smiled as they shook hands. "Yes. I remember. Such a sad time."

They headed out of the office, leaving the principal behind. Ellen said, "Ms. Toutov told us you were Frederika Blais' teacher."

"Yes, I had her in my class for two years." Leslie blushed.

Christy knew why. Having the same teacher in consecutive years was against VRA policy. Fred Jarvis must have pulled strings to keep his granddaughter in Leslie's class.

Christy realized that she'd seen Leslie around the school when Noelle had attended VRA, and that was why the woman had seemed so familiar when they met at the funeral. She also remembered other parents complaining about Frederika Blais getting special treatment —field trips tailored for her, the lead in school performances, front row seating at school events. If Leslie Bankes was one of Fred's mistresses and followed the patterns of his other women, she'd have done anything she could to please him.

"I was on the parents' council when my daughter attended VRA," Christy said as they walked down the wide hall. It was quiet now, as the children were all in class. "I didn't realize Frederick Jarvis's granddaughter was a student here. I don't remember her mother, Candis, being involved in our activities." That wasn't true, but Leslie wouldn't know that.

"Candis is the CEO of her family's charitable foundation," Leslie said. "She has a very busy schedule. Mr. Jarvis, Frederika's grandfather, was much more involved in Frederika's program."

And an elected official who was a provincial cabinet minister didn't have a busy schedule? From Ellen's expression, she had the same thought in mind, but neither of them voiced the comment.

Instead, Christy said, "You and Mr. Jarvis had a warm relationship." When Leslie shot an alarmed look her way, she smiled reassuringly. "I saw your pain at the funeral. The way you spoke ... You were more than teacher and parent, weren't you?"

Leslie opened a door, peeked in to make sure the room was empty, then gestured for them to come inside. "This is the music room. I think Principal Toutov told you that it's recently been renovated?"

"She did," Christy said.

Leslie flicked on the lights and they moved deeper into the room. "Principal Toutov doesn't know," she said on a rush.

"Well, well, well," Ellen whispered in Christy's ear.

Christy smiled at the head teacher, encouraging her to continue.

"Fred—" Leslie wrung her hands, agitation in every tense muscle. She stared at the wall, not meeting Christy or Ellen's gaze. "He was a lovely man. At first, I didn't want to get involved with him, but somehow ... I don't know. Somehow I did." She looked at Christy then, defiant. "I don't regret our affair."

"No one who was involved with Fred Jarvis does," Ellen said. There was a bite to her tone that made Leslie flinch.

"Fred was special that way," Christy said, hoping Leslie would continue.

"He was." She drew a deep breath. "We had to stop seeing each other when I became head teacher. Ms. Toutov would have realized and she wouldn't have understood."

"It must have been exciting to become head teacher. I don't mean to offend, but you're much younger than the previous head teacher." And a lot less self-confident and authoritative, Christy added silently to herself.

Leslie smiled, looking relieved. "I've only been teaching for ten years, so it did come as a surprise when Ms. Toutov asked me to apply." She relaxed a little and moved closer to Christy. "When Fred and I first became friends, it was only because of our shared mutual interest in ensuring Frederika received the best possible education. Then we became closer. I had a boyfriend at the time. He worked for a law firm downtown. Fred thought he was a great guy and tried to help him move forward, but he didn't understand that my relationship with Fred was very different from my relationship with him. We split. Then, when Ms. Toutov insisted that Frederika couldn't have the same teacher for three years running ... . Well, I was going to miss her." She sighed. "And Fred. Even then, he was planning to run for the leadership of his party. He had a lot to do and his time with me became shorter and shorter." She smiled and headed for the door. "Becoming head teacher has been a godsend. I have so much to do that I don't have time to miss ... anyone." She flicked off the lights as they all returned to the corridor.

They continued the tour, but Leslie Bankes didn't add anything to her revelations about her relationship with Fred Jarvis. Christy had the sense that she had truly cared for Fred and thought he cared for her. That she'd never really understood that she was part of Fred's greater network. She wondered, though, if Principal Toutov was as unaware as Leslie thought. Perhaps she too had once been one of Fred Jarvis' women.

Now that was an interesting thought.

She hadn't been at the funeral though. The mistresses were all seated together in the rows behind the family. If Toutov had been there, Christy would have recognized her, and she hadn't.

When they returned to the principal's office, Ms. Toutov dismissed Leslie with a curt thank you, then said to Christy and Ellen, "I've arranged for tea in the conference room while we finalize the arrangements. I'm sure you remember where it is?"

Christy glanced at her watch. "Thank you, Ms. Toutov, but I'm afraid I have already spent more time than I intended here at VRA. Staying for tea is out of the question." She held out her hand. "I will be in touch if I decide to re-enroll Noelle in the school."

"I beg your pardon?" Toutov said as she automatically shook Christy's hand. She looked thunderstruck.

"Good day, Ms. Toutov." Christy turned away. "Coming, Ellen?"

"Absolutely," Ellen said.

CHAPTER 27

V RA was located in the Point Grey area of Vancouver, across town from Christy's Burnaby townhouse. She'd taken the precaution of asking Rebecca Petrofsky to pick up Noelle this afternoon, but she wanted to be home as soon as possible. Tonight was the first night of the end of year school concert. It began at seven and the students were expected to be in their classrooms by six pm, which meant she needed to have dinner ready much earlier than usual. She also planned to go to the concert both nights, so she wanted the kitchen cleaned up before she left.

Though it was only two-thirty, traffic was already heavy on West Broadway, the main street to and from Point Grey. She tapped on the steering wheel as she waited for a light to turn green and diverted herself by thinking about the murder. "Have you noticed that Fred Jarvis' mistresses are getting younger and younger?"

"Hardly unusual," Ellen said. "Men like Jarvis have inflated views of their own virility. Most likely he thought he was God's gift to women."

Christy laughed. "I never thought I'd hear you use that particular phrase."

"I use it with considerable distaste," Ellen said.

Christy glanced over. Ellen was staring out the windshield. There were blooms of pink on her cheeks. Okay then, time to move on. Ellen had relaxed a lot of her prickly ways since she'd moved into the Burnaby townhouse, become a second parent to a pre-teen, and started a romance with a man who teetered on the edge of swash-buckling. The old Ellen still lurked within her, though, prim, precise, and proper. Back to the investigation.

"Leslie Bankes was what, early thirties maybe?" The light changed and the car edged forward.

Out of the corner of her eye Christy saw Ellen nod. "She said she'd been teaching for ten years. It fits."

"I got the impression she and Fred were still friends, but they weren't casual lovers the way he was with Marian Fleming."

Ellen was silent for a minute, then she said, "You're right. I hadn't considered that. I did notice, though, that her boyfriend wouldn't play Fred's game. He split with her when he found out she was having an affair with another man."

"Yeah. Now that is a distinct change from Fred's usual pattern. Leslie said the boyfriend was a lawyer and that Fred had offered to help him move up in his law firm. The boyfriend apparently rejected his help." She slowed as a car from the inside lane booted it to jump ahead of her into her stream of traffic. "I wish we'd found out the boyfriend's name. Do you think he might have been angry enough at Fred to be the killer?"

"We don't know anything about him," Ellen said. "But I think it's unlikely."

Traffic bunched up at yet another red light, this one at a Skytrain station corner. Pedestrians streamed across the intersection. The light would probably be a long one. Christy turned to look at Ellen. "Why?"

"Timing," Ellen said. "Leslie became Head Teacher a year ago. She began her affair with Fred at least a year before that, maybe two. If the rejected boyfriend was angry and wanted revenge he would have acted sooner."

Christy tapped the wheel again. "Good point. Still, it would be nice to be able to check him out and cross him off our list."

"I'll talk to Trevor. He knows most of the law firms in town. He can investigate."

"A big list to process when you don't have a name." Christy pursed her lips. "I could talk to Patterson. She may not be aware Leslie was one of Fred's mistresses. It would be easy for her to interview Leslie, find out her boyfriend's name, then interview him."

"Patterson said the case was closed, remember? She won't help us."

Christy thought she might, but she knew Ellen would never forgive the detective for arresting her and forcing her to spend a couple of days in lock-up. The memory skewered her perception of the detective.

"Besides," Ellen said. "We do have some clues. The law firm has to be one in which Fred felt he would be able to exert influence. That means either the firm was the one he used for his personal legal needs or one that supported him politically. Trevor can work with that."

"Trevor it is, then." The light changed and the last pedestrian made it safely to the other side. Christy inched slowly forward. Officially, jaywalking wasn't allowed, but it happened. She passed the station and picked up speed. "If Trevor connects with the boyfriend, we'll have to find out if he rejected Fred's help because of his personal values or because he just thought it was odd."

"A generational thing, you mean?"

"Yeah. Archie doesn't seem to have had a problem sharing his wife with Fred. Both men were Baby Boomers or Gen Xers. Free love, all that sort of stuff. What if Archie and Fred shared a bunch of unwritten expectations and Fred knew how to tap into them? But Fred wouldn't be able to do that with a man who was half his age. Maybe that's why Fred's charm didn't work on the boyfriend."

Ellen made a *tut-tut* sound. "Roy and Trevor are the same generation. Can you see either of them participating in Fred's bizarre lifestyle?"

Christy laughed. "No, I guess not. Okay, let's follow the mistress connection then. He split with Leslie once she was head teacher. Do you think she was jealous? That she might be angry enough to kill him?"

"I see the same problem with that theory as I do with the boyfriend as the killer. The timing is off. It's too long between the break up and the murder. Think, Christy! If she wanted to kill Fred, she would have had more opportunity before he entered the leadership race and was surrounded by extra security."

"Okay. We move on. He always had a woman at hand. Who did he turn to next, then?"

"Another teacher?" Ellen suggested.

"Maybe, but ... " Christy shook her head. "I don't think he needed to. With Leslie as head teacher he could be sure that little Frederika would still get the special treatment he wanted her to have. He didn't need her classroom teacher. Besides, it would have looked very odd if Frederika continued to have the same teacher for another two consecutive years, when it contravenes VRA rules. Questions would be asked."

"Fred Jarvis used women," Ellen said. She sounded disapproving. "He was able to make them like it, but he chose women for their usefulness not their appearance or their personalities. So what was important to him a year ago? If we can figure that out, we might be able to discover who his latest mistress was."

"Something going on in his family? He used his relationships to smooth his children and grandchildren's paths."

"Possibly," Ellen said. "I think his political career is a more likely target, though. When did he start his run for the leadership?"

"About six months ago," Christy said.

"Perhaps not from his leadership campaign, then. I expect he was the kind of man who needed constant female companionship. He would have had a new woman in the wings when he set Leslie up in the head teacher position."

A memory tugged and Christy frowned. "What if he was putting his campaign team together long before he threw his name into the contest?"

"You think the new mistress is someone involved in his leadership campaign?"

"Yeah," Christy said. "Remember Fred's funeral? The girl who guided us to our seats? She was close to tears, obviously broken up by Fred's passing. At the time, I thought it was normal upset. You know, the kind someone feels for a friend or a co-worker they're close to. But I didn't know Fred's habits then." She tapped the wheel impatiently. "Do you remember if she ended up sitting behind the family row, with the rest of the mistresses?"

"Let me think."

Christy shot her a quick look and saw that Ellen had her eyes closed as she tried to visualize the scene. Christy dealt with traffic and let her ruminate.

Finally, Ellen said, "I'm sorry. I can't remember."

Christy sighed. "Well, it was worth a shot."

They drove on, passing Boundary Road where East Broadway became Lougheed Highway. Traffic flowed easily now. They'd reach home in plenty of time for Christy to make dinner and get Noelle to her classroom on time.

"I wonder what she's doing now," Ellen said suddenly.

Christy shot her a quick look. "Who?"

"The young woman. Assuming she was one of the mistresses, I wonder if Fred's network has looked after her and found her a new job?"

"If it didn't, she'll be out of work," Christy said, speaking slowly as thoughts formed.

"I doubt Letitia will keep in contact with the mistresses. It would fall to Olivia Waters or Marian Fleming, the most senior and influential mistresses, to help her out."

"I doubt Olivia would do it. She had feelings for Fred, but I don't think she was ever bought into the broader mistress network thing."

"Marian and Archie might, especially if she has skills Archie could use for his campaign."

"Possibly. I wonder if she'd talk to us?"

Ellen laughed. "No harm in asking."

FRED JARVIS' campaign office was located in a repurposed ware-house in Yaletown. It was a large space, and once had probably bustled with people. Now it echoed with the clang of movers shifting metal desks, while others packed up paper files from tall filing cabinets. The crash of empty metal drawers closing brought Stormy's head popping out of the tote bag Christy carried him in. The cat's eyes were wide. Though Frank assured Christy that Stormy was fine, Christy kept her arm tight against the side of the tote.

Ellen immediately took control. She looked around the room, zeroed in on one of the workers who was better dressed than the others and was holding a clipboard. "You," she said, pointing at him in an imperious way.

The young man looked up, his eyes open in surprise. Then he frowned at Ellen. "Are you talking to me, ma'am?"

"Indeed I am, young man."

He slanted a worried glance at the desk shifters, apparently to make sure they would be able to continue their task without his careful observation of them, then he hustled over to the doorway, where Ellen and Christy stood. "I'm sorry," he said. "The office is closed due to Mr. Jarvis's ... " His voice drifted off as if the word death was too difficult for him to utter.

"We are not here to find Mr. Jarvis," Ellen said. The young staffer looked bewildered and opened his mouth to speak, probably to ask them why the hell they were there then. Ellen forged on, not giving him an opportunity to interrupt. "We wish to speak to his assistant. The young lady who planned his events."

"Phoebe?"

"Possibly," Ellen said, looking down her nose with regal authority, as if that would be enough to silence any doubts this young man would have about strangers who didn't know Phoebe's name wanting to see her.

Good one, Aunt Ellen. Way to get us kicked out.

Ellen sniffed and glared at the young man.

Who was now frowning heavily. "I'm sorry, but—"

"We're friends of Letitia Jarvis," Christy said, smiling at the young man, who really wasn't all that young, she thought. He was looked to be close to Frank's age, if Frank was still alive. There were lines around his eyes, and brackets at the corners of his mouth. His air of incompetence was probably the result of being overwhelmed by the rapid, cataclysmic changes in his life.

At Letitia's name the young man's round, undistinguished face, cleared. "Of course," he said. "Phoebe's clearing out her office. Back corner." He pointed to the far end of the big room where three cubicles had been erected using moveable fabric partitions.

Christy thanked him, Ellen shot him another of her imperious looks and the staffer scuttled back toward the desk movers, yelling as he went, because they'd apparently botched something during his absence.

Phoebe was sitting on a rickety looking typist's chair in front of a steel single pedestal desk. She was working on a computer, apparently deleting files, when Ellen and Christy appeared at the opening to her small pod. Papers littered the desk. A plaque that read Phoebe Beck (Ms.) hovered precariously on the edge of the desk, at risk of plunging to the carpeting below.

Christy cleared her throat. Ellen said, "Good morning."

Phoebe looked up. Her eyes were swimming in tears, her skin was blotchy, and her nose red, all evidence of her grief. A grief that was too strong to be for a boss she enjoyed working for or a job she loved doing. "Can I help you?"

Her voice was nasal, thick with tears, the tone flat and without energy. Christy and Ellen had planned to pretend they were interested in learning if there were any further memorial events planned for Fred, but Christy quickly adjusted her strategy. "We came to offer our condolences."

Phoebe frowned. She wheeled the rickety chair away from the desk and turned it so she could look at them directly. "Why?"

Ellen raised her brows and shot Christy a 'yes, why?' look. Christy ignored it and smiled at Phoebe. She put the tote on the floor and opened the top wide. Stormy stepped out, shook himself indignantly, then sat on his haunches and looked up at Phoebe. "We know about you and Fred," Christy said. She made her voice as soothing as she could and smiled what she hoped Phoebe would consider a commiserating smile.

Phoebe didn't notice. She looked down at Stormy and said, "This is the cat who spoke to Mrs. Jarvis during the funeral."

That's me. I didn't know you were listening. I don't think Letitia was.

"Of course she was," Phoebe said. There was energy in her voice now. She sounded indignant.

Could have fooled me. Stormy jumped up into Phoebe's lap, then put his front paws on her shoulder as he lifted his head to lick her chin.

Phoebe giggled.

Ellen glanced at Christy. "This is interesting."

Christy knew that Frank was getting better and better at projecting his thoughts. She hadn't yet seen him connect with strangers, though, and she found it disconcerting.

"I remember you from the funeral," Phoebe said. "This is your cat?"

Christy nodded.

Phoebe stroked Stormy's soft fur. "He helped me get through the service. Mrs. Jarvis told me I couldn't cry. That it wouldn't be appropriate. Hearing him promise that Fred's—Minister Jarvis'—killer would be found gave me so much comfort."

"Really," Christy said, eying the cat.

I told Letitia you were on the case and you always got your man. I guess Phoebe was the one who heard.

Christy was oddly touched by Frank's statement. There was more than a hint of pride in it. Pride she'd never heard when he had been alive and living with her.

Phoebe stroked the cat. "What do you need to know?" she asked, looking up at Christy.

"We have—" Christy hesitated, uncertain how blunt she could be with Phoebe, then decided to go for broke. "Evidence that Fred had a mistress in the months before his death." Phoebe sniffed and swallowed hard. Christy knew she was on the right track. "Was that you?"

"Yes." Her hand trailed along the cat's back, slowly, with a sensuous grace Stormy, who had begun to purr, clearly appreciated. Sniffing again, she said, "I didn't plan for it to happen. Barry—" She indicated the main part of the office with a jerk of her head. "Barry is a friend. He knew I needed work." She sighed. "My husband was in the military, but he was invalided out after his last tour in Afghanistan. He had a disability pension, but it wasn't enough. I was laid off my last job and we were in debt. Barry was the office manager for the campaign, so when Fred said he needed a dedicated event planner, Barry recommended me. As soon as Fred and I met, we felt a connection. But he was married and so was I."

It happens.

Phoebe's mouth dropped unhappily and her eyes were clouded. Her hand moved rhythmically over the cat's body, but it was an automatic gesture. Christy had the sense that Phoebe still harbored some guilt over the affair. "Go on," she said as gently as she could.

Phoebe sniffed. "Russell, that's my husband, was deployed overseas three months after our wedding. He was gone for nearly year. We had one holiday together while he was overseas." Her mouth curled up at the edges, but her gaze remained melancholy. "In Paris. It was lovely. Then he went back to Afghanistan and I came home."

She stopped her absentminded stroking. Stormy chirped, butted her chin with his head, then settled back on her lap, this time on his back. It was a clear invitation for her to rub his stomach. Phoebe laughed.

She began stroking him again. Stormy's purr rumbled in the quiet. Finally, Phoebe picked up her story once more. "When Russell came back to Canada, he'd changed. He wouldn't talk to me and everything I did made him irritable or angry. I didn't know what to do. I thought our marriage was over. They said it was PTSD and he was getting therapy, but he hated being out of the army and he was ashamed, like he'd done something wrong. I worked late, a lot, because it was easier than going home. Sometimes, Russell was okay with that, others he wasn't. I never knew exactly how he'd react. One night when I called, he yelled at me and told me not to come home. Fred found me here, alone in the office, crying. We talked and he invited me to stay with him that night." Her gaze skittered from Christy to Ellen, then she looked down at the cat on her lap. "I shouldn't have gone, but I was so lonely. So lost!"

"You became lovers," Christy said.

Phoebe shook her head emphatically. "No. No, he took me to his home. Mrs. Jarvis made a bed up in their spare room." Her nose wrinkled. "That night, as I was getting ready for bed, I heard them arguing about me staying in their house, but in the morning, she was very kind."

"You weren't lovers?" Ellen asked. Her eyebrows were sky high with disbelief.

"Not then, but yes, eventually. A few weeks later, in fact. Fred had arranged for Russell to see a topnotch specialist and Russell was doing better, but he still didn't want me, you know?"

No sex.

Phoebe blushed and nodded. "Fred was thoughtful and kind, and when he kissed me, well, I responded." She gulped and rubbed her eyes. "I told him it would only be one time, and he agreed, but ... " She shrugged. "It wasn't."

"Russell must have been furious," Christy said.

Phoebe shook her head. "He never knew. He liked Fred. Fred helped him get a job as well as paying for his therapy. Working again, being needed, gave him a sense of accomplishment, of still being a capable person." A smile trembled on her lips. "For a while things went smoothly. We were a couple again, and Russell was closer to the man I married than he had been since he returned."

For a while ... This sounded ominous. Christy glanced at Ellen

214

who gave her a small nod. Evidently, she was thinking the same thing. "What happened?" Christy asked.

"We had to go out of town for the campaign. I worked long hours, often out of Fred's suite and often alone. Russell did as well, but our hours off rarely coincided. When we came back to Vancouver he was grumpy again, snapping at anything I said. I asked him to go back into therapy and that made him even more angry. Fred helped me to understand that it was the illness reoccurring and that he needed to heal, then he'd be better again. And he was. He's fine now." She sighed. "Fred was so important, to both of us. And now he's gone."

It was Ellen who said what Christy was thinking. "You both worked for Fred Jarvis' campaign?" Her tone said this was even weirder than Fred Jarvis' usual strange relationships.

Phoebe's eyes opened wide in surprise. "Yes, of course. Russell was part of Fred's security team."

CHAPTER 28

"Sergeant Russell Beck, retired, served two tours in Afghanistan. In between postings he married Phoebe Cummings." Quinn was reading from notes he'd made on his iPad.

They were in Christy's kitchen—Christy, Ellen, Roy, Quinn, Trevor, and Sledge—discussing the latest opening in the case. Stormy had taken up a post by his food dish.

Quinn paused to scroll forward, then continued. "During his second posting Beck was injured and was unable to return to duty. He was diagnosed with PTSD after he left the service, for which he received some treatment. He began working for a high-end security firm and was assigned as one of Fred Jarvis' personal security team." Quinn looked up from the tablet and around at the group gathered at Christy's kitchen table. "That's it. His record is excellent. He has no red flags against his name."

"He was part of Fred's security at Fred's request, I imagine," Ellen said. She shook her head disapprovingly. "The more I learn of this man, the more I think he was the architect of his own demise."

Roy rubbed his chin as he scrutinized Ellen. "You and Christy think this Russell Beck killed Jarvis?"

Ellen nodded. "Yes. He had access. He had weapons training. He is unstable. His wife was having an affair with Fred."

"As were a lot of other women," Sledge said. He'd tagged along to the strategy session with his father, who was nodding.

"Fred had a way of minimizing the reactions of the men in their lives. He must have felt he could trust the man when he had Beck put on his personal security team."

This time he got it wrong. Stormy pawed at his food bowl, which contained only the crumbs of his crunchy kibble. *When's dinner? The cat's hungry.*

"Not yet," Christy said. Quinn shot her a look and she smiled and shrugged. Conversations with Frank were part of her life. Quinn knew that. "Ellen and I think the men involved with Fred's most recent mistresses didn't buy into his 'family' network idea. Leslie Bankes' boyfriend split with her, even though Fred offered to help his advancement within his law firm."

"Were you able to find where the man worked, Trevor?" Ellen asked.

Christy noticed that she was smiling in a hopeful—no, approving —way at Trevor, as if she expected him to have succeeded in finding a man whose name they didn't know, working for an unidentified law firm. When Trevor straightened and cleared his throat, she figured that matters between Trevor and Ellen were progressing nicely. She almost laughed when Sledge's eyes widened.

"I did." Trevor caught his son's gaze, but looked away quickly. His cheeks reddened. "The boyfriend's name is Kevin Howarth. He is employed by the firm that handled Fred's legal work. The firm also contributed to Fred's leadership campaign. While Kevin Howarth may have split with Leslie Bankes and refused Fred's career help, it hasn't stopped the firm from believing that he's Fred's protégé. He's being fast tracked for a partnership position."

Roy stirred uneasily. "If he and Leslie had split, I wonder why Fred continued to help him?"

"Perhaps Fred thought Leslie and Kevin would get back together once his affair with her was over," Ellen suggested.

Roy pursed his lips thoughtfully as he nodded. "Could be."

"It's a networking thing," Sledge said. When the others looked at him, he shrugged. "You help with a problem here. Say a quiet word in an ear there. Put this person who's looking for work together with a company that needs his skillset. The more you can help people out, particularly when you don't get anything immediate out of it, the stronger the relationships become. Vince used to do it all the time and he didn't have the weird sexual stuff happening. It worked too. When he needed to call in favors to give SledgeHammer a boost, they were there."

Since SledgeHammer was the most successful Canadian band in the last decade, his observation had weight.

"You think Fred helped Kevin even though he knew Kevin had left Leslie," Roy said.

Sledge nodded.

"That kind of networking works if everybody buys in," Trevor said. He tapped his finger on the table. "Until I told him, Kevin Howarth was unaware that Jarvis had identified him as a protégé. He was furious. He told me he suspected Leslie was having an affair with one of the parents at her school. He thought it was unethical on her part, but he had no proof. Then one night he canceled on a dinner date with her because he had to work late. He finished earlier than he expected, so he dropped by her place. He found Fred Jarvis there and realized that there was something going on between them."

Christy made a face. "That must have been creepy to walk in on your girlfriend in bed with an older man."

"Any man," Quinn said.

Christy shot him a questioning glance. He met it with a serious one of his own. A shiver prickled down her spine. She knew that Quinn had split with her because he thought she was still in love with Frank. She assumed, particularly after Tamara arrived, that there was no hope for them.

But that serious look—did it mean Quinn still had feelings for her? That he wasn't gladly walking back into Tamara's arms?

The thought enticed and for a minute she lost the thread of the conversation. Then she shook herself back to attention. This was an idea she needed to ponder when she had quiet and privacy.

"They weren't in bed, at least not when Kevin walked in," Trevor was saying. "He could tell that there was something going on from the way Fred touched Leslie and how she smiled at him. He said he knew at once. Then Fred started talking to him, asking what he did, where he worked. He said it was odd, like he and Fred were friends, or had the potential to be really close friends. He got out as soon as he could and split with Leslie the next day."

"Jarvis never actually spelled the situation out—I'm sleeping with your girlfriend, but that's okay because I'm going to put your career into overdrive and we'll help each other get ahead," Quinn said.

Trevor shook his head. "No. Like I said, Kevin had no idea. He swore that if he'd known he would have told Fred to take a hike."

"Maybe," Roy said. "Maybe not." He sipped coffee and his raised eyebrows said that he was the ultimate cynic.

Quinn glanced at his father, then looked at Trevor. "Does Howarth have an alibi?"

Trevor sighed. "Unfortunately, yes."

"Too bad," Quinn said.

Christy shifted uneasily in her chair. She held a coffee mug in her hands, but she wasn't drinking. "Which brings us back to the most recent girlfriend and her husband, Phoebe and Russell Beck. What if Russell was like Kevin and didn't realize that his new job and his position on Fred's security team was all because Fred was having an affair with his wife? What do you think he'd do if he found out?"

"I know what I'd do," Quinn said grimly.

Sledge stirred. "Russell was caught between two really important parts of his life. Which does he choose? Wife or job? He'd have to make a decision."

"I think he did," Ellen said, nodding briskly. "Phoebe says she never told him about the affair, so she assumes he doesn't know, but she said their relationship was rocky for a while. I think he found out and reacted."

Christy added, "Phoebe told us that things between them are

good again, and they probably are. For now. Fred is gone, and Russell still has both his job at the security firm, and his wife. From his point of view, he's been incredibly successful. But by Phoebe's own admission, he's volatile and unpredictable. His mood could change." Christy grimaced. "Especially if Phoebe continues to grieve over Fred's death." She looked around the table. "I think she's in danger."

Quinn eyed her steadily. "I hope you're not suggesting some kind of intervention."

"Well ... "

"Christy!"

"Quinn, all I was planned to do was talk to Patterson." Still, his concern gave her a warm feeling and had a smile hovering, almost ready to break free.

He nodded. "Not a bad idea. I'll come with you. If Russell Beck is the killer, I want to make sure they release Tamara as quickly as possible."

"Right. Tamara." The smile died, unborn. "I'll call Patterson and make the arrangements."

They met Patterson at Burnaby Mountain Park. The day was overcast, but not raining. Clouds wreathed the peaks of the North Shore Mountains. The threat of rain kept the temperature cool and added a softness to the air.

Patterson's car was already parked at the edge of the big parking lot when they arrived. She got out as Christy drew her van up beside the car. The detective was rounding the back of her car when Christy and Quinn emerged from the van. "Mrs. Jamieson," she said, nodding a greeting. She raised her brows at Quinn. "Mr. Armstrong. I did not expect to see you here."

"We have your killer," he said. His voice was heavy with what Christy knew was frustration and worry. She wondered, though, if Patterson would hear a threat in the rough tones.

Patterson leaned against the trunk of her car. She crossed her arms and said, "Do you now?"

Quinn frowned at the challenge in her voice. There was a hard gleam in his eyes. "Yeah, we do and it's not Tamara."

Christy didn't give Patterson a chance to reply. An exchange of hostilities was not what was needed at this moment. "You were right, Detective, when you said the killer was in his family circle. Or I should say, his extended family."

Patterson narrowed her eyes and said, "Extended family. You're talking about his mistresses?"

Christy nodded.

Patterson raised her brows and looked at Quinn. "Tamara Ahern was part of his extended family."

A muscle leapt in Quinn's jaw, but all he said was, "Tamara is not the killer."

Patterson shrugged. "Perhaps not. So what are we talking about, Mrs. Jamieson? If not Tamara Ahern, then who?"

"We uncovered five mistresses," Quinn said.

"I've spoken to four of them, but we think there may have been more," Christy added.

"Five? I know about a couple but who are the others?"

"The first was Olivia Waters. The next one we know about is Marian Fleming, who seems to be the most long lasting of Fred's women. Then there was the principal of his son's high school—I didn't speak to her, nor do I have her name, but Colin Jarvis can probably provide it. The next woman we know about is Leslie Bankes, head teacher at Vancouver Royal Academy."

Patterson's jaw dropped and she uttered a little sound of disbelief, cutting Christy off. "The posh private school for girls? Why would he get involved with a teacher?"

"Feathering his granddaughter's nest," Quinn said. There was amusement in his eyes. He was enjoying Patterson's discomfort.

Christy nodded. "To make sure his granddaughter got the richest school experience possible—the lead in school productions, field trips that were perfect for her, the best teachers at her school."

Patterson was now standing very still. She reminded Christy of Stormy when he stalked the squirrel that was his nemesis—focused, still, ready to pounce, but patiently waiting for the perfect moment. "Are you suggesting this teacher killed Jarvis? Because if you are, I don't buy it."

Christy shook her head. "No. I mention Leslie because she was younger than the earlier mistresses, a different generation. She was as deeply involved with Fred as the earlier women. What was new was that her boyfriend didn't buy into Fred's extended alliances concept the way Archie Fleming did. Instead, he refused Fred's help and split with Leslie."

Patterson rubbed her scar, a sure sign that she was thinking deeply and that she considered the information significant. "You think the boyfriend killed Jarvis?" She shook her head. "I can't see it."

Christy glanced at Quinn, then looked back to Patterson. "Leslie wasn't Fred's most recent mistress. They split up when Leslie became head teacher at VRA."

"His current woman was Phoebe Beck," Quinn said. He watched Patterson, narrow-eyed.

"The event planner?" The detective's gaze turned inward. "She'd know his schedule, but ... " She shook her head. "It doesn't wash. Jarvis was at his Yaletown office, in a meeting with his senior people —his communications guy, his strategist, his campaign manager. He got a phone call and said he had to take it privately. He exited the office and didn't return. Half an hour later he was found in the parking garage, not far from the elevators, dead from a clean head shot. Phoebe Beck might have known about the strategy session, but she wouldn't have known about his unplanned trip to the garage. Besides, she has an alibi for the time of death."

Quinn shifted uneasily. He shoved his hands in his pockets. "We weren't talking about Phoebe being the killer."

"She is genuinely upset at his death," Christy said. "It's her husband who is the murderer."

"Russell Beck?" Patterson was shaking her head. "The man had an exemplary record in the Forces. He is employed by a top-notch security company that thoroughly screens its personnel. If there was anything to find in Russell Beck's background, they'd have seen it and he would never have gotten the job."

"Jarvis asked for him," Quinn said. The words hung in the quiet that followed.

"Jarvis was doing his network thing again," Christy said. "Helping his mistress's husband find success. In the beginning all Russell Beck knew was that his wife worked for Jarvis, so he was fine with Fred's help. He didn't know about the affair. But when he found out he was furious. He decided to eliminate Fred."

"He has an alibi. He was with his wife. They were going to a party."

"Where?" Christy asked.

"Yaletown."

"Were they apart at any time?" Quinn asked.

"He let her off at the front entrance to the building where the party was being held while he went to park the car."

"How long did that take?" Quinn demanded.

"A half an hour. He claimed he had a hard time finding a spot." Patterson shifted uneasily. "Okay, so it's not far from the apartment building to Patterson's office space. But ... " She broke off, realigned her thoughts and said, "It is possible, I suppose. I'll check it out."

"And you'll release Tamara," Quinn said. "She isn't your killer."

"She is until I can prove otherwise," Patterson said. "Look, Mr. Armstrong, as far as Inspector Fortier is concerned, we are looking for the other members of Dr. Ahern's cell. The taskforce has its primary suspect. The scenario you and Mrs. Jamieson have presented me is plausible, but you don't have any proof."

"Beck was a skilled marksman in the army!" Quinn said.

"Not proof."

"What about Jarvis's history of sexual misconduct?" Christy asked.

"You said that Phoebe Beck believes her husband was unaware of her relationship with Jarvis?"

Christy nodded. "Yes."

"Then you have no evidence Beck targeted his boss. All you've got is a hunch. It's not good enough."

"You can't keep Tamara caged for something she didn't do!"

Christy heard the anguish in Quinn's voice. Patterson must have heard it too. "Counsel has insisted she have regular medical checks and her doctor reports that Dr. Ahern is dealing with her incarceration with remarkable composure."

Quinn narrowed his eyes. "Composure? You mean she's gone inward? Like catatonic?"

"No, she's simply calm." Patterson shook her head, then she laughed. "She's driving Fortier nuts. No matter how often he questions her, she refuses to confess. She continues to assert that she didn't commit the crime and she says that time will absolve her."

"She trusts the system," Christy said.

Patterson shot her a look. "Maybe."

"Well, I don't," Quinn said angrily.

"I'm not surprised." Patterson glanced at her watch. "All right, Mrs. Jamieson, I'll check out your leads." She hesitated, then added, "Don't expect much, though. The case is pretty much closed."

She moved around the car, to the driver's door, and slid inside.

Christy caught Quinn's hand and squeezed as she watched Patterson drive away. "She may not promise much, but she's thorough. She'll check out what we've told her."

Quinn stared at the retreating car as it turned onto the narrow road that exited the park. "That won't be enough. You heard her. They have their killer."

CHAPTER 29

Christy listened to Isabelle Pascoe, the office manager at the Jamieson Trust, as she listed the current holdings of the Trust. Less than two weeks ago, she had been amazed that Harry Endicott had found the Jamieson fortune. Now that the funds were beginning to trickle back into the Trust's accounts she was in the office to review the Trust's public persona, its mandate and official goals.

She and Isabelle were deep in the discussion when Bonnie King, who manned the front desk, poked her head in the door and said, "Sorry to interrupt, but ... " She paused. Her eyes were wide and she shook her head, as if she couldn't believe what she was about to say. "There's a policeman in reception."

Christy had looked up when Bonnie arrived. Now she frowned. "Did he say what he wanted?" She wondered if it was Fortier come to chide her for getting involved in the investigation.

"Her. It's a woman. She said her name was Detective Patterson."

Christy sat back in the big, leather covered executive chair. "Detective Patterson and I are old friends." She looked at Isabelle. "Can we finish up later?" When Isabelle nodded, Christy said to Bonnie, "Send the detective in."

Bonnie disappeared and Isabelle gathered up her papers. When

Bonnie returned with Patterson, Christy stood and came around the desk. "Detective Patterson, this is Isabelle Pascoe, who manages the day-to-day working of the Jamieson Trust. Isabelle, Detective Patterson was the officer in charge of Frank's murder case."

"Yes, I remember," Isabelle said. "A pleasure, Detective," she said as she slipped past Patterson and through the door. She closed it behind her, ensuring Christy and Patterson had privacy for their conversation.

"Please sit down, Detective," Christy said. She indicated the conversation area by the window that looked out on the spectacular view of Vancouver's harbor.

Patterson looked around the office as she settled in one of the comfortable chairs. She had the faintest of smiles on her lips as she said, "I seem to remember that this was Gerry Fisher's office."

Christy perched on the end of the leather sofa. She nodded. "It's the office of the CEO of the Trust, which is now my position."

Patterson raised her brows and her smile deepened. She took another look around, then got down to business. "I spoke with Colin Jarvis, Leslie Bankes, and her boyfriend, Kevin Howarth. They all confirmed the stories you and Mr. Armstrong told me yesterday. I also dug more deeply into Russell Beck's background. It turns out he has a history of violence issues stemming from a volatile temper."

Christy leaned forward. "Does that mean you believe he's the killer?"

"It means there's a possibility he could have done it. He had the opportunity, the shooting skill, the personality, and, if he knew about his wife's affair, the motivation. What I don't have is proof. I don't even have enough evidence to request a search warrant to look for the murder weapon in his home or vehicle."

"What do you need by way of proof?"

"Something concrete. A witness who saw his car in the garage. A tape from a surveillance camera that shows him entering or exiting the garage during the murder timeframe."

"There were no video cameras in the garage?"

"Not where Jarvis was shot, which suggests that his killer knew the building's security system and the location of the cameras. That's a point incriminating Russell Beck, but it's only circumstantial. The exit and entry cameras show no vehicles coming in or out of the garage during the time in question. Again, this implies the killer knew the security set up and parked outside the garage. However, if the killer was a professional he would have scoped out all the security measures ahead of time and created a plan to deal with them, so that's no proof."

Christy tapped her chin. "What about the phone call that drew Jarvis down to the parking garage?"

"Made from an anonymous pay-as-you-go phone."

"That's strange," Christy said, frowning. "Why would Fred Jarvis go down to the parking garage if he received a call from someone he didn't know?"

"The assumption is that the call was from Tamara Ahern and that she asked to meet with him." Patterson made the statement blandly. Her eyes were watchful. "Since Dr. Ahern is currently using a pay-as-you-go phone, rather than a smart phone with a monthly account, Inspector Fortier believes she and her network had access to a number of completely anonymous cell phones."

"Her network," Christy said scornfully. She shot Patterson a sharp glance. "Does Fortier still believe Quinn is part of that network?"

Patterson pursed her lips. She looked, to Christy's mind, like a woman who had to apologize for something she hadn't done, and didn't like it. "I cannot confirm that statement." She paused and her eyes narrowed a little. "I can't deny it either."

Which meant that Quinn was still on Fortier's suspect list and that he might, at any time, be suddenly hauled in for questioning and who knew what else. Christy drew a deep breath. "Do you think Fortier would consider reexamining Russell Beck's testimony?"

Patterson shook her head. "Not with the evidence I have now."

Christy felt a nasty sinking feeling in the pit of her stomach. "What will happen to Tamara?"

"Dr. Ahern will be held without bail until her trial, then her fate will be up to judge and jury."

"How long will that be?"

Patterson shrugged. "Several months. A year, perhaps more."

A year was a long time to be held in custody for a crime you didn't commit. The knowledge that Tamara was again locked in a cell, though this time in a very different situation, would tear Quinn apart.

In these past few months, since they had split in March, Christy had come to realize how much she cared for Quinn. How much she wished she could redo those days after they returned from California.

That's all the redo was, though—a wish. Even though that look the other day had given her some hope, she knew Quinn was involved with Tamara now and the best she and he could be was friends. And if that was what they were to be to each other, well, friends helped friends.

She looked at Patterson. "What kind of evidence do you need?"

Patterson frowned. "What do you mean?"

"What if Phoebe Beck admitted Russell knew about the affair? That he'd taken way longer than anyone would expect to park? That she suspected Russell of killing Fred? Would that be enough to get a search warrant?"

"It depends how the information was provided. If Phoebe came to me and told me this, yes, I could act on the information. If she told you and you came to me? No, it's hearsay and not enough."

"What if I recorded the conversation with her and gave you the recording? Would that work?"

"It might, particularly if we were able to confirm the allegations with substantive evidence." Patterson hesitated then said, "Look, Mrs. Jamieson, I didn't come here to convince you to put yourself in danger to acquire proof that Russell Beck is a murderer. I wanted to let you know what I'd found out. That was it."

"You haven't asked me to do anything, Detective." Christy stood up. When Patterson followed suit, she extended her hand. "I'll be in touch if I have anything further for you. Good day, Detective."

SHE THOUGHT a lot about that conversation on her commute home from the Trust's downtown offices. The more she thought, the more strongly she felt that confronting Phoebe with what Russell had done was the only way he would be apprehended and Tamara freed. She ran into a glitch when she floated the idea by Ellen, who thought she was crazy to even consider revealing Russell's deed to Phoebe. She took the critique seriously, but after an almost sleepless night she was more certain than ever.

Now it was the next morning and she was standing on the sidewalk in front of her townhouse defending herself. "I'm going down to Fred's campaign office this afternoon. I spoke to the office manager yesterday. He said Phoebe would be there today, finishing up a few details." She meant to sound determined, but she knew there was an edge of defiance to the statement.

"Not a good idea," Roy said.

"It's a bloody stupid idea," his son muttered.

"Thank you very much," Christy said. She lifted her chin in a disdainful way and added a disapproving sniff to her tone.

Quinn simply raised his brows and said, "You don't have a plan, Christy, you have an idea, and it's a bad one."

"It is not!" She looked around at the assembled group. They were waiting for her when she returned home from dropping Noelle for her second to last day of school. "Russell Beck is the murderer, but Patterson can't touch him unless she's got evidence. My plan," she emphasized the word, "is to push Phoebe into believing Russell is dangerous."

"Exactly," Ellen said. She was the one who had organized this intervention. She was of the opinion that there had to be another way, a better way, to bring Russell Beck down.

But there wasn't. Christy was sure of it. "Look, school ends tomorrow with a special assembly for the kids. Parents are invited to attend, and I want to go. That means I need to clean this up today. This afternoon."

Trevor McCullagh's car drove down the road and parked in front of the Armstrong's driveway. Trevor and Sledge piled out. "I got here as quickly as I could," Trevor said. "What's up?"

"Christy wants to confront Phoebe Beck in the hopes of acquiring enough evidence against Russell Beck to prove to Patterson that he's the killer," Ellen said.

Trevor's brow wrinkled thoughtfully. "Russell Beck is ex-military, isn't he?"

They all nodded.

"Dangerous man," Trevor said. He shook his head. "What if Phoebe is in on it?"

"I don't believe that's possible. She's genuinely distraught about Fred's death," Christy said.

"She could be a good actress," Roy offered. His eyes had the wild, glittery look that suggested he'd been in the midst of one of his creative binges before the intervention call came. He'd probably been up all night, lost in a world of his own creation. "Maybe Fred was about to dump her, so she and Russell conspired together to get their revenge. She, because she'd been tossed aside. Russell, because Fred had cuckolded him. She told him where Fred would be and organized an alibi by going to the party. He called Fred, arranged to meet him in the garage, and shot him. Then he joined Phoebe at the party and explained his tardy arrival by saying he had trouble finding parking."

"That's probably what happened," Christy said.

Roy brightened. "Really?" He sounded pleased.

"Yes. Except that Phoebe didn't plot revenge with Russell. He planned it all. He took her to the party, dropped her and said he'd find a place to park and he'd meet her at the party. He then called Fred, arranged to meet him in the garage, then shot him. Phoebe is innocent." Christy glanced at each of them. Trevor still looked worried. Beside him, Sledge was half sitting on the edge of the flower box at the end of the walk, relaxed, but watchful. Ellen was standing on the porch stairs glaring at her. Stormy the Cat sat beside her, observing, though Frank was saying nothing. Roy and Quinn stood on the sidewalk, between their house and hers, watching. Quinn's expression was disapproving. Roy's was interested as he observed the scene.

"I can make Phoebe talk," Christy said, quietly, for emphasis. "I'm sure of it."

"To what end?" Trevor said. "Unless Phoebe goes to the cops herself, Patterson can't use her information."

"Phoebe loved Fred and I think she's afraid of Russell. If I can make her see that Russell is the killer, I think she will go to Patterson."

"It's too dangerous," Quinn said.

Christy put her hands on her hips. "What's so dangerous about going to an office and talking to someone? I'll be fine."

"You're probably right," Roy said. His son glared at him and he shrugged. "What? Are we supposed to gang up on Christy when all she's doing is speaking the truth?" He turned away from Quinn to smile at Christy. "You're a smart, capable woman and more than able to handle yourself with this Phoebe person."

Christy smiled back gratefully. "Thank you, Roy."

Roy held up a forefinger. "Not finished yet. I've got a but in there. Quinn's right. Going in on your own is dangerous. You need backup."

"I'll go," Quinn said. His voice was rough with suppressed emotion. He looked Christy in the eye, his expression daring her to refuse his help.

Which she had no intention of doing. "Thank you, Quinn. I'd like to leave about twelve-thirty, so I can get there by about one. Can you be ready then?"

Quinn nodded.

Trevor said, "Wait."

They all looked at him.

"Quinn can't be Christy's back up. Didn't Patterson say that Fortier still suspects him of being part of Tamara's network?"

Christy nodded.

Trevor shrugged. "If Quinn is involved, anything that comes out of the interview could be seen as tainted, coerced even. Someone else has to be backup."

An exchange of looks passed amongst the men. Christy gritted her teeth. "You guys are being ridiculous. If it's inadvisable for Quinn to come, I'll take Stormy. Phoebe can hear Frank and she associates the cat with Fred's funeral. His presence will help make her talk."

Not enough, babe. Stormy hopped down the porch steps to twine around Christy's ankles. *I'll go and I'll help, but you need human back up.*

"Looks like the job's mine," Sledge said. He remained half sitting on the edge of the planter, his legs stretched out in front of him, his hands thrust into the pockets of his jeans. The sun glinted down on his shaggy, perfectly styled hair and he smiled a lazy, got-it-under-control smile.

"Excellent," Ellen said, following the cat down the steps. "Rob's —" She stopped, pursed her lips, then started again with careful deliberation. "*Sledge's* fame will ensure that Mrs. Beck is not on her guard. She'll be more open and speak more freely with him around."

Trevor nodded. Christy had the distinct impression he approved of his son's involvement.

"Good point," Roy said.

"Now, what is your excuse for barging into the office?" Ellen said to Christy. "It should be reasonable, but something that will get her talking."

Christy blinked. "I hadn't thought ... "

"Then we had better do so." Ellen glanced at her watch. "We have time. Come inside, all of you. We'll have coffee and plan out this operation."

CHAPTER 30

Christy pushed the door to the Jarvis campaign office open at the same time as she knocked. "Hello? Phoebe? Are you here?" She strolled into the office. The last time she'd been here the movers were busy removing desks and emptying filing cabinets. Now the vast space was virtually empty. Even the partitions that created small cubbyholes for privacy were gone. Christy's voice reverberated off the high ceiling and pictureless walls.

"Doesn't look like anyone's here," Sledge said, pushing the door wider, so that the automatic return latched to keep it open. He followed her into the office space.

"No. I guess we missed her." Christy wrinkled her brow. "But the door was unlocked. Maybe she's gone to the washroom or something."

There was the sound of movement in the walled office at the opposite end of the room from where Phoebe had once sat. Christy headed that way and called again, "Phoebe? Is that you?"

A large male figure appeared in the doorway and took up a protective stance, legs wide apart, hands hanging loosely at his side, ready for any kind of action. "Who's asking?" There was an edge to his deep authoritative voice.

Christy stopped abruptly. The man could only be Russell Beck. Dark haired, with a round face and heavy features, he was wearing a T-shirt that showed off his wide shoulders and muscled chest. Worn jeans clung to his narrow hips. His eyes, dark and deep-set under heavy brows were narrowed as he spoke. He looked dangerous and his presence here was definitely not part of the plan.

Behind her, she heard Sledge swear quietly.

Drawing a deep breath, Christy pinned a smile to her mouth and stepped forward, her hand outstretched. "I'm Christy Jamieson. I'm a friend of Marian Fleming."

Russell Beck didn't move. He watched her with an impassive expression and hard, assessing eyes. "So?"

Charming. What did Phoebe see in this jerk, beyond the obvious physical attributes? Smiling apologetically, Christy let her hand drop. "I feel like a complete fool. I've forgotten the address of the party."

Phoebe appeared in the doorway, her way out of the office hindered by Russell's big body. She peeked over his shoulder and said, "Oh, hello, Mrs. Jamieson. What can I do to help you?"

Christy slid the tote she carried off her shoulder and set it on the floor. The bag fell open and Stormy the Cat stepped out with careful, fastidious steps. He arched his back in an energetic cat stretch, then sauntered over to the couple in the doorway. He sat down in front of Russell and looked up, his green eyes wide and unblinking.

"Oh," said Phoebe, pleasure in her voice. "You've brought your cat."

Russell shot a suspicious look Christy's way. "If you're looking for a party, why'd you bring your cat?"

Cause I'm a party animal.

Now ranged up beside Christy, Sledge snorted. Russell shifted his gaze to Sledge and glared at him. Then he frowned, apparently recognizing the rock star hidden beneath the well-tailored dark suit, white shirt and navy-blue tie Sledge was wearing.

"What party were you talking about, Mrs. Jamieson?" Phoebe asked, squeezing past her husband so she could crouch down to pat the cat. She started by rubbing the sensitive area behind his ears. Stormy purred. Phoebe laughed delightedly.

"The one Marian Fleming is giving in honor of Fred Jarvis," Christy said with what she hoped sounded like unthreatening good cheer. "I knew you'd be invited too, so I thought Sledge and I would stop by and get the address from you."

Phoebe stood abruptly. There was a stricken look in her eyes and her mouth drooped. "I wasn't invited."

"Oh," Christy said, and tried to look bewildered, as if she wasn't sure what she should do next. In fact, that wasn't so far from the truth. With Russell Beck standing in front of her, there was no way she could play on Phoebe's feelings for Fred Jarvis. The careful plan concocted in her kitchen this morning was now about as useful as stale donuts.

Russell was still eying Sledge. "You're Rob McCullagh? Sledge of SledgeHammer? The Sledge?"

Of course he is. Who else would he be? Didn't you hear Christy call him Sledge?

Russell's eyes widened. He looked around, then down at the cat, who was still sitting primly at his feet. "Was that you?"

Yeah. Who else?

Russell took a step back, bringing him in contact with the door-frame. That little act of vulnerability was only momentary, though. His eyes narrowed again and his mouth set in a hard line. He looked angry, and with it, dangerous.

Sledge stepped forward, within arms' length, and shot out his hand. He flashed his trademark smile and said, "How are you doing, man? I'm afraid I didn't catch your name."

Russell dragged his gaze away from the cat. Meeting Sledge of SledgeHammer and sharing conversation with him was not an opportunity to be missed, after all, no matter what the situation was. "Beck. I'm Russell Beck."

He moved as if to take Sledge's hand, but Stormy stood up at that moment and stretched. *Yeah, yeah, yeah. Polite bullshit. Listen up! I want to talk to you.*

Russell's arm fell back to his side. "You do?"

Sledge unobtrusively stepped back and away, out of range.

Yeah. This is between you and me. The others can't hear—

"I can hear," Phoebe said. She sounded indignant.

Christy and Sledge exchanged a quick look. Frank clearly didn't want Russell to know that she and Sledge were also in on the conversation. "Phoebe, I'm so sorry to have bothered you. It's just ... " She shrugged. "I know how close you were to Fred Jarvis, so I assumed—"

"What do you mean, close to Jarvis?" Russell demanded, sounding hostile.

Christy moved back a step, closer to Sledge. "Well ... " She didn't have to pretend to be unnerved by the anger in Russell's voice.

Come on! Who are you trying to kid? You know exactly what close to Jarvis *means.* There was a taunt in the voice. Stormy sat down and licked a front paw, the picture of blasé indifference.

They all knew that Russell Beck had a volatile temper, that he was psychologically fragile, and they believed he had killed Fred Jarvis. There was no telling what he would do if pressured. What was Frank up to?

Russell's jaw moved, his chin jutting forward, while his eyes narrowed to slits. All his attention was on the cat. "I know she was sleeping with the bastard. So what?"

Phoebe slowly stood. "You knew?" Her voice wavered, whether from fear or anguish, it was hard to tell.

Of course he knew.

"Shut up! Yes, I knew." He turned his attention to his wife. His expression didn't soften, though his voice lost the edge of outrage. He sounded almost bewildered as he said, "Jesus, Phoebe, how could you betray me by sleeping with the boss? Our boss? I worked for the guy. Do you know how humiliating it was to look into his eyes and know he was screwing you? That he was laughing at me every moment of every day?"

"That's not true!" Phoebe cried. Her hands were bunched into fists at her side. There were tears in her eyes. "Fred knew how much I love you. He wanted to help you, to get you back on your feet with a job and rebuild your self-esteem."

"My self-esteem?" Russell roared. It seemed he'd reached his breaking point. He moved in on Phoebe.

The cat bounded away. Sledge took Christy's arm and eased her back so that she was behind him and they were both to one side of the open doorway, leaving the Becks in full view of anyone in the corridor. Christy frowned. The hall outside was quiet and she couldn't see anyone, but Sledge's move had been quite deliberate. What was up?

Russell was inches away from Phoebe now. She was staring up at him, her gaze locked with his. Dismay had her eyes wide and her lips parted. "Yes! Your self-esteem. You came back from your tour of duty changed and I wanted the man I married back. The doctors said that having a job would help, so Fred checked with his contacts. He found the opening, but you landed the job."

"How long were you sleeping with him?" Russell asked. His voice was dangerously low.

The tears in Phoebe's eyes trickled down her cheeks. She sniffed, then said in a low voice, "Months."

Russell's menacing expression changed to one of shock. "Months? I thought it began with that trip out of town."

"Yes," she whispered, and hung her head in a guilty way.

Russell lifted his hand to strike. She cringed back, raising her arms and putting her hands in front of her face to ward off a blow.

The cat wandered over and sat down on one of Russell's feet. He looked up, green eyes wide. *Such a tough guy, hitting a woman.*

"Shut up!" But Russell's raised arm was frozen, the blow unde-livered.

Bet it was more fun putting a hole in the old man's head.

"When I asked Jarvis if he was sleeping with you, he told me I was family. That he cared for me." Russell was still staring at Phoebe with anger in his expression, but he slowly lowered his hand. "Can you believe it?"

"Yes," said Phoebe. She shifted her hands to rub the tears from her cheeks.

Russell's lips turned into a sneer. "Well, you're an idiot. He just wanted me to let him go on screwing you. He came up with some bull about being allies in a tough world. He thought he'd convinced me it was okay, but he hadn't. I told him I was quitting." He shot a smoldering look at Phoebe. "And so were you."

When?

Russell frowned and looked down at the cat.

When did you tell him you were quitting?

"I gave our notice on Friday. He told me he wouldn't accept it. Bastard." Russell glared at his wife. "Then Phoebe works late that night, with him, here in this office." His voice had hardened. There was anger and outrage in the sound, but most of all there was betrayal. "I knew what was going on. I knew you'd never leave him."

"Russell." Phoebe reached out. Her tears were falling faster now, but she ignored them. "Russell, I loved Fred, but not the way I love you. He was kind to me. He made me feel special. He recognized how difficult your life as a soldier was. He helped me understand you, because he knew you came first. If you'd just asked me, I would have stopped seeing him!"

"Sure you would," Russell said, scornfully.

Why did you kill him?

Russell glanced down at the cat, who stood up, freeing his foot, then butted against his leg. Russell automatically took a step back and away from Phoebe. "I'd suspected something was going on between Phoebe and Jarvis for a long time, but on that Friday, I knew. There was only one way Phoebe would ever be mine." He looked up and his eyes locked with those of his tearful wife. "Fred Jarvis had to be dead and gone."

Phoebe uttered a little gasp of dismay and lifted her hand to her mouth. Russell's gaze hardened and his lip curled.

The cat started to purr. He twined sinuously around Russell's ankles, drawing the man's attention away from Phoebe, back to the confession he didn't know he was making.

How did you do it?

Frowning, Russell glanced down at the cat, who paused to stare back, green eyes unblinking. Accusing.

"After I dropped Phoebe off at the apartment building on Saturday afternoon, I called Jarvis from an untraceable phone. I told him I needed to talk to him about Phoebe. Said I was down in the garage. I asked him to come alone. He trusted me, so he did." Russell's tone was matter-of-fact, calm.

Chilling, Christy thought. Sledge must have felt the same way, for he slipped an arm around her waist and eased her further from the door, well away from the action taking place at the far end of the room.

Russell didn't notice. Or if he did, he didn't care. He was talking to the cat and no one else in the room seemed to matter. Even Phoebe. "I disabled one of the video cameras the day before, so I was able to come in through a side door undetected. Then I got into position and waited. When he reached the meeting place, I stood up. As soon as I knew he'd recognized me I lifted my weapon and let him see what I planned to do. He begged me not to. Said I didn't understand and that Phoebe would always be mine." Russell's lip curled. "Yeah, sure, like I was stupid enough to believe that." He stared deep into his wife's eyes. "I let him think he'd won me over. And then I shot him."

"Oh, Russell, how could you?"

Phoebe's anguished wail masked the sounds of activity by the main doorway. Christy saw Patterson dart into the room, with Quinn following behind. He paused in the doorway, using his cell phone.

Patterson held her service weapon in both hands and had it trained on Russell as she advanced toward him. "Mr. Beck, step away from your wife and hold your hands away from your body."

Stormy turned his attention to Phoebe, butting her leg with his head, easing her out of the way. *Come on, Phoebe. Let's go over to Christy and Sledge.*

Wide-eyed, her skin blotchy from her tears, Phoebe backed away from her husband. Stormy twined around her, shifting her so that her stumbling footsteps moved her out of the danger zone, to the relative safety behind Patterson, with Christy and Sledge.

Quinn came into the room to stand beside them. "Back up is on the way," he said.

Patterson nodded. "Russell Beck, you are under arrest for the murder of Frederick Jarvis."

CHAPTER 31

T he gym doors opened at precisely nine o'clock, allowing parents to file inside to find seats on the chairs that had been set up in the big, echoing room. It was the last day of school and time for the end of year wrap up. In a few minutes, once the family members were all seated, the student body would be allowed to enter, by class, with the littlest students first.

There was hot competition amongst the parents for prime seats, so after a quick consultation, Christy and Ellen decided to find a place against the wall and stand. Christy was carrying Stormy in her tote. Ellen had her tablet and was prepared to film the whole event. Both Stormy, whose head had just emerged from the mouth of the tote, and the tablet would benefit from the improved view over the heads of seated parents that standing would give.

The excited chatter died off as parents settled and it became obvious that there were no more adults waiting to enter. The principal and her staff busied themselves making sure that everything was set-up as it should be. Then one of the kindergarten teachers, her class in a somewhat orderly queue behind her, entered and paused. The principal nodded. The students began to file in, to settle in front of the rows of seating for the parents.

"They are surprisingly well behaved," Ellen said from behind the tablet where she was monitoring the scene she was filming.

You do know that everything you say will be picked up by the mic, don't you?

"Of course I do."

Christy chuckled. Frank's comment hadn't been recorded, of course. Good thing only family would be watching the video.

Since Burnaby worked on an elementary and high school only model, with no middle school between the two, this was the last year the grade seven students would be in this school. They all shuffled into position at the front of the gym, on stage, as it were, as the senior students.

The ceremony began with one of the teachers presenting a slide show, featuring pictures taken of the children at events throughout the school year, then songs were sung, retiring or transferring teachers were thanked, and finally the grade seven graduating class received diplomas and medals as reminders of their years in the school. With that completed, all the students cheered, the principal wished them a happy summer, and the assembly was over.

The children filed out of the gym with a good deal less decorum than when they'd come in. They would go back to their classrooms to pick up the last of their belongings and receive their final report cards. Their parents would join them there.

Christy and Ellen let the rest of the parents exit before them. Not only were they hugging a side wall with parents exiting the rows all around them, but Christy wanted to give Noelle as much time as she could to savor the day.

Rebecca Petrofsky found them as the crowd thinned. "Wasn't that fun? I love the last day of school assembly. The kids are so full of enthusiasm and the teachers are mellow and everyone is nostalgic for the year passed. I always shed a tear or two," she said, grinning with rueful amusement.

Christy laughed. "I did enjoy it. Thanks for suggesting I come." Rebecca hadn't suggested, she'd announced that Christy couldn't miss it, but no matter. The result was the same. She turned to Ellen. "How about you, Ellen? What did you think?"

"This was nothing like the end of the year at VRA."

That was certainly true. There the last day of school was a full day. The morning was regular classes, while the afternoon featured a lecture by someone worthy of note. Final report cards were handed out as the students exited their classrooms for the last time, along with study assignments to be completed over the summer months so that the children would be prepared for the new year in September. No one cheered and there was no loud babble raised by excited voices.

"I like this better." Ellen tucked the tablet into her purse and missed Christy's look of relief.

"Do you have plans for the summer?" Rebecca asked. They had reached the corridor by now and were halfway to the girls' classroom.

Christy shook her head. "No. How about you?"

"We have a trailer we keep down in Washington State, by a beach. We spend most of the summer there." They reached the classroom. Rebecca smiled before they went in. "Noelle is welcome to come down for a visit."

"Thanks," Christy said. "I'll talk to her about it."

In the classroom, the girls were ready to go. Mary Petrofsky was regaling Noelle with stories about summers at the trailer, and their teacher, Mrs. Morton, was smiling, looking more approachable than Christy had ever seen her. Rebecca and Christy organized the girls and they all walked home together, chatting about summer plans and the school year just past. At Christy's house, they parted company. Mary and her mother were off to shop for their summer at the beach, while Christy, Ellen, Noelle, and Stormy had been invited to an end-of-the-school-year barbeque at the Armstrongs' house.

The barbeque was an Armstrong tradition, according to Quinn. It was a transition from school to vacation, when the family made their summer plans, with everyone offering up suggestions, and final decisions made after all ideas had been thoroughly discussed.

In reality, Quinn had said the previous day, as they waited to give their statements after Russell Beck's arrest, his parents had made the plans long before and just presented them in an egalitarian way to make Quinn feel he was a valued and important part of the process. Christy thought that would be rather off putting, but Quinn had slid her a long look, smiled in a way that made her heart turn over, and said, "Life with Dad. You get used to it."

Roy had asked them to arrive around noon, which gave Christy time to bake a batch of brownies, with Noelle's help, of course, and Ellen to put together the fancy quinoa salad she'd proudly made herself from a recipe she'd worked on in her cooking class. They were all looking forward to the party as they made their way out their back door, then along the path to the Armstrong's backyard.

They found Roy standing at his barbeque, with Trevor peering over his shoulder. Sledge was opening a bag of chips at the table. A bottle of beer stood beside a large bowl, which apparently was the destination of the chips.

"Roy! Mr. Three. Sledge!" Noelle shouted, announcing their arrival. She did a little dance, careful not to upend the plate of brownies she was carrying. "School's out!"

All the adults laughed and Ellen said, mildly for her, "There is no need to shout, Noelle."

Sure there is! Didn't you hear her, Aunt Ellen? School's out! She's free for the summer.

"Yeah," said Noelle nodding.

Ellen made a disapproving sound in her throat. She placed her bowl of salad on the table beside the chips. The cat suddenly froze, then leapt toward the trees that marked the point where the yard ended and the greenbelt began.

"What's he up to?" Sledge asked.

"He's probably caught sight of the squirrel," Christy said. Her contribution was a bowl of coleslaw, which she put on the table beside Ellen's salad. She watched as Noelle carefully put her brownies down and pretended not to notice when she snuck a square from the pile.

"Hey," Sledge said, smiling at Noelle. "Aren't you supposed to wait until after you've had your main course before you have dessert?"

Eyes full of mischief, Noelle said, "Oops!" The word came out a little blurry as her mouth was still full of brownie. Sledge laughed.

"Where's Quinn?" Christy asked, trying to sound casual.

"Upstairs with Tamara, putting together the hot dogs and hamburgers," Trevor said. His attention was on the barbecue, which used charcoal briquettes, not propane, for fuel. Roy was carefully tending the blaze so that the briquettes would be hot coals when the meat arrived. Trevor was supervising.

Of course Tamara was upstairs with Quinn. What had she expected? "Will Olivia be coming?" Christy asked. She tried to sound as if she was making conversation, and her interest was only casual, when in fact the answer was terribly important to her.

"We didn't invite her," Roy said.

Relief rushed through Christy. Olivia was Tamara's birth mother. If she was part of the festivities, that would mean Quinn and Tamara were a confirmed couple. That Olivia wasn't there gave her hope that a future for Quinn and Tamara wasn't inevitable.

Roy crouched down to blow on the coals. "I was prepared to, but Tamara asked that we not."

"Oh." That blew her assumption that Olivia's absence meant Quinn and Tamara weren't a couple.

"I'll go up and help the young people bring down the food," Ellen said. "Come with me, Trevor."

Trevor looked up from the barbeque and blinked. "Okay." They disappeared into the house.

"Well," said Sledge.

Aunt Ellen and Trevor? Really?

Roy stood up. "Coals are ready." He dusted off his hands and winked at Noelle as he grabbed a brownie.

Quinn appeared in the doorway carrying a platter of hotdogs and hamburgers. He was followed by Tamara, who held a bowl of pasta salad in one hand and a green salad in the other. Christy quickly went to help Tamara, taking one of the bowls, while Quinn delivered the meat to his father and held the platter as Roy carefully placed each piece on the grill. Ellen brought a tub containing plates, cutlery and glasses, while Trevor hauled a cooler filled with beverages.

Since the food took up most of the table they all settled on deck chairs and ate from plates held on their laps. Conversation eventually rolled around to the unmasking of Russell Beck the day before.

"What I don't understand is why Patterson was there," Christy said. "She told me she couldn't be involved." She passed around the plate of brownies. At the rate they were disappearing, she should have made a double batch.

"I convinced her," Quinn said. Christy frowned at him and he laughed. "Don't forget, I know your habit of diving into the thick of things. I figured you were right that Beck was the killer. I also thought there was a good chance something would go wrong."

"Thanks," Christy said. "I think. How did you convince Patterson?"

Quinn sobered. "I worked on her conscience. She suspected you planned to confront Phoebe. She didn't like the idea. In fact, she intended to step in and stop you, once she had the when and where. I let her know Sledge was with you and I convinced her to hold off and see if our plan worked."

Christy took the last brownie and sat down. "Well, I'm glad you were there. How did it, um, sound from the other side of the door?"

Since Quinn and Patterson couldn't hear Frank's mind speak, this was a valid question. Quinn knew about Frank, of course, and by now he'd pretty much accepted that many and varied people were able to communicate with him, but Tamara hadn't a clue, so they were all being cautious about what they said and how they responded when Frank talked.

"Like Russell was having a breakdown. His voice was raised. He sounded defensive, angry, overwrought." Quinn stopped, glanced at Tamara, then said slowly, as if he was picking his words, "He seemed to be responding to questions, as if some unseen being was prodding him into a confession."

Way cool. I did good work. The voice was lazy, half asleep. The cat was now sunning himself curled up in Noelle's lap in the middle of the patch of grass between the patio and the trees.

Christy laughed and was glad that she had a mouthful of brownie so she couldn't blurt out something inappropriate. Instead, she swallowed and raised her brows. "Like Fred's ghost?"

"Someone's ghost, anyway," Quinn said. Sledge laughed and Tamara looked at him thoughtfully.

Roy stirred. "Now that this case is over and school's out, we all must be thinking about the summer."

"Here it comes," Quinn said.

Roy frowned at him. "What comes?"

"Summer plans."

Roy brightened. "Good point. What's everyone got arranged?"

Sledge shifted restlessly in his seat. "Hammer and I have to finalize new management for SledgeHammer." He shook his head. "We've been letting it drift, both of us. Vince's firm is handling our day-to-day for now, but we need to make a decision. The trouble is, neither of us wants to do it." Their manager's death coming at the end of their last tour had taken a deep emotional toll and Sledge didn't look happy about the task. Not surprising as it sounded more like work than vacation.

Roy nodded, looking pleased. Raising his brows, he looked around. His gaze fell on Christy. "How about you and Noelle?"

"We don't have any big plans. Rebecca Petrofsky invited Noelle down to their place in Washington State for a visit. I might drop her there and continue on to Seattle for a couple of nights."

"Mary says the beach there is beautiful," Noelle said from the grass. "She wants me to come for the whole summer."

The whole summer? Seattle? What about me?

At her father's comment, Noelle frowned. Christy said hastily, "Not the whole summer, kiddo. Maybe a couple of weekends. Or a week-long visit."

Noelle looked at the adults, focused for a minute on Tamara, then studiously patted the cat in her lap. "Stormy would be lonely."

Christy smiled at her daughter, relieved she'd minded her words. "Yes, he would."

Roy cleared his throat. "Anyone else have plans? Three? Ellen?"

"Salt Spring is nice this time of year. My garden will need tending." Trevor glanced around the table. "The deer tend to go after the herbaceous borders. You need to be vigilant."

"Vigilant? How?" Tamara asked. Coming from a life in urban Toronto she didn't have a lot of experience with wildlife.

"Applying, um, a natural repellant to the perimeter." He reddened.

His son laughed and took pity on him. "Fluids that smell like a predator has been in the area and marked his territory."

Like dog pee?

"Yuck," Noelle said.

"Um, yes," Trevor said. He focused on Ellen and shifted the conversation away from indelicate subjects. "My house has a spare bedroom. Have you ever been to Salt Spring, Ellen?"

"Of course," she said. "I have several friends who have taken up residence on the island." She looked thoughtfully at Trevor. "I suppose a summer visit would be nice. Catching up with people."

"We could give a party."

"We?"

Trevor backtracked hastily. "I mean, I. I could give a party."

"Hmm. Perhaps."

Roy observed this with a frown. Christy saw Quinn watching him with amusement and thought of his comment about his father's tendency to arrange summer vacation.

"What about you, Tamara?" Sledge said. "Do you have anything planned?"

Tamara glanced at Quinn. "No. I suppose I'll go back to Toronto now that I'm no longer a suspect in the Jarvis murder." She looked around the table. "I want to thank you, all of you, for believing in me." She hesitated, then said, "I had a lot of time to think while I was in detention. About who I am and what I want to do in my future. I realized I can still be myself. That I can take risks and give back." A smile quirked up one corner of her mouth. "I just can't take the same kind of risks." She drew a deep breath. "I'll never go back to CMSA and work in danger zones, but I can fundraise, and I can bring awareness of what is happening to the world."

She looked over at Quinn and smiled. The implication was clear. Her experience working to save the innocent in tragic conflicts, together with Quinn's media profile, would make them an unbeatable team for good.

"You're heading back to Toronto, then?" Sledge said, surprising Christy. She expected Quinn to be the one to comment.

Tamara hesitated. "I'm not sure. I came here to find my birth parents—and I did—but now? With all that has happened? I'm not sure that I should ever have done that. My parents, my real parents, are in Toronto. That's where I'm from. That's where my family is." She shrugged, looking guilty. "Still, something tells me I should stay here in Vancouver At least for a little while and see if I can get to know Olivia. And ... stuff."

And Quinn. His expression was non-committal, but Christy wondered if he could resist the lure of working with Tamara on the international stage. Christy swallowed the lump in her throat. Probably not.

Roy cleared his throat. "Sounds like everybody has bits and pieces going on."

"You could put it that way," Quinn said. There was amusement in his voice. "Why don't you tell us what you have planned, Dad?"

Roy looked at him gratefully. "All right, I will." He jumped up from his seat, then hurried into the house. A couple of minutes later he returned. He was holding what looked like a thin, tabloid newspaper in his hand. He cleared a place on the table and spread out the newsprint. They all gathered around, including Noelle.

The cat hopped up onto the table to look. He put his paw on the paper, above a diagram that appeared to be a map of some kind. *What's this?*

"This is a map of the campground at Clan Ranald Beach." Roy beamed as he looked at each of them in turn. "The most beautiful beach on the West Coast." He stopped, frowning. "One of the most beautiful beaches. Anyway, it's a great beach. Long and sloping, perfect for kids who want to paddle in the shallows. No undertow." He shot a significant look at Christy, then Noelle. "Family friendly."

"Okay," Christy said, wondering what he was plotting.

"As good as Mary Petrofsky's beach?" Noelle asked.

"Better," Roy said. "It's in BC."

"Dad," Quinn said.

Roy ignored him. "Reservations for the campsites at Clan Ranald open in February and book up really quickly." He looked around and beamed with pleasure. "I booked three sites for the first two weeks of August. The sunniest two weeks of the summer."

"Three sites, Dad?"

He nodded. His finger stabbed down onto the diagram, which apparently was a map of the facility. "Back end of the campground. A double just before the curve of the road, and a nice little space opposite, across the way."

They all looked at the map and Roy's pointing finger. Christy could see a squiggly line that indicated a path down to the beach starting not far from the double site. Roy was right. It was a great location.

"The double sites are large ones, and they can each handle two family sized tents. I thought Christy and Noelle could share a tent over on this side of the double, with a pup tent for Ellen." He looked up in time to see Ellen's expression of shocked disbelief, so he added hastily, "Or we could do one big tent for all three of you." Ellen's expression didn't change. "Well, we can work out the details later. On the other side, Quinn and I would share, with a small tent for Tamara. The site across the road is nestled in the trees. It isn't as big, but there's room for two small tents, so Trevor and Sledge wouldn't have to share."

Sledge laughed. "I'm invited too?"

Roy raised his brows and nodded. "Each site comes with a picnic table, so we could wrestle the two tables on the double site together to make one long one. That should seat all of us. We'd set up a covered area at the back of site for chairs and conversation." He nodded again. "So that's the plan. Who's in?"

Sledge said, "What happens when one of my fans recognizes me and has a freak out? The whole campground will know who's sleeping in the site round the corner."

Roy studied him thoughtfully. "You've got a good beard. Grow it out, shave your head, and wear a ball cap. No one will recognize you."

Christy almost laughed. Sledge looked astounded.

"Shave my head?" He fingered his signature tousled, carefully styled locks.

Trevor did laugh. He poked his son and said, "I'm in. What about you, rock hero?"

After a moment, Sledge's inherent sense of humor took over and he shrugged. "Why not? Sure I'm in. But I'm not shaving my head."

Roy nodded. "Your choice."

"We're going camping?" Excitement glittered in Noelle's eyes. "Mom? Are we going camping too?"

Sharing a campsite with Quinn and Tamara was not Christy's idea of an ideal vacation, but the hopeful expression on her daughter's face chased away her reluctance. She smiled and indulged in a mom ruffle of Noelle's hair. "Yes, sweetheart, we're going camping." She looked at Roy. "My parents and I camped at a beach on Lake Ontario when I was a kid, so I've got some experience. I'll help you organize the set up."

"Great. We'll need tents, sleeping bags, air mattresses—"

"Air mattresses and sleeping bags?" Ellen said. "As in bedding down on the ground?"

Again, Christy wanted to laugh, this time at the astonishment in Ellen's voice. "That's pretty much how it works."

Quinn's lips twitched. "Don't forget the communal bathrooms."

"They're flush toilets, not pit toilets," Roy said indignantly. "And there are showers available as well. What more would you want?"

"An en suite bathroom, a king-sized bed, fresh sheets and towels daily, room service," Ellen said tartly.

"This is camping," Roy said. "Being one with nature. Pitting yourself against the elements ... "

Quinn took a look at Ellen's horrified expression and said, "Dad, you're not helping."

Roy sighed gustily. There was disappointment in the sound.

Ellen frowned. "Well ... " She was clearly wavering.

Roy brightened.

Before he could say anything else that might deter Ellen, Trevor said, "New experiences, Ellen. Think of it. Walks on the beach in the moonlight. The sound of the wind ruffling the tree tops as you fall off to sleep—"

"Mini golf with your great niece," Christy murmured.

Ellen had been looking at Trevor, her expression softening, but at Christy's words she glanced sharply at her and then at Noelle, who was listening to everything the adults said with big eyes and an avid expression. "All right," Ellen said. She took a deep breath. "I'm in."

"Yeah, Aunt Ellen!"

"Tamara?" Roy said.

Tamara glanced at Quinn. Their gazes locked and Christy saw him incline his head just a fraction. "I'm no stranger to sleeping on the ground," Tamara said. "I'm not sure ... I may not be a good campmate. I ... Sometimes I have flashbacks."

"We'll look after you," Quinn said. There was warmth in his voice, but Christy couldn't tell if it was affection or friendship that caused it.

Whichever it was, there was relief in Tamara's smile. "All right. I'll come."

"Good!" Roy said. "We're all accounted for—"

What about me? I've never been camping.

There was immediate silence. Everyone at the table, apart from Quinn and Tamara, looked at each other, consternation in their expressions. Quinn raised his brows. The sudden silence would have alerted him that Frank had made a comment. Tamara simply looked bewildered.

Stormy crouched down on Roy's map and meowed plaintively.

The excitement in Noelle's expression clouded over. "We can't go, Mom. We can't leave Stormy alone for two weeks."

Christy looked at her daughter. The light of adventure was gone from her eyes, replaced by an oddly mature acceptance of sacrifice. She drew a deep breath. "Stormy can come with us."

I can? I'm in?

"Really, Mom?" When Christy nodded, Noelle high-fived Roy, who was next to her.

Stormy stood, arched his back, then rubbed against Christy's hand. She patted him absent-mindedly as she watched the joy return to her daughter's expression. "Really. We'll have to take Stormy's harness and leash, though."

What? The leash? No!

"Yes," said Ellen. "The leash is a necessity."

"We're taking a cat camping?" Tamara asked. Then she began to laugh. So did Sledge. Trevor smiled indulgently and Quinn shook his head.

Roy looked around at all of them. He beamed. "Then it's settled. We're going camping!"

The End

CAT AMONG FISHES

THE 9 LIVES COZY MYSTERY SERIES, BOOK FIVE

"Offshore fish farms are lethal to other marine life." The environmentalist pitched his voice to a conversational level, but his eyes flashed with outrage.

"Progressive Salmon Farms Worldwide has pioneered eco-friendly open water salmon pens. Our site here in Loyal Scotsman's Bay is perfect for our new technologies and takes into account all of the environmental concerns that surround older fish farms."

Stormy the Cat wiggled his shoulders free of Christy's tote bag. *I don't care if it's raining. This reminds me of the time Gerry Fisher insisted I go to the official opening of the new Jamieson Ice Cream factory when I was sixteen. Stupid speeches and a ribbon cutting. Boring! I'm out of here.*

"Prove it!" the environmentalist said.

The PSF representative reddened. "If you read our literature—"

"Your literature is spin doctored and full of falsehoods!"

The small audience, bored by the sales pitch, perked up at the possibility of a battle, but Stormy wasn't interested. Nor was Noelle. As the cat stepped daintily out of the tote Christy had lowered, Noelle tugged on her sleeve. "I want to go too, Mom."

Christy nodded. "Okay. Keep an eye on Noelle, Frank." She was whispering, though she didn't have to. Voices were raised as the arguments heated up.

Sure. Tail high, Stormy trotted away. Noelle skipped along beside him. Together they slipped through the door, still open wide, welcoming everyone to the information meeting. Their destination was a Plexiglas tank the size of a swimming pool. Visible through a big plate glass window, it was a mock up of the projected fish farm and designed to show PSF's environmentally friendly features. Noelle and the cat paused before it, apparently fascinated by the juvenile salmon swimming lazily in their small ecosystem.

Christy turned away from the window and glanced around the room. She saw that Ellen was standing close to Trevor. Were they holding hands? She couldn't quite see from her position, but she hoped it might be. Tamara was between Sledge and Quinn. Her expression was one of interest, while Sledge appeared to have drifted off into another dimension. Quinn was watching the door.

Christy's heart leapt. Was he worried about Noelle being out on her own?

The rain that had driven them inside had stopped now and the clouds were slowly drifting away. Mellow late afternoon sun glinted off Plexiglas tank. Christy was contemplating ways of leaving this charged and very political meeting without causing too much of a stir when there was a splash and the sound of a body hitting water. She heard Noelle scream, "Daddy!"

Christy whirled about. In the Plexiglas tank the juvenile salmon were now swimming in an agitated way, while Noelle was charging up the stairs to the wooden walkway that encircled the tank, a mock up of the floating docks that would be the visible evidence of the real thing. Before Christy could even begin to move, Noelle arrived at the walkway, tore across it, and leapt into the water. Inside the tank the salmon swam about even more frantically than before.

Christy headed for the door at a run, but Quinn got there first. Sledge followed him out and as Christy burst from the doorway, she saw that Quinn was at the stairs. He took them two at a time, reached the top and was across the walkway in one stride. He dove into the tank and swam for Noelle.

Sledge followed closely behind Quinn and with a whoop, he too jumped into the tank.

There was a gasp from the crowd. Now at the base of the staircase, Christy heard the PSF rep shriek, "My fish!"

She glanced back at the demonstration building. The PSF rep was leading the charge out and he looked ready to kill.

He shook his fist as he shouted, "Stop this immediately. You're traumatizing my fish!" His face was red as he rushed toward the tank. Christy ignored him and ran up the stairs.

As she reached the walkway Quinn surfaced with Noelle in his arms. He swam over to Christy and together they maneuvered Noelle out of the water. She wiggled, trying to get back in. "Mommy, Stormy is still underwater. He'll drown! We have to help him!"

At that moment Sledge surfaced. He held the cat high, one hand under his shoulders, the other at his back end. Stormy's fur was plastered to his body, his eyes were wide and a little manic, and in his mouth was one of the juvenile salmon. It flopped up and down, frantically seeking escape, but Stormy's jaws held it fast.

Noelle leapt to her feet, then hopped ecstatically up and down, clapping her hands. "Stormy! You're safe. And you caught a fish. Good for you!"

Quinn made a snorting sound that could have been a disguised laugh and hauled himself out of the water. Sledge shifted the cat so he could paddle over to the walkway. He deposited Stormy beside Noelle, then pulled himself out and sat beside Quinn.

As soon as the cat was on the walkway, Noelle dove for him. She snatched him up into a tight hug. The salmon gave one last desperate flop and Stormy lost his grip. The fish flew over the side of the tank, onto the ground.

Twisting out of Noelle's grasp, Stormy raced to across the walkway, then leapt off the edge to the ground below. He landed almost on top of the fish, mere inches away from the feet of the outraged PSF rep. Snatching up the tail of the fish, he bolted, the salmon bouncing along behind him. He headed for the makeshift parking lot where he took refuge under Christy's van.

"If looks could kill," Quinn murmured in Christy's ear.

She glanced at the PSF rep. He was staring at the van, fury in every tense muscle in his body. From his expression, it was clear he had murder on his mind.

CAT AMONG FISHES
Available in eBook and Print

ALSO BY LOUISE CLARK

The Nine Lives Cozy Mystery Series

The Cat Came Back

The Cat's Paw

Cat Got Your Tongue

Let Sleeping Cats Lie

Cat Among Fishes

Forward in Time Series

Make Time For Love

Claim Time For Love

Discover Time for Love

A Turbulent Time for Love

ABOUT THE AUTHOR

The author of the 9 Lives Cozy Mystery Series, Louise Clark has been the adopted mom of a number of cats with big personalities. The feline who inspired Stormy, the cat in the 9 Lives books, dominated her household for twenty loving years. During that time he created a family pecking order that left Louise on top and her youngest child on the bottom (just below the guinea pig), regularly tried to eat all his sister's food (he was a very large cat), and learned the joys of travel through a cross continent road trip.

The 9 Lives Cozy Mystery Series—*The Cat Came Back, The Cat's Paw,* and *Cat Got Your Tongue* —as well as the single title mystery, *A Recipe For Trouble*, are all set in her home town of Vancouver, British Columbia. For more information please sign up for her newsletter at http://eepurl.com/bomHNb. Or visit her at www.louiseclarkauthor.com or on Facebook at LouiseClarkAuthor.

CPSIA information can be obtained
at www.ICGtesting.com
Printed in the USA
BVHW072150020321
601492BV00004B/297